# Praise for Diann

CW00551249

"Book after book, Duvall brings her readers romance, danger and loyalty."

"Duvall's storytelling is simply spellbinding." —Tome Tender

"Dianne Duvall does an amazing job of blending paranormal with humor, romance, action, and violence to give you a story you won't want to put down." —The SubClub Books

## Praise for Dianne's Immortal Guardians Books

"These dark, kick-ass guardians can protect me any day!" —Alexandra Ivy, *New York Times* Bestselling Author

"Fans of terrific paranormal romance have hit the jackpot with Duvall and her electrifying series." —*RT Book Reviews*

"Crackles with energy, originality, and a memorable take-no-prisoners heroine." —*Publishers Weekly*

"Full of fascinating characters, a unique and wonderfully imaginative premise, and scorching hot relationships." —The Romance Reviews

"Fans of paranormal romance who haven't discovered this series yet are really missing out on something extraordinary." —Long and Short Reviews

"This series boasts numerous characters, a deep back story, and extensive worldbuilding… [Ethan] boasts the glowing charms of Twilight's Edward Cullen and the vicious durability of the X-Men's Wolverine." —*Kirkus Reviews*

"Paranormal romance fans who enjoy series like J.R. Ward's Black Dagger Brotherhood will definitely want to invest time in the Immortal Guardians series." —All Things Urban Fantasy

"Ms. Duvall brings together a rich world and a wonderful group of characters… This is a great series." —Night Owl Reviews

*"It was non-stop get-up-and-go from the very first page, and instantly you just adore these characters... This was paranormal at its finest."*
—Book Reader Chronicles

*"Full of awesome characters, snappy dialogue, exciting action, steamy sex, sneaky shudder-worthy villains and delightful humor."*
—I'm a Voracious Reader

## Praise for Dianne's
## The Gifted Ones Books

*"The Gifted Ones series is nothing short of perfection itself. I can't wait to see where she takes us next!"* —Scandalicious Book Reviews

*"I enjoyed this world and can't wait to see more crossover as the series continues... You will smile, swoon and have a lot of fun with this."*
—Books and Things

*"Full of danger, intrigue and passion. Dianne Duvall brought the characters to life and delivered an addicting and exciting new series. I'm hooked!"* —Reading in Pajamas

*"The Gifted Ones by Dianne Duvall combine paranormal romance with historical medieval keeps, magic, and time travel. Addictive, funny and wrapped in swoons, you won't be able to set these audios down."*
—Caffeinated Book Reviewer

*"Ms. Duvall excels in creating a community feel to her stories and this is no different... A Sorceress of His Own has a wonderful dynamic, an amazing promise of future adventures and a well-told romance that is sure to please."* —Long and Short Reviews

*"I loved this book! It had pretty much all of my favorite things — medieval times, a kick-ass heroine, a protective hero, magic, and a dash of mayhem."*
—The Romance Reviews

*"Dianne Duvall has delivered a gripping storyline with characters that stuck with me throughout the day and continue to do so long after I turned that last page. A must read!"*
—Reading Between the Wines Book Club

*"A great beginning to a new and different series."* —eBookObsessed

## Titles by Dianne Duvall

*The Gifted Ones*
A SORCERESS OF HIS OWN
RENDEZVOUS WITH YESTERDAY

*Immortal Guardians*
DARKNESS DAWNS
NIGHT REIGNS
PHANTOM SHADOWS
IN STILL DARKNESS
DARKNESS RISES
NIGHT UNBOUND
PHANTOM EMBRACE
SHADOWS STRIKE
BLADE OF DARKNESS

*Anthologies*
PREDATORY
(includes *In Still Darkness*)

ON THE HUNT
(includes *Phantom Embrace*)

# AWAKEN THE DARKNESS

NEW YORK TIMES BESTSELLING AUTHOR

# DIANNE DUVALL

*Immortal*
*Guardians*

AWAKEN THE DARKNESS
Copyright © 2018 by Dianne Duvall

Published by Dianne Duvall, 2018
www.DianneDuvall.com
Editor: Anne Victory
Cover Art: Syneca Featherstone

E-book ISBN: 978-0-9864171-6-0
Print ISBN: 978-0-9864171-7-7

**All Rights Reserved.**
No part of this work may be used or reproduced in any manner whatsoever, printed or electronic, without written permission except in the case of brief quotations embodied in critical articles and reviews. Thank you for showing the author your support by only purchasing authorized editions of this book and by complying with federal copyright laws and not reproducing, scanning, or distributing any part of it in any form without permission.

This book is a work of fiction. Names, characters, places and incidents are either products of the author's imagination or used fictitiously. Any resemblance to actual events, locales, or persons, living or dead, is entirely coincidental.

*For my family*

# Author's Note for Immortal Guardians Fans

Dear Reader,

The initial events in the Prologue will seem familiar to those of you who have read all the books and novellas in the Immortal Guardians series. I considered beginning the story with Chapter One and letting you discover who the hero was when the heroine did. But that would've required a lengthy tale of how he had come to be there near the end of the story. I much preferred showing you instead. So if your inclination is to skip the Prologue, I highly recommend that you do not. It will show you exactly what so many of you have been speculating about: what happened to Stanislav.

I would also like to thank all of you who have asked me for Stan's story and who have fervently hoped his role in my Immortal Guardians family has not come to an end. I've wanted to tell his tale ever since I wrote *Night Unbound* but had to wait for the right time. When I released *Blade of Darkness*, Stanislav leapt forward and informed me that the time had come.

Like Richart's and Yuri's stories, Stanislav's began as a novella. But since I've gone indie, I didn't have to adhere to a strict word count this time and was able to give it full rein. I hope you will enjoy reading or listening to his tale as much as I enjoyed writing it.

Thank you always for your support. If you'd like to chat with me and other readers who enjoy this series and/or The Gifted Ones series, I invite you to join my new *Dianne Duvall Books Group* on Facebook. We've been having so much fun in it. I hope I'll see you there.

—Dianne Duvall

# Acknowledgements

I'd like to thank Crystal and my fabulous Street Team for your continued support and the many smiles you inspire. You all rock! I'd also like to thank the members of my Dianne Duvall Books Group on Facebook. I'm having so much fun with you. If you haven't joined yet and enjoy my Immortal Guardians and/or The Gifted Ones series, we'd love to see you there.

Special thanks go to Anne Victory, who is such a joy to work with, and to Syneca Featherstone, who brings the covers I imagine to vivid life. I also thank the proofreader, formatter, and other behind-the-scenes ladies who helped me bring you *Awaken the Darkness*.

More thanks go to the bloggers, reviewers, and wonderful readers who have picked up copies of my books and helped spread the word about them. I appreciate you all so much. And, of course, I'd like to thank my Facebook and Twitter friends and my blog followers who share in my excitement with every release and make me laugh even when I'm stressing over deadlines. You're the best!

# Prologue

"**H**OOOOOOOLY SHIT!" ETHAN EXCLAIMED.

Stanislav glanced at Ethan, an American immortal who was around three hundred years younger than his own four hundred and thirty-seven years. Ethan's eyes were wide as he took in the men and machines in front of them.

A new vampire army had arisen. One more skilled and armed with the only sedative known to affect immortals and vampires. An army aided by an immortal betrayer they had yet to identify. But the Immortal Guardians *had* finally located the new vampire army's base and discovered — much to their astonishment — that the betrayer had given the vampiric virus and the sedative to a huge mercenary group that had already begun infecting their own men.

No wonder the damned vampires he and his brethren had been encountering recently were so skilled in battle. An army of men with superspeed, superstrength, perfect night vision, and accelerated healing abilities that left them nearly unstoppable on the battlefield would bring the mercenary group billions of dollars. And all evidence suggested this group didn't care who hired their vampire army. They would make it available to the highest bidder worldwide.

Vampire mercenaries. Stanislav shook his head. After hunting and slaying psychotic vampires every night for centuries, anything new — particularly if it offered a challenge — he usually embraced with eagerness, happy to escape the same-old, same-old. But this would irrevocably change the world in dangerous ways. It had to be stopped. *They* had to be stopped.

Stanislav followed Ethan's gaze.

And it sure as hell looked as though he and his brethren would stop them today.

Chris Reordon, head of the East Coast division of the human network that aided Immortal Guardians, had chosen the rendezvous point for immortals, their Seconds, and the humans he commanded: a dense forest several miles distant from the mercenary compound, well beyond the sight of the compound's surveillance equipment and far from any isolated country homes that might produce curiosity seekers. It also bore a heavy enough canopy to protect the immortal warriors from the sunlight that gleamed above them.

Since half the mercenaries they would be fighting were vampire, the immortals had decided to attack in force that afternoon. Vampires couldn't withstand any sun exposure at all. Immortals could. Youngsters like Ethan, not so much. At full strength, Ethan could probably only withstand a few minutes of direct afternoon sunlight before his skin would begin to pinken with a burn, then blister and worse. But the older the immortal was, the more daylight he or she could tolerate. Yuri, a hundred years older than Stanislav, could tolerate half an hour. Stanislav could withstand fifteen minutes or so. More if the sky bore a few clouds. David, who had seen thousands of years, could stand in the sun for hours. And Seth, the eldest amongst them and leader of the Immortal Guardians…

As far as Stanislav knew, Seth could stand in the sun all day without suffering any ill effects.

How they all envied him.

"What?" Chris asked belatedly as he spread a large map on the hood of one of many Humvees outfitted with a variety of mean-looking weapons.

"You think you have enough men?" Ethan asked, motioning to the multitude of rough-hewn Network special-ops soldiers garbed in camouflage.

"This is just half of them," Chris responded absently. "The other half are already in place, observing the compound's perimeter."

Stanislav shared a concerned look with Yuri. If even one

Network soldier's presence had been detected, the mercenaries would know they were coming.

"None have been discovered," Seth said as though Stanislav had spoken the thought aloud. "I monitored their approach myself."

"What the hell is that?" Sheldon—Richart's Second—asked as he pointed at something atop the Humvee.

Stanislav was a bit curious about that himself.

Chris followed his gaze. "A TOW missile."

Yuri caught Stanislav's eye and raised his brows with a smile, his expression saying *Cool!*

Stanislav grinned. It *was* cool. Neither of them had seen such up close before, since immortals tended to use blades to hunt and slay vampires.

"And that?" The French immortal Lisette pointed to a weapon atop another Humvee.

"Flamethrower," Chris answered.

Bastien, the British black sheep of the Immortal Guardians family, stared up at it. "What's its range?"

"It can light up vampires two hundred and fifty feet away," Chris said. "But since it'll also light up immortals, we plan to use them primarily on the gate and on the grounds away from the main structures."

The other military vehicles all boasted high-caliber automatic weapons. Stanislav would have thought it overkill if the compound they intended to destroy didn't encompass four thousand acres.

"Now," Chris said, pointing to an area on the map, "these are the training fields that will be active. Live ammo is used on the target ranges, so you'll face a lot of firepower there. The gates will be heavily guarded. Patrols walk the fence. There will be a changing of the guard in half an hour, so the soldiers on duty now will be tired and likely not as vigilant. Surveillance cameras are mounted on the fences here, here, and here, near the main structures and training fields. But they're sparse on the rest of the grounds. These red circles indicate where you'll find them.

"Once more, you'll find an assload of vampires in this building. The human mercenaries who work the night shift will be sleeping here in the building next to it. This over here is the armory. Anyone you let go in there will come out packing major weaponry. There's only the one door, and a hell of a lot of them are going to want to use it, so I suggest you park a couple of immortals in front of it."

"I'll do it," Yuri volunteered.

"Me, too," Stanislav swiftly added.

Seth nodded his approval.

The eagerness with which Yuri approached this battle filled Stanislav with unease. Yuri was like a brother to him. When vampires had transformed Stanislav against his will four centuries ago, Seth had plunked him down on Yuri's doorstep and assigned Yuri the task of training and mentoring him. The two Russian immortals had been best friends ever since. As close as brothers by blood. Hell, even closer than Stanislav had been to his own brothers while they had lived. Stanislav and Yuri bore such similar personalities. The same quiet temperament. The same likes and dislikes and sense of humor.

Seth had always stationed the two together in the same cities over the centuries. So they'd hunted together nightly. Enjoyed quiet hours reading together before dawn. And had kept at bay the loneliness this life could breed.

But lately things had changed. *Yuri* had changed… in ways that alarmed Stanislav. Yuri had begun taking unnecessary risks. He was an exceptional swordsman and, in the past, had escaped most hunts relatively unscathed. Usually if either of them was injured, it was Stanislav. In recent weeks, however, his friend had racked up one wound after another on a nightly basis. Not superficial wounds. Not paltry scratches that healed or faded to scars before the two of them even made it home. But gashes so deep Stanislav saw bone when he inspected them. A throat nearly slit. Fractured limbs. Broken ribs that punctured lungs. Stab wounds deep enough to damage internal organs.

It scared the hell out of Stanislav, because he knew the only way Yuri would incur such injuries was if he *let* the vampires wound him.

"Try not to blow up the building, guys," Chris implored. "We could use the stuff that's in there."

Stanislav faked a long-suffering sigh. "You're forever spoiling our fun, Reordon."

Yuri laughed and clapped him on the back as several of the other immortals chuckled.

But Stanislav's worry remained. When he had confronted Yuri about the multitude of wounds that had led him to fear his friend had grown weary of this existence, Yuri had stunned him by admitting he had fallen in love with a woman who couldn't safely be transformed.

A woman who must not be a *gifted one*.

*Gifted ones* like himself and his fellow immortals were men and women who had been born with advanced DNA that lent them special gifts. Yuri could see spirits. Stanislav could read others' emotions and manipulate those emotions if he so desired. Lisette and her brother Étienne were telepathic. Roland could heal with his hands. David could do all of the above and shape-shift, too. Seth could do the same *and* teleport. The older the immortal, the more gifts he or she bore. And the DNA that lent them those gifts also protected them from the more corrosive aspects of the vampiric virus that infected them, transforming them into immortals.

Humans were not so lucky. Ordinary humans infected with the virus suffered progressive brain damage that drove them insane and compelled them to prey upon innocents. Ordinary humans turned vampire.

Which meant the woman Yuri loved could not spend the rest of eternity with him. If he transformed her, she would turn vampire and have to be destroyed in just a few short years.

Was the knowledge that Yuri would either have to watch the woman he loved die from old age or lose her to bitterness when she inevitably aged and he remained youthful simply too much for him to bear? Yuri had denied he had a death wish when asked directly. But the sparkle of excitement Stanislav saw in his friend's eyes now, the eagerness with which Yuri anticipated this battle, unnerved him.

He would have to keep a close eye on him.

With Seth's aid and approval, Chris assigned each immortal an area of the compound to tackle. "Seconds," Chris ordered, "park your asses behind the nearest bulletproof structure and guard your immortals. Shoot anyone with a tranquilizer gun."

Stanislav glanced at Alexei in time to see him nod.

Alexei met his gaze. Narrowing his eyes with exaggerated intensity, the Second pointed the index and middle fingers of his right hand at his own eyes, then swung them around and jabbed them toward Stanislav in an aggressive *I'll be watching you* gesture.

Stanislav grinned, amusement taking the edge off his anxiety. Alexei had served as his Second, or human guard, for almost three decades now and had never let him down. Not once. Stanislav would keep an eye on him, too. Alexei was tough. Brave as hell. But he was mortal. Stanislav didn't want to lose him to a stray bullet.

"If your immortal is tranqed," Chris instructed the Seconds, "use your walkie to call it in and cover them until we can get them out of harm's way."

"Should that happen," Richart said, "I can teleport the immortal to David's place."

"Good. The rest of the injured, mortal and immortal, should be taken to Network headquarters. Our emergency medical team is standing by." Chris raked them all with a glance. "Any questions?"

Silence.

He nodded. "Seth, let me know when you and the other immortals are in place, ready to strike, and I'll make the call." He turned to his men. "Helmets on."

The Network soldiers all donned helmets with chinstraps.

Seth eyed the immortals and arched a brow. "Well?"

Every movement broadcasting either reluctance or belligerence, the immortals around Stanislav dutifully donned a head covering that resembled a ski mask and shielded everything but their eyes. Even their mouths were covered except for small breathing holes. Like Stanislav, they had already squeezed their bodies into specially designed rubbery suits that resembled a diving suit and would protect them from the sunlight that would soon bathe them.

"Go ahead," Chris said. "Get it out of your system."

Grumbles and complaints erupted from several as Stanislav shared a long-suffering look with Yuri, then pulled the damned mask down over his head.

"I hate this thing," Yuri grumbled.

"Feels like I'm suffocating," Stanislav agreed.

"Is this damned thing thicker than it was before?" one of the

Brits groused.

"Yes, it is," Chris said as he rolled up his map. "Now suck it up and get moving."

Only Chris Reordon could get away with talking to immortals like that.

Stanislav and his fellow Immortal Guardians made their silent way through the forest until they clustered together in the evergreens across the street from the mercenary compound's front gate. Thick trees and a bounty of chest-high weeds hid them from the guards' view and stymied the sunlight each time it tried to penetrate the dense foliage and hint at their presence.

A few immortals had not yet donned their masks, waiting until the last minute. Those that had, however, were difficult to tell apart. Seth, David, and Zach were all so old that they didn't need to wear suits or masks. The rest of the men, however, were all of a similar height—in the six-feet to six-feet-four-inches range—and muscular build. The only way to distinguish one from another was the unique weapons each bore and, in the case of the married males, the size of the females they stuck to like glue.

Stanislav had no difficulty identifying Yuri. He had given Yuri the weapons his friend bore and even in battle would be able to identify him simply by his fighting methods.

Eyeing his friend, he bit back a curse.

Yuri shifted his weight from one foot to the other, practically dancing in place he was so damned eager for the coming violence.

*Okay, everyone,* Seth told them mentally, *Chris is making the call.*

On Chris's mark, all cell phone reception would be disrupted and the landlines cut. Satellite phones would still function though, so Stanislav and the other immortals had been instructed to keep their ears open and prevent any calls from going out. The electricity would also be cut. Seth would take out the backup generators with several grenades.

Seth vanished.

Stanislav slid two katanas from their sheaths.

*Wonk! Wonk! Wonk!*

The soldiers at the gate jumped when an alarm began to blare and gripped their weapons tighter as they tried to look in every direction at once.

*Boom!*

Flames and debris appeared to fly from four different locations as Seth teleported from generator to generator with lightning speed and tossed the grenades. Chaos erupted as the alarm ceased blaring. Mercenaries ran about the compound, trying to figure out what the hell was happening.

Two grenades skipped across the ground toward the gate that blocked the only entrance and exit.

One of the guards caught the movement and looked down as the objects came to rest at his feet. "Ah, shi—"

An explosion cut off the man's words. Stanislav winced as the thunder pierced his sensitive ears like needles and left them ringing for several seconds. Bodies and body parts flew. The gate blew open and broke apart, flinging shrapnel across the two-lane street.

Stanislav and the others ducked as pieces of metal flew past and embedded themselves in the trees around them. Then they raced forward, David in the lead, to confront their enemies.

From the corner of his eye, Stanislav saw Chris's Network battalion surge forward in their armored vehicles.

Shouts rang out.

Mercenaries opened fire.

Sticking close to Yuri's side, Stanislav sped toward the armory, taking out every mercenary he could along the way. The front of the main building on the right exploded into chunks of granite and glass as they passed it.

David crashed through it all—Lisette, Zach, and Marcus on his heels.

Stanislav swung his katanas, cutting down mercenaries as he raced past the training fields. Screams erupted. Bullets flew through the air like swarms of bees. But the suit he hated so much stopped a hell of a lot of them.

Beside Stanislav, Yuri sheathed one of his katanas and yanked an automatic weapon from the hands of one of the mercenaries. As he continued toward the armory, his pace never slowing, Yuri sprayed the enemy with bullets.

Stanislav laughed. Sheathing his own weapons, he did the same.

The armory rose before them. Two stories high. Large enough

to store a hell of a lot of weapons and ammunition. As expected, many of the human mercenaries scampered toward it like rats scenting cheese.

He and Yuri took out dozens before they ran out of ammo.

Yuri tossed his weapon down, grabbed another, and started for the door.

Stanislav beat him to it. "I'll clear it out," he called. Because of Yuri's recent self-destructive behavior, he didn't think it wise to let him loose in a building full of explosives while he carried an automatic rifle. Dropping his own rifle, he drew both swords and dove inside.

Shouts erupted as men frantically grabbed weapons and ammo and swung around.

Damn, they'd moved fast. There were more crammed inside than he had expected, but it didn't slow him down. Stanislav cut a swath through them, inspiring such terror that some decided to risk firing their weapons.

Swearing, he hoped like hell those bullets wouldn't hit any grenades or other explosives as he slew one after another until only he remained standing. He swept through the building—upstairs and downstairs—one last time before he headed outside.

The mercenary compound had transformed into a war zone. Stanislav didn't know how in hell Chris Reordon was going to keep this from appearing on the news but didn't doubt the human would do it.

Yuri stood with his back against the wall, spraying mercenaries with bullets.

"Clear," Stanislav called and backed up to the wall on the opposite side of the doorway.

The number of humans charging toward them, though substantial, had dwindled a little. Immortals Bastien and Melanie swept through the mercenaries, inflicting fatal wounds and sparking terror. Network soldiers, all clad in black, swarmed in their midst too, picking off any mercenaries the immortals missed and guarding the immortals' backs.

This was not their first clash with mercenaries, but all were determined to make it their last. Not one man would be left alive to resurrect the outfit in the future.

From the corner of his eye, Stanislav saw Yuri drop his rifle and go to work with his swords. Alexei and Dmitry—Stanislav's and Yuri's Seconds—approached in a crouch, barely recognizable beneath their helmets and body armor. Alexei took up a position at the corner of the building on Stanislav's side, his automatic rifle spitting fire and bullets that kept mercenaries from sneaking up behind Stanislav. Dmitry did the same, parking himself at the opposite corner and protecting Yuri.

A tank rumbled forth from one of the hangars that Immortal Guardians Étienne, Krysta, and Sean were clearing out.

*Shit.* The mercenaries must have—

Two missiles struck the tank, launched by Chris's men. Flames reached high into the air.

Dmitry whooped.

Alexei laughed.

Stanislav grinned. He might be concerned about Yuri and Alexei's safety, but he nevertheless enjoyed a good fight.

Yuri grunted.

Stanislav did, too, when a bullet penetrated his suit where the material thinned along his neck. Fortunately, it missed his carotid artery. "How many of these bastards are there?" he grumbled. He had slain dozens on the way to the armory and inside it. But more kept coming, each one determined to get his hands on the weapons the two immortal warriors guarded.

Explosions overshadowed the gunfire in occasional bursts.

In the distance, flames spewed forth from the flamethrower atop Chris's Humvee as vampires darted out of the building that housed their sleeping quarters, deciding sun exposure posed less of a threat than the powerful immortals inside.

Another bullet struck Stanislav in the side. The uncomfortable suit he wore stopped several where it was thickest. But some areas were thinner so it wouldn't restrict his movements. And every once in a while a bullet would find a weak point and penetrate it like a blade.

Centuries of fighting enabled Stanislav to compartmentalize the pain and continue swinging his swords. Some vampires who had miraculously evaded the flamethrower's reach joined the mercenaries he and Yuri faced, surging forward. Their skin blistered in the sunlight as they ducked Bastien's swords.

Dmitry's weapon quieted as he hastily reloaded.

Stanislav kept an eye on the vampires zigzagging through the combat as his sword spilled another human mercenary's blood.

Alexei suddenly swore and fired a frenzy of bullets toward the back of the building. Eager to take advantage of the opening, three mercenaries altered their paths and lunged toward him.

Stanislav leapt over to guard his friend's back, killing those who meant to slay Alexei while his Second dispatched the mercenaries creeping toward them from the rear.

"Behind you!" Dmitry suddenly shouted.

Stanislav spun around.

Mercenaries had taken advantage of his brief inattention and surged toward the doorway. One of the men aimed a tranq gun at Yuri and fired.

The dart hit Yuri in the neck as he turned at Dmitry's warning.

Inside his mask, Yuri's eyes rolled back in his head. His knees buckled. His swords fell from hands that went limp as Yuri collapsed, hitting the ground hard.

Stanislav grunted when a blade bit deep into his side.

The vampire wielding it shouted in triumph. His skin charring, he yanked the blade out and raised it high.

Dmitry's gun resumed fire. "Shit!" he shouted. "Yuri's down! Yuri's down!"

Stanislav blocked the vampire's next swing and struck a blow of his own. Then another and another, putting on a burst of preternatural speed despite the blood loss that drained his energy. He heard Alexei move away behind him, still firing his weapon furiously.

More mercenaries must be coming around the back corner.

Stanislav swept the vampire's head from his shoulders, then swiveled to aid Yuri.

He couldn't remember the last time he had felt true fear, but—in that moment—it struck him with the force of a quarrel from a crossbow.

Yuri lay on the ground, unmoving, the tranquilizer dart sticking out of his neck where the suit was thinnest while Dmitry fought off a wave of mercenaries.

Another blistering vampire darted forward and grabbed one of Yuri's fallen swords.

Stanislav lunged forward. "Nooooo!" he bellowed, swinging his blades wildly as he fought past four more blistering and burning vampire mercenaries.

Too late.

The vampire struck fast, cleaving Yuri's head from his shoulders.

All the air left Stanislav's lungs, sucked away in an instant by grief and horror and disbelief. It couldn't be.

It couldn't *be*.

Yuri couldn't be dead. He *couldn't* be dead.

But he was.

A suffering greater than that spawned by all of his wounds combined crashed through Stanislav. They'd killed him. They'd killed Yuri. They'd taken his fucking head!

"*Yuri!*" he roared, rage igniting his insides as tears blurred his vision.

He pushed forward, cutting and knocking bodies out of his way, feeling as though he were wading against a swift current in chest-deep water. Bullets struck him. Blades bit deep. But he paid them no heed.

Something round flew at him. Stanislav knocked it aside, his only desire to get to his friend—his brother—before the symbiotic virus inside him devoured Yuri from the inside out and left nothing behind for Stanislav to hold and bid farewell.

Yuri was dead. His brother was dead.

A sob caught in his throat.

The object he batted aside flew through the armory's doorway and skittered across the floor with a clatter he barely heard over the pulsing heartbeat in his ears and the gunfire and bullets that peppered him.

Just a few more feet…

Thunder shattered his eardrums. Flames and shrapnel slammed into him, knocking him off his feet.

Agony engulfed him.

Blessed darkness.

A hand clamped around the raw flesh of his wrist, rousing Stanislav.

Torturous pain battered him.

Difficult to breathe.

Razor blades in his lungs. Smoke in his nostrils.

Something abraded him from his ass to his boots. Rough. Almost rhythmic in its repetition. The hand manacling his arm stretched it above his head. A thousand knives seemed to stab him in the shoulder.

Thunder rumbled. Distant gunfire split the day. Flames seemed to sear his skin.

He struggled to open his eyes.

"Hurry," a voice hissed.

Something kept hitting his legs… or what was left of them. It felt as though little flesh remained on his shattered bones.

What was it? Where was he?

He drew in a wheezy breath and nearly passed out from the pain it generated. Liquid rattled in his lungs. His right eye wouldn't open. The left he cracked enough to see daylight flickering behind a dense canopy of leaves.

The ground swept past in a blur.

His head lolled backward, giving him an upside-down view of a man dragging him across the ground, a second man at his side.

They moved swiftly. Too swiftly for humans.

Vampires?

A large, hazy object abruptly loomed before them.

His captors stopped. A thunk sounded. Hands gripped him, magnifying the pain. Then Stanislav went weightless, rising into the air before he hit a hard surface with a thud that produced such agony the darkness returned.

⟫◈◈◈⟪

Movement shook Stanislav awake, then rocked him in a manner that might have been soothing if he didn't feel as though his body had been put through a meat grinder.

A rhythmic rumble penetrated the pools of blood in his ears.

A car?

Again he cracked an eyelid open and tried to make sense of his surroundings.

He was in the trunk of a car?

How had he gotten there? Who had put him there?

The car jumped as it hit a bump, tossing him up an inch or two, then slamming him back down.

He moaned. His head swam. Nausea rose.

Darkness.

<hr/>

*Shick. Thud. Shick. Thud. Shick. Thud.*

Something settled upon Stanislav's legs, fanning the burning flames that seemed determined to devour them. He gritted his teeth, knowing only pain for several moments as consciousness beckoned.

Moaning, he tried to open his eyes. One was swollen shut. The lid blanketing the other lifted just a bit.

What…? What had happened?

*Shick. Thud. Shick. Thud.*

Where was he?

"Stop pacing and dig, damn it," a male ordered. "He's starting to wake up."

Curses filled the air.

More of those pats on his legs, like David's cats leaping down on him and settling in for a nice nap. Every touch sent new agony coursing through him.

He tried to focus, tried to clear his vision, his mind. He wiggled his toes, alarmed by how difficult the task was. Managed to make the fingers of both hands twitch, too.

He hadn't lost any limbs. His whole body hurt so much that the knowledge came as a surprise.

Something hit him in the face. Dust invaded his nose.

He coughed, then damn near passed out again at the suffering that seized his body.

"Shit!" someone swore.

The *shick-thuds* sped up.

More weight pounced on his raw, burning legs. His stomach. His chest. His broken arm. His face.

Again he coughed.

Dirt. Someone was burying him.

*Two* someones.

"Are you sure he won't be able to get out of this?"

"Yeah. Look at him. He looks like barbecued ground beef that's been chewed up and spit out. With that much damage and no blood supply, no way in hell is he going to claw his way out of this."

More dirt. More torturous coughs.

"Won't he suffocate if we bury him?"

"Nah. I heard the higher-ups say nothing short of beheading will kill an immortal. They're like fucking water bears."

"What the hell is a water bear?"

"Forget it. Just keep digging."

Why were they burying him? Why weren't they beheading him? Why not just take his sword and…

Ice clawed its way through the pain.

*Yuri.* Something had happened to Yuri. Someone had decapitated him.

Grief tore through him.

He had to get to Yuri. Had to get to what was left of him before he lost him forever.

He rolled onto his side. Moaned.

"Fuck the shovels! Just push it in!" an anxious voice barked.

Stanislav dragged an arm up. A bone protruded from the skin.

He growled in agony as he curled the arm over his face and head.

A mountain of dirt showered down upon him like a never-ending tidal wave, the weight of it growing and digging into his battered form. The light dimmed. Then darkness blanketed him, this time not triggered by unconsciousness.

The landslide ended. Quiet fell.

Stanislav tried to move.

Dirt trickled down into the pocket of air his arm had trapped around his face.

He stilled.

The voice was right. His wounds had left him too weak to burrow his way out and kill… whoever the hell had put him here.

A rumble of voices overhead told him what his beleaguered

senses couldn't. The two vampires remained on the ground above him.

Fighting the pain, he called upon his gift and scrutinized their emotions. Both felt fear. But as minutes passed and Stanislav didn't burst from the ground and attack them, relief crept in, followed by triumph.

Well, fuck that. For all he knew, one of the men above him had slain Yuri.

*Both* would pay for it.

He seized their triumph and warped it, morphing it into distrust, suspicion, and anger.

Their voices rose, the words they spoke running together as they argued.

Weakness teemed within him while he fed their fury, their need to commit violence, fueling it with every ounce of energy that remained in him.

Thuds and crashes sounded above. Scuffling feet. More shouts.

A heavier thud sounded. Dirt shifted as a body hit the ground above him.

Two shuffling footsteps. Then a second body hit the ground.

Silence.

No voices. No emotions. No heartbeats save Stanislav's, which slowed to one beat per minute. Then one beat every five minutes. Then less.

*Yuri.*

*Forgive me, my brother.*

His breath stopped as darkness claimed him.

# Chapter One

*Two years later*

Susan guided the car to a halt in the driveway and shut off the engine. Leaning forward, she peered through the front windshield. "Wow. I was kind of hoping the pictures online didn't do it justice, but it looks even worse in person."

The beagle beside her barked his agreement, then poked his nose out the partially lowered window.

Sighing, Susan pocketed the keys and opened the driver's door. Stepping out into the brisk fall air, she closed it behind her and walked around to open the door for her furry companion. "I don't know, Jax." Bending, she grabbed the end of his leash and looped it around her wrist before he could dart away. "This isn't looking so good."

A two-story home rose before them. Nice sized. Larger than any home she had ever lived in, that was for sure. But the canary-yellow paint was starting to peel, the front porch clearly needed a few boards replaced, and the yard…

Well, there *was* no yard really. Just patches of weeds here and there.

She glanced around, squinting against the bright sunlight. "I mean, I like the location." Loved it, actually. "It's isolated. No neighbors or any other structures for miles." A boon. For reasons that still escaped her, Susan had been born with the ability to hear other people's thoughts. Out here she would be able to enjoy blissful silence instead of having to constantly tune out her neighbors' mental noise.

She returned her attention to the house. "But I really wasn't planning on buying a fixer-upper." She noted the crooked spindles in the porch railing. "And this place looks like it needs a *lot* of fixing up."

Jax woofed and wagged his tail, unperturbed. Nose to the ground, he explored with great excitement all of the unfamiliar scents he could drink in as he tested the reach of his leash.

"You like it, huh?" Smiling, she turned in a slow circle. Forest bracketed the house on the west and east sides. A small field sprang into forest after a few yards across from it to the north.

When Jax woofed and gave the leash another tug, Susan walked him over to the trees.

Rustling sounded as some creature she couldn't see scuttled away. Jax barked, his tail wagging at warp speed as he drew her forward into the brush.

She laughed. "Yeah, you'd love it here." So many scents and creatures to investigate. "But I want to look around a little more before the real estate agent gets here."

Gently urging him back, she strode up a faded brick path. Someone had made a half-assed attempt to remove some of the weeds that had grown up between the pavers, but most were already reclaiming their territory. She stopped at the foot of the steps. "Sheesh. I don't even know if this is safe to walk on."

Placing a foot on the lowest step, she tentatively applied her weight to it.

*Hmm.* It felt surprisingly sturdy. Didn't squeak. Maybe it just needed a coat of paint.

She continued up another four steps, still taking care, and stepped onto the porch.

*Creeeeeak.* There it was. And nearly every other board she trod upon did the same. But like the steps, they felt strong beneath her feet. The railing and spindles that rose up from them would definitely have to be replaced though. They wobbled under the slightest pressure.

She and Jax followed the porch around the side of the house and onto a back deck. Like the porch, the boards there looked old and weathered but were firm beneath her feet.

"Maybe this isn't as bad as I thought," she murmured.

A closer examination of the wood siding revealed no evidence of rot or termites or foundation issues.

Hope rose.

A lovely meadow—or what *could* be a lovely meadow if she cleaned it up and did a little landscaping—extended a good fifty yards from the back deck. Resting her hands on the railing, which was steadier back here, she closed her eyes and turned her face up to the sun.

Jax's claws clicked against the wood as he explored the deck.

"You hear that, Jax?"

The beagle paused as though listening with her.

"Utter silence," she breathed reverently, soaking in the peace, the wonder of not having to listen to the thoughts of all her neighbors.

A breeze lifted her auburn hair, drawing it away from her face. And as it did, the strangest feeling came over her. As if the house behind her were awakening from a long nap.

Gravel crunched as a car approached out front.

Shaking her head at herself, Susan retraced her path to the front of the house.

A plump woman with glasses and dyed blond hair that brought to mind the puffy hairstyles from the eighties stepped down from a dark gray SUV. "Hi!" she called cheerfully, slamming the door. "You must be Susan."

Returning her smile, Susan skipped down the steps. "Hi. I got here a little early and was just looking around a bit. I hope you don't mind."

"Not at all." Juggling her keys, the woman strode forward and offered her free hand with a smile. "I'm Rhonda."

Susan shook her hand. "Nice to meet you."

"What do you think?" the woman asked, gesturing to the house. "Nice, huh?" She motioned to the field behind her. "Beautiful view. Lots of privacy. I believe peace and quiet were high on your list of priorities, weren't they?"

Susan nodded. "Yes, they are. And the view is lovely." She gestured to the weed patches on either side of the brick walkway. "The yard… not so much."

The woman winced. "Yeah. The owner hasn't done much with the place since she inherited it. I tried to tell her it would sell faster if she added a little curb appeal, but…" She shrugged.

"Is it okay if I bring Jax in with us?"

"Sure, honey. I don't mind. I love dogs." Leaning down, the woman patted Jax on the head. "And you're a cutie, aren't you?"

Jax licked her hand and wagged his tail.

Smiling, Rhonda straightened and headed for the front door. "Reminds me of the dog I had when I was a little girl, except mine was a basset hound."

Much to Susan's surprise, the real estate agent used an alarm trigger on her own key ring to deactivate an alarm, then used the key next to it to open the door instead of using one of those key box things the other homes she'd shown Susan had borne.

"There's an alarm system?"

"Yes, but it's only temporary and will be deactivated when the house sells."

"Have there been problems?"

"Oh, you know how it is. When houses are listed online, sometimes people who want something for nothing will check them out just to see if there's anything in them that's worth stealing." *They did so more than once with this place, probably because it's out in the middle of nowhere and clearly unoccupied.* "And sometimes teenagers like to stir up trouble. One time, I went to show a house in Chapel Hill and the interior of the place was trashed. Teenagers had gotten the address online and decided to make it their little hangout. Left food wrappers and beer bottles all over the place. Sprayed graffiti on the walls. So the alarm is just precautionary."

Susan had seen similar things on some of those house-flipping shows.

Rhonda swung the front door open. "Now," she said as she entered, "it's gonna smell a little musty in here because the house has been closed up for a while."

Susan followed her inside.

"Leave the door open, would you? The breeze will help air it out."

Susan glanced up. Directly in front of her, a staircase rose to a second-floor landing. The ceiling above was two stories high. Traditional railing formed a rectangle above her, letting her see open doors to several rooms above them. *Wow. This place is huge.* "What did you say the square footage is?"

"Twenty-six hundred."

Twenty-six hundred? That was twice as big as the place she was renting now.

"Stay put for a minute and let me turn on some lights."

While Rhonda wound her way in and out of rooms, flipping switches, Susan looked around.

On her left lay a sizable living room with a ceiling that must be eleven or twelve feet high. A large fireplace with an outdated cover dominated one wall. No way would she light a fire in that thing without getting it inspected first. But once she did, it would be nice to have a cozy fire snapping and crackling and keeping her warm on chilly nights.

On her right lay what she suspected had once been a formal dining room. She stepped inside it just as Rhonda turned a light on in the room adjacent to it, revealing a kitchen.

Yep. Definitely a dining room.

"Shall I show you around?" Rhonda asked brightly. A little too brightly, perhaps. The woman seemed nervous now that they were inside. "As you can see, there are hardwood floors throughout."

Scuffed and faded hardwood floors that needed sanding, restaining, and Susan wasn't sure what else to restore their former glory. That would be a big expense, because she wasn't up to performing the task herself.

"This would make a great dining room," Rhonda gushed. "And look at this spacious kitchen!"

It *was* spacious. And needed serious updating. "How old is the house?"

"It was built in 1943." Smile still in place, Rhonda knocked on a cabinet door. "They built 'em strong back then. These are solid wood cabinets. Not that plywood crap they used in my place."

Susan laughed. Solid wood was good. But like the floors, they needed some sanding and staining or a coat of paint at the very least. New hardware, too, but that was doable on her budget. Unfortunately, the countertops were Formica. Worn and stained.

Warped in one place. Ideally, she'd like to replace those with granite. With so much square footage of countertop though, that was something she'd have to put off for at least a couple of years.

"What did you say you do for a living, dear?" Rhonda asked.

"I'm a writer," Susan commented absently. And she would have to sell a hell of a lot of books to accrue enough royalties to replace those countertops. "How long has the house been on the market?" Since kitchens and bathrooms tended to sell homes these days, she wondered if this wasn't one of the chief reasons the place hadn't sold.

"Two years," Rhonda admitted reluctantly. She patted the countertop near her and wrinkled her nose. "It could use some updating, huh?"

Susan nodded, mentally calculating the cost. New sink. New fixtures. New appliances all around, because that stove would have to go.

"It has a nice breakfast nook though, don't you think?" Rhonda said, backing around the bar and waving her arm at the connecting room.

Hell, the breakfast nook was larger than the entire kitchen in Susan's current abode.

As she followed Rhonda through the home, that odd feeling returned. The *house waking up from a nap* feeling. As though it were a living, breathing entity sluggishly opening its eyes and blearily following their progress through its domain.

It wasn't a bad feeling. Or a creepy feeling. It was kind of hard for her to pin down. But she wondered if perhaps Rhonda felt it, too, because the woman steadily picked up speed as she showed Susan a kitchen pantry the size of a walk-in closet, a half bath that needed as much updating as the kitchen, then the four bedrooms and two bathrooms upstairs. The expense of the multitude of things Susan would have to do to turn this into her dream home far exceeded what she could afford to spend. And it would take years.

Disappointment settled upon her shoulders.

She had so hoped this would be the one. She desperately needed the peace and quiet this place could provide. And newer homes — even those half this size — parked on this much land were nearly impossible to find and way beyond her budget.

They returned to the ground floor. As Rhonda hustled her toward the front door, Jax dug in his heels and snuffled at the base of a closed door beneath the staircase.

Susan stopped. "What's that? A closet?"

There was no mistaking the dread that filled Rhonda's features then, though she tried very hard to keep her smile in place. "No, that leads to the basement."

Susan's eyebrows flew up. "The house has a basement?"

"Yes."

She'd always wanted a basement. "Is that included in the square footage you gave me?"

"No."

*Cool. Bonus footage.*

When Rhonda made no move to show it to her, Susan asked, "May I see it?"

"Of course," the woman replied and crossed to the door. *Why'd the dog have to stop, damn it? We were almost in the clear.*

Susan blinked when that thought came through. It was the first unrehearsed thought she had picked up from the real estate agent since meeting her.

"Excuse me, cutie," Rhonda told Jax, then opened the door.

Jax lurched forward, nearly knocking the woman down and yanking the leash right out of Susan's hand.

"Oh! I'm so sorry," Susan apologized as Jax clattered down the stairs into the darkness.

Rhonda grabbed the doorjamb and righted herself. "No problem, honey."

"Are you okay?"

"I'm fine," she insisted, then resolutely straightened her shoulders and peered through the dim doorway. *You can do this.*

Susan stared at her. Perhaps the basement was small and the woman was claustrophobic.

Or maybe basements just creeped her out.

Rhonda leaned her upper body in and felt around for the light switch as if she feared something would leap out and grab her. Light flickered on, illuminating the stairs. Giving Susan another of those false smiles, Rhonda stepped inside and clomped down the steps.

*Ooookay*. Susan followed. *Wow!* The basement was almost as huge as the first floor. But… "Oh." She didn't even try to hide her disappointment. "It has a dirt floor?"

Jax sure didn't mind. He was racing around, nose to the ground, his breath raising little puffs of dust.

"A lot of the older homes around here do." Rhonda remained by the staircase, poised for flight, while Susan walked around. "My brother-in-law bought a place with a basement like this. He hired a contractor to help him pour a concrete foundation, fixed the rest up, and turned the basement into a two-bedroom apartment. Ended up renting it for more than the cost of his monthly mortgage payments."

Susan had no interest in renting any part of her home. The whole purpose of finding a place parked on a lot of land out in the middle of nowhere was to get *away* from people, not invite them in. "That would be way outside my budget."

"Well, there's certainly no harm in leaving it like this."

Susan grunted. "Not if you don't mind bugs and rodents and snakes in your basement." No doubt that was why Jax was so excited. He had definitely caught something's scent. He kept returning again and again to a central portion of the floor.

"I've never run into any critters while showing the house to other interested parties," Rhonda replied. *Not the ones who made it this far*.

Susan wondered what *that* thought signified.

"If you see any, I'm sure an exterminator could get rid of them for you. I can give you the number of a good one," Rhonda offered.

Crossing to Jax, Susan knelt beside him.

Wagging his tail, he woofed and scratched at the dirt.

"What'd you find, boy?" As she watched him, a strange compulsion seized her. Reaching down, she rested a hand on the ground—fingers splayed—and closed her eyes.

Peace settled upon her. As did a wondrous warmth that seemed to settle in her chest, then flowed outward to the rest of her body. Longing followed. But longing for what?

*That's right where they found them.*

Susan's eyes flew open when she caught that thought from

Rhonda. The woman was definitely creeped out. Rising, Susan faced her. "You told me the woman who wants to sell it inherited it. Did the previous owners die here?"

Rhonda's eyebrows rose. "What? No."

"What happened to them?"

"Him," she said, then shook her head. "The current owner's cousin inherited it from his parents. But he was killed shortly thereafter."

Susan frowned. "Here?"

"No. He worked for that big mercenary outfit that was destroyed a couple of years ago and was one of the casualties. Shadow something."

Shadow River. Susan had heard about that. Apparently some disgruntled members of a private military company had bombed the hell out of the place and shot everyone in sight. It had been the biggest mass shooting in the country's history.

She gave Rhonda a wry smile. "For a minute there I thought maybe he'd died here."

Rhonda laughed. "No, honey. No one died here." Her gaze strayed to the ground Jax continued to examine. *It was weird though, what the workers found down here when they came to clear out the place. Two pairs of clothing laid out like chalk outlines at a crime scene. Socks tucked into the shoes. Underwear inside the belted pants. What looked like bloodstains on the lot of it.*

Susan eyed the ground beneath her feet uneasily. *Really?*

Her unease abruptly morphed into warmth and peace and a strong feeling of well-being, coaxing her into shrugging it off. Maybe the guy had been a budding independent filmmaker or something. Her college roommate's boyfriend had made two short films while she'd known them, and both had involved liberal amounts of stage blood.

She followed Rhonda back upstairs and waited on the front porch while the woman turned off all the lights, then locked the front door.

"So?" Rhonda asked with a *give me some good news* grin. "Are you interested?"

Susan shook her head. "I don't think so."

Her face fell. "Really? I'd think this place would be perfect for a writer."

Susan looked around wistfully. "It would be. But it just needs too much updating."

"That's too bad, but I understand."

"Is there anything else you could show me in my price range?"

Nodding, Rhonda mentioned a house on the outskirts of Carrboro and started listing its attributes as they slowly descended the front steps and meandered down the brick path.

*Please.*

Susan frowned. That thought hadn't come from Rhonda.

Glancing around, she saw nothing but fields and trees swaying in the gentle breeze. No indication of human life other than themselves.

She looked over her shoulder. It seemed almost to have come from the house itself, which made her question whether or not she had actually heard it.

Shrugging mentally, she nodded as Rhonda mentioned a second property that might interest her. But the farther they strolled down the path, the more Susan's steps began to lag. Sorrow filled her, surprising in its intensity, as did regret and a sudden overwhelming conviction that she was making a huge mistake.

Stopping, Susan faced the house and studied it.

The sorrow faded, replaced by peace and happiness and that wonderful warmth.

She could do this. She could buy this house and fix it up. It didn't matter if it took years. It would be worth it. She would be so happy here. Just looking at it filled her with joy and hope and excitement. She wanted this house. She had to have this house!

Turning to Rhonda, she interrupted the woman midsentence. "I changed my mind. I'll take it!"

Rhonda's mouth fell open. Then her eyes widened and a huge smile dawned. "Wonderful! You're going to love it here, honey. I just know it."

⋙◈◈◈⋘

The thuds of car doors closing and the rumble of engines told him the women were leaving.

Despair filled him. He had done everything he could to make

the woman stay. Not the one who had come before with males. (He had filled those males with such fear that they had scampered away like cats being chased by wild dogs.) But the *other* woman. The new one.

He had awakened to the sound of her voice, low and so appealing that it had coaxed him into braving the pain and remaining conscious. How long had he been out this time? Weeks? Months? He had no way of knowing down here in the dark with nothing but constant agony.

Did he know her — the new woman? The one with the voice that seemed to stroke the very marrow of his bones? Did she know he was down here? Did she know *why* he was here? Who had put him there?

He couldn't remember anymore, if he had ever known at all.

He couldn't even remember his name.

But there was something about her… this stranger… or not a stranger…

He had called upon his gift and manipulated her emotions to try to coax her into staying. But she had still left.

She would be back though. He knew she would.

And he would be waiting.

⟫◈◈◈⟪

As soon as Susan got home, she panicked. What the hell had she been thinking? She couldn't buy that place! It needed too much work! And it would take *so* much money. Money she didn't have.

She hadn't even looked at the roof. Or the attic. Or asked if the house had ever flooded or if it rested in a one-hundred-year or five-hundred-year floodplain. Had it ever had mold problems? How old was the air-conditioning unit? The heater? The hot-water heater?

She couldn't buy that place! What about the plumbing and the electrical? In a house that old, there were bound to be problems. Big problems. What if it turned into a freaking money pit? Or what if it didn't but something went wrong with her writing career and she ended up not being able to afford the updates? The publishing industry had changed in huge ways in recent years. There was no telling what would happen next.

Rhonda was very understanding when Susan called her but somehow managed to talk her into taking another look at the place.

The same thing happened when she did. Warmth filled Susan as soon as she stepped onto the front path. Warmth and an incredible feeling of welcome, of coming home. And as she walked through the house, noting the same flaws that had made her doubt the wisdom of purchasing the place, that feeling of excitement returned. Happiness. Hope. The certainty that this was where she was meant to be. That this was where she belonged.

"So?" Rhonda gave her an encouraging smile. "Are you interested?"

"Yes!" Susan declared.

Then questioned her sanity again when she got home.

What the hell was wrong with her? What was it about that place that made her throw all common sense out the window?

Rhonda showed her the house again. And again. The fifth time she just stayed in the kitchen, working on her laptop, while Susan wandered from room to room with Jax.

The old place really called to her. Seemed even to speak to her, but not in a creepy *holy crap, it's haunted* way. She never once felt uneasy. On the contrary, she felt safe. Content. As if she belonged there.

*Please*, a voice seemed to whisper.

So much longing. Her own desire calling to her, perhaps, trying to override all doubt?

Well, if that was the case, it worked. As long as Susan was at the house, she *felt* no doubt.

Returning to the kitchen, she waited while Rhonda tucked her laptop away and grabbed her keys. The real estate agent closed and locked the door, then stared at Susan. "Listen, honey. Clearly you want this place, so I did something I don't usually do. I went ahead and had the place inspected." She pulled a sheaf of papers out of her large bag and handed it over. "The roof is in great condition. Unless there's a hail storm or something, the inspector said it should last another decade or so."

"Really?"

Rhonda smiled. "I know. I admit I was surprised. The electrical checked out just fine. The plumbing, too. He said the plumbing isn't nearly as old as the house is and guessed the cousin's parents updated it around the time they replaced the roof. He found a little rust on the wire thingies in the dishwasher, but I've got the same in mine at home and mine's only two years old."

Smiling, Susan skimmed the pages in her hand.

"He said the AC is only a few years old. The heater, too. The water heater will likely have to be replaced in the next couple of years though. He said the air ducts need cleaning. He recommended replacing them but said you could get by with just a cleaning if that was out of your budget. The porch railing needs work, but you already knew that."

Susan's heart began to pound as she listened and read and listened some more. It was shockingly good news. To have so little wrong with a place this old? Amazing.

"And…" Rhonda paused dramatically. "I talked the owner into coming down on the price."

Susan tilted her head to one side. "How far down?"

"Way down. This house has been on the market for two years and is priced higher than other homes in the area. Homes with remodeled kitchens and bathrooms. I told her there was no way she would sell it at the current price, especially with all the updating it needs." *And that this was probably her last chance to sell the place. Everyone else I've shown the damned house to practically ran out the front door and never looked back.* "So she agreed to knock twenty thousand off the asking price."

Susan stared.

Rhonda leaned in and lowered her voice as though she feared being overheard, which Susan found amusing, considering there was no one around for miles. "Between you and me, she's *really* eager to get this thing off her hands, so I may be able to talk her down another ten."

"Ten thousand?" Susan asked, finding it hard to believe and needing clarification.

"Yes."

*Do it.*

Susan didn't know if that was Rhonda's thought or the inner whisper that kept compelling her to buy the place, but as excitement bubbled up inside her, she blurted, "I'll take it!"

Grinning big, she threw her arms around Rhonda and hugged her.

Rhonda laughed and hugged her back.

"*If,*" Susan qualified, "the owner knocks off the extra ten thousand."

"She will," Rhonda said. "But…"

Susan waited for her to continue. "But?" she questioned when the woman hesitated.

"But this time I'm afraid I'm going to have to ask you for an EMD."

"A what?"

"An earned money deposit to demonstrate your commitment to the offer you're making."

Susan laughed. "No problem. I'm sorry I dragged you out here so many times."

Rhonda waved off the apology. "It'll all be worth it once you're in your new home."

# Chapter Two

THUDS ROUSED HIM.

Pain assaulted him as it always did. He could no longer remember the cause and had long since given up on identifying it. Hunger and thirst flayed him, too. But the woman he could hear moving around beyond his dirt tomb soothed him like a healing balm.

Her soft footfalls padded across a wood floor somewhere above him. She was barefoot again and fretting over something. He didn't know what, but could feel her emotions and almost see her nibbling her lower lip or chewing a thumbnail.

Concentrating, he weakened her worry and replaced it with warmth. He had done so each time he had awakened to her presence in whatever structure rested atop him, filling her with the relief she brought him, the happiness. He didn't know who she was. Hell, he didn't even know who *he* was. But her being there...

Well, he just knew he needed her. She made this—whatever this torture was—bearable.

His heart beat once. He drew in a breath. The agony the slight movement fostered nearly plunged him into unconsciousness again.

Where *was* he? *Who* was he?

When his disquiet began to infiltrate the woman upstairs, he again filled her with warmth and welcome and happiness. She was the only thing that kept him sane.

He *was* sane, wasn't he?

"When love," she began to sing softly, "into my dreams was

creeping." Her voice was low and sultry. "I gave my heart into your keeping."

Pure ecstasy. How he needed her.

As she continued to sing, he wanted to weep with gratitude.

How long had he been down here, suffering alone? It seemed an eternity.

How long had it been since he'd last roused? An hour? A week? A year?

How was he even still alive? What *was* he that he could survive this? He might not be thinking quite right, but he knew his remaining alive for so long after being buried underground wasn't normal.

The pain that racked him crescendoed, eliciting a moan.

A clickety-clack sounded above as her dog trotted down the stairs, then began scratching at the dirt.

*Find me*, he willed both the dog and the woman. *Please.*

Darkness swallowed him.

*Find me.*

Susan stilled. Her voice trailed off at the sound of that whispered plea in her head.

*Please.*

Today's mail still clutched in her hand, she slowly turned and looked around.

As usual, she found herself alone. But that hadn't been the first time she'd heard a voice, stronger this time than the whisper she had initially mistaken for some inner voice that guided her.

Assuming she was picking up on someone else's thoughts, she had checked to see if she had acquired any new neighbors. But she hadn't.

When the voice didn't surface again, Susan was surprised to feel a little disappointed. Though few words had been spoken, the feelings that had accompanied those she'd heard had wrapped around her like a warm blanket and made her feel good.

Sighing, she headed into the kitchen.

*Night surrounded her, as comforting as an old friend, while she strode along a wide sidewalk. Pools of golden light illuminated the path, but she could see with complete clarity areas that lay in darkness.*

*A college campus rose up all around her, quiet and deserted, most students in their beds.*

*Someone walked beside her, their long strides in sync. When he said something that amused her, she turned her head and found a handsome man with short dark hair. Laughter lurked in his sparkling brown eyes. Both of them wore black pants, black shirts, and long black coats.*

*She was as tall as he was. And male. But it felt natural.*

*She drew in a breath… and could smell* everything. *The grass. The trees. The Dumpster behind the building up ahead. The cat creeping around one corner of the building they passed.*

*And blood.*

*The metallic tang hit her at the same time she heard a scuffle break out in the distance.*

*She shared a look with her companion.*

*In unison, they drew long katanas and picked up their pace.*

*The scenery around them blurred, then swam back into focus.*

*Four men knelt over two prone males on the ground. Spinning around, they regarded her and her companion with glowing eyes, some blue, some green. Their lips drew back into snarls of fury, flashing long fangs coated with crimson liquid.*

*Raising the sword in her right hand, she lunged forward and swung.*

A dog barked.

Susan jerked awake, her heart slamming against her ribs. Eyes wide, she sat up and examined the bedroom around her. What a weird-ass dream. Maybe she shouldn't have watched that *Blade* marathon right before going to bed.

Glancing at the clock, she groaned. 4:32 a.m. She had only been asleep for an hour. What had woken her?

A bark echoed through the house.

She sighed. Apparently a certain beagle had. "Damn it, Jax," she grumbled as she rose. "You'd better not have woken me up because you saw another opossum waddling by. That's the third time this week."

Grabbing her cell phone, she used it to light her progress as she shuffled out of the bedroom and headed downstairs. She shoved her mussed hair out of her face and tucked it behind her shoulder.

A shiver shook her as she descended the last step. The first real cool snap must have swept through while she had slept. A chill had settled upon the house, causing gooseflesh to pepper the skin exposed by her soft tank top and pajama shorts.

Rubbing her arms, Susan glanced at the front door, then the back. "Jax?"

*Woof!* came his muffled response.

Where the hell was he?

It took a couple more barks for her to determine he was in the basement.

"Oh, man. I really don't want to go down there at night."

Both of the exterminators she had called had spent mere seconds in the basement before they had come running back up, faces ashen, and said they needed to leave. Immediately. No explanation given. So who knew *what* scuttled around down there after the sun set?

Flipping the switch just inside the entrance, she squinted against the light, dim though it might be. "Jax?"

More barks, accompanied by scratching sounds.

Turning the phone off, she headed downstairs, wishing all the while that she didn't have a fear of creepy crawlies. It was such a stereotypical girlie thing, but she'd never been able to shake it.

"What the hell?" she blurted when she spotted the busy beagle. He'd dug a hole big enough for her to stretch out in near the center of the floor. "What are you doing?" she cried, hurrying forward. "No! Bad dog! Bad Jax! Stop that this... instant..." Her voice trailed off as the alarm and dismay that had rushed upon her disappeared. In its absence, curiosity arose.

Overwhelming, burning, must-be-appeased curiosity.

Tilting her head to one side, she watched Jax scratch, scratch, scratch at the dirt. "What have you found, boy? What's down there?"

She wanted to know. She really, *really* wanted to know. No, she *had* to know what was down there. She didn't know *why* she had to know, but she did. Curiosity continued to build within her until it conquered everything else. She had never in her life wanted to solve a mystery as much as she did this one.

Looking around, she crossed to the area that housed a jumble of gardening tools. Setting her phone down, she picked up a shovel.

———⊸◈◈◈⊶———

Elation filled him. She was doing it. She was looking for him. Coming to free him.

He concentrated what little energy he had on feeding her curiosity and dampening her fear.

Dust sifted down into his little world as the soil above him shifted.

His heart beat once inside his chest, the pain the slight movement sparked excruciating.

He sucked in a breath. Coughed. Moaned in agony as his head swam.

———⊸◈◈◈⊶———

Jax barked.

Susan grinned, as excited as the dog. "I know, right?"

She didn't know how long they had been digging. Long enough for her legs to acquire a nice coat of dirt, for blisters to form on her hands, and for her bare feet to grow cold and hurt from stepping up onto the shovel to push it down into the cold hard ground.

Ignoring her tired back, she tossed another helping of dirt onto the large mound outside the hole. It was so deep now that she'd had to step down inside it in order to keep digging.

Setting the point of the shovel back on the ground, she hopped up onto it.

*Ahhhhhhhh!*

Susan jumped as the deep roar reverberated through her. Dropping the shovel, she covered her ears to silence it but couldn't. It was in her head, which spun suddenly. Heart pounding with fear, she staggered to one side and looked all around.

Jax whimpered and leapt out of the hole, his tail tucked between his legs.

She glanced down at the dirt beneath her feet, all excitement gone.

What the hell was she doing? Digging a hole in her basement in the middle of the freaking night? What had…?

Her heartbeat slowed as calm sifted through her.

Jax stopped cowering behind her and stepped up to the edge of the hole.

She returned her gaze to the dirt. What was down there?

Curiosity seized Susan once more. Jax, too.

As the beagle jumped down into the hole, she reached for the shovel.

A deep voice, full of pain and carrying a… Russian?… accent, filled her head. *Careful. Please.*

It should concern her. Should actually send her fleeing up the stairs and out of the house. But it didn't. She had to know what was down there. The curiosity was killing her!

Gingerly, she poked at the dirt with the shovel.

Jax's claws caught in something just under the surface.

Kneeling, Susan set the shovel aside and reached out to explore Jax's find.

Something rubbery, with a texture similar to a car tire. Weird.

But *very* intriguing.

Forgoing the shovel, she shooed Jax back and began to scoop the dirt away with her hands. More rubber. Rounded. Sliced and torn in places. Definitely not a tire. It was more like a rubber cover encasing something solid that gave a little when she tested it. Some of the dirt she scraped away from it was rust colored.

Her heart leapt as her fingers brushed something different. Something harder. She could feel the outline of it beneath the loosened soil and—

"Oh shit." It was a man's boot.

*Keep going*, that mysterious voice whispered. *Don't stop.*

It compelled her as much as the curiosity riding her did.

"Why the hell am I doing this, Jax?" she murmured, uncovering another boot beneath the first.

Jax leapt out of the hole.

"Great," she muttered. "You started this. Now you're going to abandon me?"

But he didn't. The faithful beagle stood above her, tail wagging wildly, making happy little whining sounds as he watched her.

Susan continued to scoop dirt away.

Legs came into view. The odd rubber that encased them looked as though someone had peppered it with buckshot or something. Lots of ragged tears and holes she couldn't see into for the dirt that had settled in them.

Then a hip. A man lying on his side?

Fear struck, almost instantly obliterated by that strange calm and inexplicably intense curiosity.

*Mannequin*, the voice whispered in her head.

Doubt rose, again vanishing as eagerness replaced it. She *had* to see what else the dirt concealed.

A narrow waist. An arm drawn up over a head, concealing a face.

"Please let this be a mannequin or some bizarre art project abandoned by the previous owner," she murmured.

Why the hell was she even still digging? Why was common freaking sense not kicking curiosity's ass and hightailing her out of there?

*Because you have to know*, that deep voice murmured. *You* need *to know*.

"I do," she agreed. "I need to know."

Her fingers tangled in soft hair.

She stilled, rubbing the short dusty tresses between her fingers until the midnight color was revealed. Flying into motion, she brushed dirt away from the head those soft strands hid. Careful, but urgent, her heart slamming against her ribs.

Breathing heavily, she sat back on her heels and stared down with utter amazement at the treasure she had uncovered.

A man—a very tall man—lay curled on his left side, facing her, his right arm drawn up over his face, a large hand sporting numerous lacerations shielding his head.

He was thin. So thin as to be almost skeletal. But his skin…

It didn't look leathery or decayed or mummified.

Nor did it appear to be plastic. This was no mannequin.

So why wasn't she afraid? She *should* be very afraid. She should be shaking in her proverbial boots right now.

Cautiously, she grasped his wrist and lifted the arm a couple of inches, slowly drawing it down away from his face.

"Oh no," she breathed. Lowering his arm to his side, she leaned in close and brushed his dark hair back from his dusty face. "What did they do to you?" she whispered.

He was handsome… or would've been were it not for the

wounds that scored his compelling features. His eyes were closed, his brow furrowed as though he still suffered. His ears had bled, as had his nose. His cheeks, coated with perhaps a week's worth of dark stubble, were sunken and marred by *so* many deep gashes and scratches. What had happened to him?

Tears welled in her eyes.

How long had he been buried there? She glanced down his long length. And how had he remained so well preserved? As though he had just lain down and breathed his last breath five minutes ago?

She returned her attention to his face, drew her fingers across his forehead, carefully avoiding the jagged line carved into it.

His skin was gritty from the dirt. Cool to the touch.

She shook her head. "What did they do to you?" she whispered again.

One of his eyelids lifted.

She sucked in a breath.

His brown eye blinked, then focused on her.

Amber light flashed in it.

The fear that she should have been feeling all this time now struck with a vengeance.

Her heart doing its damnedest to burst from her chest, she yanked her fingers back and tried to scoot away.

His hand shot out and clamped around her wrist, preventing her from withdrawing.

"Oh shit!" she cried, struggling to free herself from his hold while Jax began to bark.

Agony contorted the man's features as she strained against his grip. A moan rumbled forth from his throat.

Glancing down, she saw bone protruding from his forearm and stilled. She returned her wide-eyed gaze to his face, breathing heavily.

His brows drew down as he squeezed his eyes shut. A muscle flexed in his jaw as he clenched his teeth and hissed in a breath.

"This isn't happening," she whispered shakily. "This so isn't happening."

*I'm sorry.*

She could hear the pain that afflicted him even in his thoughts.

*I'm sorry. Don't leave. Please.*

—◈◈◈—

Drawing in a ragged breath, he fought the pain. Excruciating. Unbearable.

*Don't leave me. Please don't leave me. Please don't leave me*, he chanted over and over again, wishing he could speak the words aloud.

*Shouldn't have grabbed her. Didn't mean to frighten her. Hurts so fucking bad. I just didn't want her to leave.*

He tightened his hold on her wrist. Not to restrain her, but because he needed the contact. *Been so long.* He rubbed his thumb against her soft skin. *Been alone for so damned long. Just didn't want her to leave. Please don't leave me.*

The dirt shifted near him.

He opened the eye that wasn't swollen and damned near wept when he saw she had stopped straining to get away from him and had actually inched a little closer.

Every movement hesitant, she reached out with her free hand and brushed his hair back from his face. Moisture sparkled in her eyes as her throat worked in a swallow. "I won't leave," she promised softly. "It's okay. I won't leave you."

The courage it took for her say that and to remain with him when the pain pounded him so hard that he could no longer dampen her fear…

Gritting his teeth, he slowly brought her hand to his lips and pressed a fervent kiss to her knuckles. *Thank you.* He met her gaze, tried to speak, but couldn't. *Thank you*, he thought again, wishing he could convey his gratitude.

Smiling through her tears, she nodded and again drew her free hand over his hair in a caress that was pure ecstasy.

*Forgive me*, he pleaded silently.

She shook her head. "It's okay. It didn't hurt. You just caught me off guard."

Surprise struck. Could she read his thoughts?

*Not for grabbing your wrist*, he thought.

She tilted her head to one side. "Then for what?"

She could. She could read his thoughts.

*For this*, he told her. Altering the angle of her arm, he brought her wrist to his lips and sank his fangs in deep.

The woman cried out in protest, her pretty features creasing with pain as she tried to free herself from his grasp. A few seconds later, she swayed. Her eyelids lowered as her brow smoothed and her struggles ceased.

He moaned as his fangs siphoned her blood directly into his parched veins. Sweet relief.

The dog began to growl.

*Calm your pet*, he thought, knowing somehow that she would comply with his request.

The woman murmured something that seemed to soothe it. The growls ceased.

*Sleep*, he encouraged her.

Eyes closing, she sank down beside him, her face inches away from his own.

She smelled so good, so fresh after an eternity of being surrounded by the scents of dirt, blood, and smoke.

When her skin grew cooler and her heartbeat picked up a bit, he withdrew his fangs. Any more and she would require a transfusion.

He gritted his teeth and moaned as the worst of his wounds began to heal. The bone in his arm slowly shifted back into position in torturously small increments. Those in his legs did the same. Organs damaged by hunger and dehydration regenerated. Flesh parted by the deepest gashes slowly began to knit itself back together. But none of it healed completely. He needed more blood.

He stared at his rescuer.

If he took any more of hers, he might have to give some of it back. Something bad would happen if he did that, wouldn't it? If he returned her blood after it had been in his body, wouldn't it harm her in some way?

Several moments' contemplation didn't recover the reason why, but he wouldn't risk it.

Releasing her wrist, he raised his shaking hand and brushed disheveled auburn hair back from her face. Her features were relaxed in sleep. Dirt-smudged. Damp with the tears she had shed for him.

At his touch, she made a sound somewhere in the back of her throat and snuggled closer with a sigh.

He didn't know who she was.

He didn't know who *he* was.

But in that moment, he loved her for freeing him.

The dog voiced a plaintive whine.

Speech still eluding him, he sent feelings of calm to the loyal animal.

Then, taking the woman's small, pale hand in his, he tucked it against his chest, pressed his forehead to hers, and succumbed to a deep healing sleep.

⟩◈◈◈⟨

*Whistling under her breath, she strode up a sidewalk toward a sprawling one-story house. Voices carried to her ears long before she entered without knocking and closed the door behind her.*

*Shrugging off a long black coat, she hung it up on a rack that held a dozen or more others. Hers bore wet patches that carried a metallic scent. Her shirt and pants did, too.*

*A chorus of greetings made her smile and turn toward a large living room with high ceilings. Several sofas and love seats held a multitude of men and women, most of whom had black hair and brown eyes and were garbed in midnight hues like her.*

*Tossing them a wave, she headed for a darkened hallway on the opposite side of the room.*

*"Stanislav!" someone called over the jumble of conversations.*

*Turning, she saw her friend claim a seat at a table in the corner. He motioned to the chessboard atop it. "Join me for a game?"*

*She nodded. "Just give me a minute to clean up after tonight's hunt," she called back, her voice deep and flavored with a similar Russian accent. The room blurred as she shot into the hallway and down to a basement bedroom. Peeling off black clothing, she crossed to the bathroom, stepped into a large shower, and turned the faucets.*

*Water struck her in rhythmic pulses, warm and welcome. Soapsuds flew as she bathed so swiftly it was all a blur.*

*Turning the water off, she stepped out, grabbed a towel, and dried her body as quickly as she had cleaned it. Her hair felt short as she rubbed it vigorously. Dropping the towel on the long granite counter beside the sink, she looked in the mirror.*

*She had showered so fast that steam had not had time to gather on the glass, leaving her view unobscured.*

*A strikingly handsome male stared back as she combed her fingers through her damp hair. Warm brown eyes. Jet-black hair and eyebrows. Dark stubble coating a strong jaw. Broad, muscled shoulders. A well-developed chest. Thick biceps.*

*Staring at her reflection, she reached out and turned on the sink's cold-water faucet.*

*It squeaked, then squeaked again as she adjusted the temperature.*

*Then squeaked again. And again.*

Frowning, Susan sighed as a persistent whining sound dragged her from sleep. "Too tired, Jax," she mumbled. "Give me another hour."

More whining.

"Thirty minutes?" she bargained hopefully. "I'll give you some beef jerky if you wait."

He barked a protest.

"All right. All right," she groaned. "I'm up." But she didn't move. Exhaustion pulled at her, urging her to go back to sleep. Soooo tempting.

A shiver shook her.

Sighing, she would've snuggled deeper into the covers to sneak in a few more minutes of rest, but something hard pressed against her forehead. She frowned. And no sheet or blanket covered her.

She tried to move her arm to search for them and couldn't.

Grumbling, she pried her eyes open.

A face swam into view, blurry at first because the man's forehead rested against hers.

*Oh crap.* Her eyes flew wide. A man's forehead was pressed against hers!

Gasping, she reared back and stared at the stranger.

His eyes were closed, his breathing long and slow with sleep. Brow furrowed, he cradled her hand to his chest as if he never wanted to let it go.

What the hell?

His cheeks were sunken and marred by scratches and gashes. She cast a frantic look down his body. He was underweight, emaciated, his form clad in what appeared to be a rubber diving suit that bore numerous tears and holes.

She looked up at the dirt walls around them and found Jax peering down at her. As soon as she met the beagle's big, soulful eyes, he barked and his body began to rock as he wagged his tail in relief.

Fear and confusion buffeted her. She remembered Jax waking her up last night. Remembered following his barks down here to the basement and finding him digging like crazy. Remembered curiosity overwhelming her, driving her to grab a shovel and start digging so she could find out what had caught Jax's attention.

She returned her gaze to the tall dirt walls. Had she dug this hole?

This was a really deep hole.

The sore muscles of her arms and legs and the blisters on her free hand told her she *had* dug it.

She looked at the man beside her. But who was *he*? Where had he come from?

He couldn't have…

She grimaced at the absurdity of the question that arose but couldn't seem to stop her mind from posing it.

She hadn't found this man down here, buried at the bottom of this hole, had she?

She shook her head, then reeled with dizziness. Throwing her free hand out, she braced it on the man's hip, then jerked it back. She didn't know what other injuries he might be sporting and didn't want to jar his wounds.

"Not possible," she whispered. "It's not possible."

She couldn't have removed several feet of dirt from her basement floor and uncovered this man. This man was alive. She could see the faint rise and fall of his chest. And he clutched her hand. *He* clutched *her* hand, not the other way around.

But she had been in the house for about a month now. No way could he have lived down here that long.

So who *was* he?

Panic rising, she tugged against his hold in an attempt to free herself.

He sighed in his sleep and drew his thumb over the back of her hand in a light caress.

Terrified now, she rose onto her knees and tugged harder. She didn't know who the hell this was, but —

His eyes opened sluggishly, as though he was having difficulty coming awake.

Susan scooted as far away from him as she could and yanked against his hold.

Brow creasing, he glanced over at her.

She froze, afraid to move now that she had drawn his attention.

He started to smile, then must have noticed the fear she radiated, because his eyes widened and he swiftly rolled onto his back.

His hand clamped down hard around hers as he closed his eyes. "Ahhhh!" His face contorted and the tendons in his neck stood out as he threw his head back and cried out at the agony the sudden movement had spawned.

Pain shot through her fingers until she worried he might break them.

The pressure immediately lessened. *I'm sorry.* He drew sharp, jagged breaths in and out through his nose. *I'm sorry. I didn't mean to hurt you. The pain just caught me off guard.*

His deep voice flowed into her head with ease, as though he had spoken to her telepathically many times in the past.

She stared at him, wide-eyed, as his breathing slowed. The taut muscles of his body relaxed somewhat.

Was the pain receding?

The fear that held her in place abruptly fell away. The tightness in her chest faded. Her shoulders unknotted. Her head still swam a bit and her stomach remained unsettled, but that awful fear was gone.

He eased his grip on her hand a bit more, rubbed his thumb over her skin in another caress. "Forgive me."

Her gaze flew to his face. His voice was deeper, rougher than the one in her head. Hoarse from long disuse perhaps?

He opened his eyes.

She sucked in a breath.

They glowed now with an incandescent amber light.

He licked chapped lips. "Please don't fear me. I mean you no harm."

She didn't fear him, though she couldn't say why. "Who are you?"

He opened his mouth to answer, paused, then closed it. The amber light in his eyes flashed brighter. "I'm…" His frown deepened. "I'm…" A sound of frustration escaped him as he carefully raised his free hand and gripped his forehead. "I don't know."

She studied him. "You can't remember?"

"No."

Now that panic didn't cloud her mind, she delved into his thoughts and kicked herself for not thinking of doing it sooner.

Usually when she read someone's mind, she found a mixture of short-term and long-term memories combined with whatever they were thinking in that moment. If she chose to delve deeper, she could often reconstruct the man or woman's past.

But she didn't find that in this man's mind. His was like nothing she had ever encountered before. Almost like a blank slate. No memories. Only the jumbled thoughts that currently buffeted him. And even those bore gaps here and there that left phrases more than full sentences. A quick look at those revealed his frustration over his inability to access something so simple as his name. Concern for her plagued him as well. He worried over her pallor and cold fingers. She found regret over inadvertently scaring her and squeezing her hand too tightly. A deep desire to put her fears to rest and convince her that he was sincere when he said he meant her no harm. And gratitude. So much gratitude.

"What happened last night?" she asked, no longer trying to pull her hand away. He needed the contact. She might not be able to access *all* of his thoughts—it was pretty chaotic in there right now—but she had found his need for the contact as well as the comfort it afforded him and couldn't bring herself to deny him. "I remember coming down here and finding Jax digging." She glanced down at the blisters on her free hand. "I remember grabbing a shovel and joining him, but everything after that…" She shook her head. "What happened?"

"You freed me," he told her, giving her hand a grateful squeeze as he stopped rubbing his forehead. "At long last, you freed me."

She swallowed, mouth dry. "Did you drug me?" It was the only logical explanation she could fabricate to explain everything.

"With what?" he countered. "I've not left this basement since…" Again she felt frustration batter him as he sought information that just wasn't there. "I've not left this basement and doubt I will be able to do so now without assistance. Why would you think I drugged you?"

"Because none of this makes sense." She motioned to the dirt walls around them. "Because my mind is telling me that last night I dug up a man who has been buried in my basement for an unspecified length of time but is miraculously still alive and I'm not afraid and I *should* be. I should be screaming at the top of my lungs and diving for my cell phone to call 911, but I'm not and…"

"And?" he prodded.

"And your eyes are really bright," she finished miserably. "I mean they're *really* bright. Like someone's holding a candle behind your irises bright. Which means you either drugged me or I've cracked."

"I'm sorry." He rubbed his eyes. "It's the pain."

"Pain doesn't make people's eyes glow."

"It does mine," he said.

"How do you know that?" She followed his mental struggle to discover where that information had originated and felt as discouraged as he did when he couldn't find it.

"I don't know," he answered finally. "But it does, and the pain is considerable. I would darken them if I could. I don't wish to frighten you. But I can't."

She would have pressed him if she hadn't been monitoring his thoughts. He really was in agony. "Do you know who did this to you?"

Silence, then a huff of annoyance. "No. I don't even know where I am."

"The basement of my house."

"In the United States? You're American?"

She blinked. "Yes. We're in North Carolina. Not far from Pittsboro."

He repeated the town name. "I can find no memory of the place."

"Do you know how long you've been down here? Or how you

came to be here?"

Another pause. More aggravation accompanied by a slew of what she suspected were Russian swear words. "No. I can remember nothing before waking up, encapsulated in dirt."

She shifted, preparing to rise. "Well, you need medical attention."

His grip tightened as panic flared in his eyes. "Don't leave me."

Her heart turned over. "I'm not. I'm just going to get my phone."

He shook his head vigorously, then clenched his teeth and moaned.

"Stop moving," she urged him.

"You can't call anyone," he gritted, his bright eyes ensnaring hers. "I don't know who put me down here. It isn't safe."

"It's okay. I'm just going to call 911."

"You can't," he insisted. "It isn't safe, I tell you. You'll be in danger. And I can't protect you, weakened as I am by my wounds."

Again, if she hadn't been privy to his thoughts, she would have feared him a criminal intent on evading the law. But the only thoughts in his head right now were for her safety. *Her* safety, not his own. He didn't know who had done this to him and feared if she told someone—even the police—the villain would hear of it and somehow be able to track her down and harm her. And until his wounds healed and he regained his strength, he would be too weak to protect her.

He didn't worry that *he* would be harmed.

He didn't worry that police might think him a criminal and arrest him.

He didn't even worry that they might think him insane.

His only desire was to keep her safe.

And though he couldn't remember who he was, he was conscious of the fact that glowing eyes were not normal and feared the reaction of authorities or anyone else when they saw his. Not just what they would do to him. But what they would do to her if they didn't believe her when she said she didn't know him.

Even more, he feared what they would do to her if they thought her different like him.

Susan had to admit, that gave her pause. She knew well the negative and sometimes terrifying reactions people could have when faced with someone who was different.

"I'll leave," he announced when she could think of no response. "If you would just let me rest here for a few more hours, I will leave and you can be safe again." *I won't let her come to harm because she freed me.*

She eyed him incredulously. "Leave? How? You can't. Where would you go?"

*As far as I must to keep the bastards who did this to me from finding her.* "It doesn't matter. I won't endanger you. I can go now if you wish it."

Susan couldn't believe she was about to do it but found herself saying, "No. You can stay here. I won't" — what the hell was she doing? — "I won't call anyone." *Yet*, she added mentally but was appalled to realize she didn't mean it. People's mouths might lie, but their thoughts didn't. And this man's thoughts told her he posed no threat to her. So, though it defied all common sense, she would help him.

Until he gave her reason not to.

He looked as though he couldn't believe he had heard her correctly. "Really?"

"I know. It's crazy, right?"

His lips turned up in a faint smile. "Decidedly. But very much appreciated. Thank you. You're very kind."

She shook her head. "Don't thank me until we're out of this hole." When she would've risen, he tightened his hold on her hand. She looked at their hands, then raised her brows.

"I'm sorry," he said, *embarrassment*? entering his features. "It wasn't intentional."

She searched his thoughts and did indeed find embarrassment. He'd been stuck down in this hole alone for so long that he didn't want to let her go and thought displaying such weakness shamed him.

She patted his hand. "It's okay. I understand. I'm Susan, by the way."

"It's a pleasure to meet you, Susan," he said with old-world charm that made her think he would bow and kiss her hand if he weren't incapacitated. "I'm..." His expression went blank, then darkened. "Damn it!"

"It's okay," she assured him. "It'll probably come back to you once you're feeling better."

Nodding, he reluctantly released her hand.

"Even as thin as you are," she said, "I think I'm going to have a hard time getting you out of here." She stood. "Maybe I could…" The room tilted and rolled. Her stomach lurched. Her vision darkened as her balance wavered. "Oh crap."

Jax's bark rang in her ears as she stumbled backward and fell.

# Chapter Three

ALARM STRUCK AS HE WATCHED Susan waver. Throwing out her arms in an attempt to regain her balance, she stumbled backward, tripped over his legs, and fell.

Swearing, he lunged upward and thrust his arms out to catch her.

Burning pain blasted every inch of him as she struck his chest. Clenching his teeth, he growled and fell back against the dirt.

Susan lay still atop him as he held his breath and waited for the worst of the suffering to pass.

"Susan?"

Her face rested in the crook of his neck, her warm breath caressing his skin. A glance down confirmed she was unconscious.

Cradling her to his chest, he cursed himself for taking too much blood. He was certain he hadn't taken enough for her to need a transfusion, but it had clearly left her weak.

"I'm so sorry," he whispered, glad she hadn't found the deed in his thoughts. He had feared he wouldn't be able to hide it from her.

The dog began to whine again.

"It's okay, boy," he murmured. "She's okay. She's just tired."

Several minutes passed while he stroked her hair and held her close despite the pain it caused. She was petite and looked as though she only weighed about a hundred pounds. After spending all damned night digging his sorry ass up, no wonder she'd passed out.

"I haven't seen it yet," she mumbled against his neck as consciousness returned, "but I'm willing to bet your ass is actually quite nice."

Startled laughter escaped him, inspiring another groan. "Don't make me laugh. It hurts too much."

"Sorry. I couldn't resist." Bracing a hand on his shoulder, she rose onto an elbow and brushed long, silken auburn hair back from her face. Her lips turned up in a mischievous smile that made his heartbeat pick up. Then her eyes widened. "Oh crap! I fell on you? I'm so sorry!"

He clenched his teeth as she applied pressure to what he suspected were broken ribs.

"Oh hell. Your ribs are broken, too?" she cried in dismay as she scrambled off him.

"You're reading my thoughts," he commented through clenched teeth. Damn, it hurt.

She stilled. And he felt her dismay at his discovery.

"You're telepathic?" he prodded.

"Could we maybe talk about that later? I really need to get us both out of here."

He nodded. "As you wish. Help me up, please?"

She regarded him with disbelief. "You can't get up!"

He slowly rolled onto his side. "How else will I escape this hell?"

"I don't know, but…"

Somehow he managed to get his knees up under him. Thrusting a hand into the dirt wall beside him, he used it as leverage and pushed himself to his feet.

There was just no suppressing the shout the torturous movement jerked from him.

Susan leapt to his side and grabbed one of his arms, dragging it across her shoulders and helping him remain on his feet.

"Thank you." His head swam. His breath came in gasps. "Just give me a moment… to get my balance."

She nodded.

A few minutes passed in silence.

He shook his head.

"What?" she asked.

"What a picture we must make. Both of us as weak as kittens and covered in dirt. Each of us trying to hold the other up."

She smiled. "Definitely not how I expected to spend my

Saturday."

Once he was confident he wouldn't collapse without her support, he took a step back and motioned for her to face the side of the hole. "Go ahead."

She watched him long enough to ensure he wouldn't keel over, then turned to the wall. "I still can't believe I dug this myself."

He nodded. It was a deep hole. He estimated he was six foot one or two inches tall, and his chin barely topped the edge.

The dog hurried over to her and lapped at her face.

Sputtering, she rubbed his head and ears and murmured soothing words, then gently shooed him away.

Though the hands she raised to grab the lip of the hole bore angry red blisters, she voiced no complaint. Gripping the edge, she tried to jump up enough to aid her arms in boosting herself out but failed as fatigue hindered her.

He stepped up behind her. "Forgive my impertinence."

"What impertinence?" Without looking at him, she again tried to climb out.

Settling his hands on her shapely bottom—covered only by short shorts—he pushed her up and out of the hole.

Emitting a yelp of surprise, she tumbled onto the ground, then spun around to look at him.

He offered her what he hoped was a sheepish smile rather than a wince. "It seemed the quickest solution."

Her lips tilted up in a wry smile. "Well, it worked. Thank you."

Nodding, he tried to draw in several deep breaths, dreading the inevitable, but couldn't because of his damned ribs. *Just get it over with*, he chastised himself. Placing his hands on the lip of the hole, he heaved himself up enough to get a knee over the edge, then tumbled out and sprawled onto his back.

He knew nothing but pain for many long minutes.

He hoped he hadn't cried out but feared he had. The room had gone very quiet.

Even the dog made no sound.

And still he didn't move. Especially when he became aware of the warmth at his back and the arms that encircled him.

While he had lain there, oblivious, Susan had dragged him back away from the edge, then sat down behind him and wrapped her arms around him, letting him rest against her. Her slender legs bracketed his hips. Her breasts cushioned his head.

Reaching up, he curled a hand around the delicate forearm resting on his chest and gently squeezed. *So kind.*

"Not really," she said dryly. "I'm just too damned tired to move. And cold, not that you're warming me up much."

He didn't know how many more minutes passed before they forced their weary carcasses upright and shuffled over to the wooden stairs.

"I'm going to take a wild guess," she huffed as they painstakingly scaled one step at a time, "at how you survived being buried alive like this."

He clutched the banister and tried not to lean so much of his weight on her slender shoulders. "Are you?"

She nodded. "I think you must be a robot."

Amusement struck. "Do you?"

"Yes. One of those super-advanced AI robots that looks and feels like a human but isn't. Because the only way a normal man in your condition would leave this basement is strapped to a gurney. You should *not* be able to do this."

He shook his head. "An interesting theory. But—at the risk of sounding like a complainer—I don't think robots feel pain."

"True." Her fingers patted his side where she gripped him. "Don't worry. I'm sure a couple of ibuprofen will fix you right up."

He laughed, then grunted. "I thought I told you not to make me laugh."

"Sorry. I shouldn't joke. I just hate that you're in so much pain. And honestly, I'm feeling a little loopy."

Both heaved a sigh of relief as they exited the basement.

Fighting for breath, he glanced around. High ceilings. Nice high doorways that would keep him from bumping his head if he forgot to duck. Worn hardwood floors. And several unpacked boxes stacked out of the way.

"Do you want to sit down and rest?" she asked, breathless.

He shook his head. "Once I sit down, I won't get up again anytime soon."

"Okay." She guided him forward, keeping one arm around his waist, her other hand holding his to keep his arm around her shoulders.

His heart sank when she led him to the bottom of another long staircase. "Where are we going?"

"Well, you need to lie down," she huffed as they started up the stairs. "And don't take this the wrong way, but…"

"But what?"

"I only have one bed."

He shook his head, then wished he hadn't as dizziness struck. "I can sleep on the sofa."

"I don't have a sofa. My old one sucked, so I ditched it when I moved and haven't had a chance to buy a new one."

He paused, gripping the banister as he drew in rasping breaths that cut like a knife. "I can sleep on the floor." Did she realize she was rubbing his side in soothing strokes? Because she was, and it felt really nice and hurt all at the same time.

She shook her head. "Jax will turn you into a pillow if you do. And I don't want to risk him hurting you. You can sleep with me."

He glanced down at her, shocked. "Are you sure?"

She nodded. "Considering the shape you're in, I feel confident all you're going to do is sleep."

"You're right, of course."

"Just don't die on me, okay?"

"Okay." They resumed their trek up the stairs. "Would you think me a fiend if I admitted that — were I in better shape — I might be tempted to try something untoward once we were in bed together?"

She grinned, her amusement trickling into him via his gift. "Untoward?"

He nodded. Was that not the right word?

"I wouldn't think you a fiend. I'd think you crazy for being tempted. I'm covered with dirt and sweat and dog slobber and am all gross."

He found a smile. "I find you quite fetching in your" — he glanced at her shorts and tank top — "summer clothes."

She laughed. "They're pajamas."

"Those are pajamas?"

"Yes."

He liked them but thought it best not to mention that.

They entered a bedroom that lacked the boxes he'd seen downstairs. This room was unpacked and boasted a modern black bedroom suite with a queen-sized bed.

Crossing to the bed, they turned their backs to it, then tumbled backward.

Quiet fell, disrupted by his rasping breaths. "I hate to sound like a broken record, but holy hell, that hurt."

"I'm sorry."

Neither moved.

"I should probably go downstairs and get you some water and something to eat," she said.

"It can wait." Sleep was already creeping up on him.

"Then I should go down and let Jax out," she uttered without enthusiasm.

"He can wait, too." She needed to rest.

"If I don't, he'll pee on the floor."

"I'm pretty sure he already peed in the basement." The scent of urine had tinted the air outside the hole.

"Oh." A moment passed. "Okay." In the next instant, her breathing evened as sleep claimed her.

He wanted to lift her and ease her up against the pillows so she could rest more comfortably but was just too damned weary.

Maybe later.

For now, he eased her arm from around his shoulders so the weight of his head wouldn't put the limb to sleep. Then, twining his fingers through hers, he closed his eyes and sank into another deep, healing slumber.

⇒◦◦◦⇐

*Darkness surrounded her, suffocated her. She tried to pierce it, but her eyes could find no hint of light. Nothing that would help her escape this prison.*

*Weight pressed down upon her, heavy enough to crush her bones. And perhaps it had. There was no part of her that didn't hurt so much that she wanted to howl with it. But when she opened her mouth, dirt and dust tried to choke her.*

*Cold.*

*Pain.*

*Silence.*

*No hope.*

*Then a voice came to her, burrowing down through the soil and coiling around her.*

*"When love," a woman began to sing softly, "into my dreams was creeping, I gave my heart into your keeping."*

*Pure ecstasy.*

*How she needed that voice, that presence to alleviate the darkness and pain and salvage her sanity.*

*Tears welled in her eyes as she let the soft song embrace her.*

*Her breath hitched.*

Susan awoke with a sob. Her first thought was that her cheeks were cold.

Reaching up, she found moisture trailing down them. When she would've raised her other hand too, to brush away the tears, she found she couldn't and turned her head.

At some point, the stranger from her basement must have moved her, because her head now rested on one of her pillows and her legs no longer dangled off the foot of the bed. Instead, she lay on her back, a blanket pulled up over her.

The stranger lay next to her, curled up on his side with her hand clutched to his chest. Surprisingly long lashes rested upon his cheeks as he slept, his brow furrowed, his body tense.

The dream that had driven her to awaken in tears had been his.

It was one of the hazards of being telepathic. She could block others' thoughts and keep them from bombarding her when she concentrated but tended to lose that ability once she succumbed to slumber. Then their thoughts and—if they slept—their dreams would often infiltrate hers as his had.

Rolling toward him, she brushed his hair back from haggard features.

Fear attempted to creep in. She was in bed with a strange man she had found buried in her basement. But compassion accompanied it.

Was that what it had been like for him? Stuck down there in the cold dirt, suffering every second of every hour of every day with no hope of rescue?

His fingers tightened around hers as he shifted. He started to stretch, then stopped with a grunt. His eyes opened, a deep warm brown that still held a hint of that amber glow. "I'm sorry," he said as he focused on her face.

"For what?" Her fear melted away as he met her gaze.

"I should have bathed before lying down. I've gotten dirt all over your bedding."

Seriously? He had been buried alive for who knew how long while she had been farting around up here, unpacking. And he was apologizing for getting her covers dirty? "How long were you down there?" Had his memory returned?

He opened his mouth, got that blank look again that held both disbelief and frustration, then shook his head helplessly. "I don't know."

"Could you hear me while you were down there? Did you know I was up here?" If so, he must hate her for not having saved him sooner.

"I remember hearing you sing."

She grimaced. "As if you weren't being tortured enough."

He smiled. And despite the cuts that marred his sunken features, she found it very appealing. "You have a lovely voice. It brought me great comfort."

"I don't suppose you've changed your mind about my calling the police, have you?"

"I fear it would endanger you," he told her with regret. "I will leave, if you wish it. You've already helped me enormously. You need not do any more."

She shook her head. "Until you remember who you are, you have nowhere to go. You can stay here." So far his thoughts — fragmented though they might be — had given her no reason to fear he would harm her.

"Thank you. Could I, perhaps, avail myself of your shower?"

"Of course." Sitting up, she glanced down at her dirt-smudged tank top and arms and grimaced. "I think I will, too." Realizing how that might have sounded, she shot him a look. "*After* you. Not at the same time."

He smiled. "I assumed as much. Why don't you go first?"

She had a feeling that once his wounds healed and he regained the weight he'd lost, he would be quite handsome. "Okay. I'll only be a minute. Can I get you anything first? Some water? Something to eat?" He must be both starving and dangerously dehydrated. She should have insisted he eat and drink something before they'd fallen asleep.

"Water, please. And you should drink some yourself. Or perhaps some orange juice."

Throwing back the blanket, she scooted off the bed. Her head still swam a bit, so she thought juice would be the better choice. "Juice sounds good. Would you like that, too?"

"Yes, please." He was so polite.

"Okay. I'll be right back."

"Careful on the stairs," he cautioned. "You were dizzy before you slept."

Oddly touched by his concern, she left the room and went downstairs.

Jax greeted her with jumps and licks and tail wags, then raced for the back door. Susan took a moment to put him outside on the long leash that let him explore, then poured a couple of glasses of orange juice in the kitchen. She took a minute to use the half bath off the breakfast nook, then headed back upstairs.

Her guest had pushed himself up enough to lean back against the headboard.

Wow. He was really tall. He had been sort of hunched over from his wounds when they'd climbed up here earlier, so she hadn't really noticed. But he made her bed look short.

She handed him a glass, smiling when he thanked her.

It took her no time to empty her own. Boy, it tasted good. She was so thirsty. Hungry, too. They had slept the day away, and she hadn't eaten anything since last night.

Opening her dresser drawers and pulling out bikini panties, a bra, some jeans and a T-shirt while he watched felt uncomfortably intimate. "I'll just be a minute," she said again as she crossed to the en suite bathroom.

Inclining his head, he followed her with his piercing gaze.

Flipping on the light, she entered and closed the door behind her. She eyed the doorknob.

"It won't hurt my feelings if you lock it," he called through the door.

Smiling, she locked it. There was a strange man in her house and she had not wanted to lock the door while showering because she had thought it might hurt his feelings. What the hell was wrong with her? Had all fear and wariness abandoned her?

If so, why now?

Grabbing her toothbrush, she slathered it with minty paste and gave her teeth a good scrub. Much better. Then she stripped off her filthy clothes and tossed them in the hamper. Leaning into the shower, she cranked the faucets and ducked out of reach of the spray until the water warmed. Once it did, she stepped under the liquid curtain and sighed as it settled upon her hair and shoulders.

It felt great until it hit her blisters. Then her hands began to sting like crazy, prompting her to grab the soap and get it over with in a hurry. The muscles of her arms, shoulders, and upper back ached as she rubbed them vigorously with a foamy sponge. Her thighs did, too. She had been pushing herself so hard to finish her latest manuscript and get it in the hands of her editor that she hadn't exercised in weeks. Now her body protested the tough workout she'd given it last night.

Despite her stinging palms and fingers, Susan was happy to be clean as she shut off the water and toweled herself dry. Her ears strained to catch any sound beyond the door but heard nothing. Nor could she hear his thoughts.

Had he fallen asleep again?

Had he left?

A chill skittered through her.

He hadn't died, had he?

Alarmed, she hurriedly donned her clothes, grabbed a comb, then yanked open the door.

Relief suffused her.

He sat on the bed, facing her. Both hands gripped the edge of the mattress so tightly his knuckles shone white. His head hung low.

She took a step toward him. "Are you okay?"

Nodding, he raised his head and opened his mouth to speak, then stared at her with an expression she couldn't read.

"What?" she asked when the silence stretched.

His lips curled up in a tired smile. "Nothing. You're just

beautiful."

Heat flooded her cheeks.

His smile broadened. "Even more so when you blush."

Grinning, she approached him. "Sweet talker."

He chuckled.

"Let me help you up."

"I don't want to get you dirty."

"First, let me say: Wow, your mother *really* raised you right, because your manners are impeccable. Second, don't be silly." Tossing the comb on the bed, she pulled one of his arms across her shoulders. He was so tall she didn't even have to bend or stoop to do it despite the fact that he was seated.

He rose, resting less weight on her than he had earlier. But his steps were slow.

His thoughts began to flow into her again, most focused around steadfastly trying to remain on his feet and not wanting to burden her with too much of his weight.

"At the risk of sounding like a perv," she said once they stood in the large bathroom, "I don't think I should leave you alone in here."

His lips curled up in another smile. "It's okay. I won't fall."

"I'm not so sure about that."

"I am." *And I don't want her to see me unclothed while I bear so many flaws.* He cast the mirror a disgusted glance. *I look like an ogre beside her beauty.*

*Awwww.* That was so sweet. "There's no need to feel self-conscious."

He swore. "You weren't supposed to hear that."

"Sorry." Things like that had ruined every relationship she had ever embarked upon.

"I'll be fine, Susan."

She seriously doubted that.

"If it will make you feel better, I'll leave the door unlocked and you can come running if you hear a loud thud."

"That isn't funny." Her lips twitched. "And yet I'm tempted to laugh, so I must be getting loopy again. I'll go make us something to eat while you shower." She hesitated. "Do you need help undressing?"

"No, thank you."

Wrinkling her nose, she gave him a look full of chagrin. "I felt so sleazy asking you that."

Amusement twinkled in his odd eyes. "Were I feeling better, I might have offered a sleazy response."

She laughed.

"You don't by any chance have some men's clothing I could borrow, do you?"

She mentally ran through her limited wardrobe. "I have a T-shirt that will probably fit you." Sometimes she slept in large men's T-shirts. "But I'm afraid nothing else will." She had never lived with a man, thanks to her telepathy. She'd kept no souvenirs from her few ex-boyfriends. And nothing else of hers would come *close* to fitting him.

"May I borrow the shirt?"

"Of course." She retrieved a shirt. "I'll grab my laptop and order you some clothes while you shower. I'm sure someone around here has same-day or next-day delivery."

"Thank you. I'll reimburse you as soon as I can. But eat first," he said as he took the shirt. "Your health is more important than my wanting to pretty myself up for you."

Smiling, she left the bathroom and closed the door behind her.

Getting out of the peculiar rubber suit wasn't as difficult as he imagined getting into it had been. It looked like the type of suit that was meant to hug one's frame. But it fit his loosely, indicating significant weight loss.

The wounds he exposed as he peeled it off were pretty gruesome. How the hell had he gotten them? Who had inflicted them? Were they—whoever *they* were—searching for him? Or had they simply buried him and left him for dead?

Knowing Susan might be monitoring his thoughts, he guarded them as best he could. He knew he was different in ways that would alarm her. Ways that already *had* alarmed her, he thought with a grimace as he noted the faint amber glow his eyes held. But her fear had diminished with less assistance tonight.

He stepped into the shower. The house's previous owner must

have been tall, because he didn't have to duck to wet his hair. The hot water pouring over him was sublime. For once, he groaned in pleasure instead of pain, though the many gashes that still marred his form stung like fire when the water and soapsuds hit them. How tempting it would be to spend an hour beneath that wonderful spray. But Susan would worry. So he washed his body and shampooed his hair. Then he washed his body and shampooed his hair again, because it felt so damned good.

Once he dried off, he studied himself carefully in the mirror.

He guessed he was about six feet two inches tall with short, jet-black hair. His face seemed that of a stranger. Not familiar at all. But perhaps that was a result of the cuts and abrasions that marred his forehead and much of the right side of his face. It almost looked as though he had been dragged face-first across a gravel driveway.

The weight loss might also be feeding the lack of recognition. He was pretty sure his stomach wasn't usually so sunken nor his ribs so prominent. As he took in the wealth of deep gashes and what appeared to be bullet holes that parted his skin, none of which bled, he was doubly glad he had not let Susan remain while he had showered. It was bad. Yet it didn't alarm him as much as he thought it should, neither the multitude of serious injuries nor the fact that he could survive them. As if such were a norm.

Who *was* he?

*What* was he?

He couldn't even tell how old he was. Though he bore no gray hair, he felt sure he was older than he looked, which was around thirty years old or thereabouts.

His head began to pound as fury rose that he couldn't remember. His brown eyes began to glow brighter amber. *Ah, hell.* Memory or no memory, he knew that wasn't normal. And unbeknownst to Susan, he had sprouted fangs, sunk them into her wrist and siphoned her blood into his veins.

Was he a... vampire?

Instant denial flooded him, strong enough to convince him he wasn't.

Then what? A lab experiment gone wrong?

Dragging the borrowed shirt over his head, he tried to calm his tumultuous thoughts. The amber glow in his eyes faded but didn't disappear entirely. The pain buffeting him was still too great.

The boxers he had worn beneath the rubber suit had deteriorated enough to not be an option. So he tossed them in the trash bin, grabbed a fresh towel and wrapped it around his hips, tucking the end in to hold it in place.

He reached for the rubber suit. When he picked it up, something clattered to the floor.

He glanced down. A cell phone. Did the suit have pockets then?

He performed a quick search and found only one inner pocket that must have held the phone. He draped the rubber suit over the shower door. He would've thrown it away with the boxers, but something told him to hang on to it in case he might need it.

Retrieving the phone, he stared down at it. Though it was cracked all to hell, he nevertheless tried to turn it on.

No luck. He clung to it, and couldn't quite force himself to toss it on top of the boxers in the bin. Had the phone worked, enlightenment would've only been a phone call away. He could've called any number stored in it and found out who the hell he was.

He glanced again at the stranger in the mirror. He could use a shave but cringed at the thought of dragging a blade down over those cuts and scrapes. So he ignored the beginnings of a beard and opened a few drawers. Upon finding a new toothbrush, he removed it from the package and availed himself of the tube of minty paste next to the faucet.

Susan began to hum somewhere below.

Leaving the bathroom, he carefully made his way down the stairs.

# Chapter Four

HE FOUND SUSAN IN THE kitchen. Something that smelled utterly delicious cooked on the gas stove beside her while she leaned against the counter and typed on a laptop.

When she glanced up and saw him, her forehead smoothed. "Oh. Good. I was just about to check on you. I stopped hearing your thoughts and was afraid you had passed out."

"I'm fine." He rounded the counter and joined her. The faded jeans she had donned after her shower hugged full hips and slender legs. His greater height—she was about a foot shorter than he was—allowed him to glimpse a hint of the shadowy cleavage bared by her V-necked T-shirt.

He slid the laptop an uneasy glance. She hadn't contacted anyone about him, had she?

She turned it toward him. A pair of men's sweatpants dominated the screen, displayed by an online store. "I figured until you're in better shape, you'd want something soft and comfortable. Will these do, or would you prefer jeans?"

He crossed to stand beside her and watched as she scrolled through a variety of men's trousers. "Those," he said, pointing to the pair that leapt out at him.

"Black cargo pants?"

"Yes, please."

"Okay. I'll get you several pair along with some T-shirts. Any color preference on the shirts?"

"Black."

She tapped more keys. "Boxers, briefs, or boxer briefs?"

He smiled when she refused to look at him while posing the question. "Boxers."

More tapping. "You'll need some socks, too. I didn't pay much attention to your shoes. Should I get you some new ones?"

"No, thank you." His boots had been in surprisingly good condition when he had removed them before repositioning himself and Susan farther up the bed.

More taps. Several screen changes. Then she smiled. "All done. They'll be here tomorrow."

"Thank you. I'll reimburse you as soon as I can." Her paying for his clothing did not sit well with him.

She waved a hand. "Don't worry about it."

But he did.

Grabbing a fork, she stirred some spaghetti in a large pot of boiling water as she gave him a once-over. A twinkle of mischief entered her light brown eyes. "You would make a great highlander."

He smiled. "Shall we pretend the towel is a kilt then?"

"Works for me," she replied with a grin. Picking up a tall glass of orange juice beside her, she held it out to him. "Here. Have some more."

"Thank you."

His fingers brushed hers as he took it from her. The juice was sweet and cold and gave him a chill as he downed it in a few swallows.

"Would you like some water, too?" she asked, her voice full of sympathy.

"Yes, please." He couldn't remember how long it had been since he had eaten or drunk anything.

When she moved away to fetch a pitcher from the refrigerator, his gaze fell to her laptop. An image of a beach at sunset decorated the screen.

His eyes went to the date in the top right corner and clung. Something about it didn't seem right. It actually seemed downright alarming, but the reason eluded him.

"Listen," she said as she returned and handed him the glass, "I've been thinking."

She smelled really good. And it wasn't just the herbal shampoo she used. It was *her*.

Raising the glass to his lips, he drank while she continued.

"I've been trying to figure out how you didn't die down there under all that dirt. I looked it up online while you were in the shower. And a person can only live about three minutes without air, so there must have been a tube or something I failed to notice while I was digging you up that provided you with air and kept you from suffocating."

He didn't remember seeing a tube. But he hadn't exactly been able to move around and check out his surroundings.

"I thought a person could only live three days without water. But apparently under certain circumstances, a person can live a week without water. Maybe even a little more in extreme cases. That's it though. So you can't have been down there for more than a week."

Setting the empty glass on the counter, he again glanced at the date on her computer. A week didn't seem right.

"I was gone all day last Sunday," she told him. "And I took Jax with me. So I think someone must have buried you down there then."

"Why would they do that?"

"I don't know. Whoever it was didn't damage or steal anything. There were no broken windows. The doors weren't marked up from forced entry. And nothing was missing. I had no idea anyone had even been in the house. So I wonder if maybe whoever did it had a key. I know I should have done it by now, but I haven't gotten around to changing the locks since I moved in. I just didn't see a need to hurry, because Jax is a great guard dog. If anyone were to approach the house, he would let me know."

He doubled down on his efforts to shield his thoughts from her. "When did you buy this house?"

"About a month ago. That's when I moved in anyway. The actual purchasing process took a month and a half."

He knew from the scratching sounds he had picked up each time she had come to look at the house that Jax had smelled him down in the basement long before she had purchased the place.

He had been buried in that basement a hell of a lot longer than a week but couldn't admit it without her knowing that his eyes weren't the only strange thing about him.

"Anyway," she said when he offered nothing more, "I went ahead and made an appointment for a locksmith to come out tomorrow morning and change all the locks, just in case. And a security company will come by tomorrow afternoon to install a security system for me." She shifted her weight from one foot to the other and bit her lip. "I know you didn't want me to call anyone and probably don't want any strangers around, but..." She shrugged. "I'm scared. I don't like to admit it, but I am. Knowing that whoever hurt you was in my house when I wasn't here makes me want to pack a bag and head for the hills."

Touching her arm, he gave it a gentle caress. "I'm sorry. I didn't mean to bring such chaos into your life."

She shrugged. "You didn't. The assholes who hurt you did."

He chuckled, his beleaguered heart attempting to pound at her nearness when she didn't move away. "I'd like to remain out of sight while the workmen are here, if you don't mind." He hadn't heard her make any phone calls while he was in the shower. He had already discerned that his hearing was uniquely sharp. So she must have made the appointments online.

He frowned. What if she was right and he had only been buried for a week? He supposed he shouldn't rule out that his mind might be playing tricks on him. His hair wasn't overly long. His beard only seemed to be about a week old. And his nails were short. Surely that wouldn't be the case if he had been buried down there a lot longer.

Unless those were all more oddities he bore.

But if men *had* just buried him in her basement a week ago, might they not have also installed spyware on her computer? He couldn't guess what they hoped to gain from such, but then he didn't understand why they had buried him in the basement either. So he thought it best not to rule out the possibility that one of them—having tracked her internet activity—would show up tomorrow in the guise of the expected workmen.

"Can you lock the basement door before they arrive?" he asked.

Tilting her head, she studied him. "Yes."

"Then do it."

"You think someone might impersonate the repairmen and—"

"I doubt it," he interrupted, not wanting to frighten her more. "I'm just trying to cover all bases. I'll stick close so I can watch over you."

Smiling, she stepped back and pulled a colander out of a lower cabinet. "Shouldn't I be the one watching over you?" She set the colander in the sink. "You were practically dead yesterday."

He shrugged, irritated by the pain the careless motion inspired. "I'm very resilient."

"I believe you."

His heart continued to work too hard while he watched her, his eyes taking in the long, loose hair that was beginning to curl where the ends dried.

When dizziness struck, he reached out and braced a hand on the counter.

She frowned over her shoulder. "You'd better sit down before you fall down."

Inwardly, he swore. He hated exhibiting such weakness in front of her. Maybe repairmen coming tomorrow wouldn't be such a bad idea. He needed more blood and couldn't partake of Susan's again. He would find a way to take some of theirs and hope it would be enough to restore his strength. As well as his memory.

Seating himself at the table, he set his broken phone on it to one side.

"What's that?" Susan asked as she set knives, forks, and spoons on the table in front of him, then added more on the other side of the table.

"I found it in my suit."

"I'm guessing it doesn't work?"

He shook his head. "The battery is dead. But even if it weren't, the phone is too damaged to be of use."

"Are you sure?" She held out her hand.

Stanislav placed the phone in it.

She examined the cracked front and back, then tilted it and picked at the center of the mangled base with one fingernail. "Oh. Yeah. You can't even plug it in. That sucks."

"Yes, it does." He returned the phone to the table.

After taking two plates down from an upper cabinet, she heaped both with generous helpings of spaghetti topped with a fragrant sauce.

His stomach cramped with sudden hunger despite the orange juice he'd downed.

"Do you think a tech guy could retrieve something off of it?" She set the plates on the table, then returned to the kitchen and filled his glass and a second one with cold water from the refrigerator.

"No. It's trashed. I just couldn't bring myself to throw it away."

"Of course not. It's a piece of your past." She handed him his glass, then set her own beside her plate.

"And it probably holds the phone numbers of friends and family I can't remember," he added as she seated herself across from him. "I apologize for not waiting until after you were seated to sit down myself." The lapse in courtesy troubled him.

She stared at him. "Really? Guys actually do that?"

"Rise when a woman enters the room and wait to sit until after she has seated herself?"

"Yes."

He shrugged. "I do." The impulse had been a strong one, so it must be a norm for him.

Twirling her fork in her spaghetti, she muttered, "I've been dating the wrong guys."

He smiled and picked up his own fork. The pasta was hot, the sauce spicy and delicious. "Mmm. This is wonderful." He had to struggle not to shovel it into his mouth as fast as he could. His body badly needed sustenance.

Her face lit with pleasure. "I'm glad you like it. I thought it best to start with something light since you haven't eaten in a while. There's plenty more if you want it. I made extra just in case."

"Thank you," he said between bites. "You're very kind."

"So are you," she said with a soft smile. Her gaze drifted to his left hand. "Do you think you're married?"

His first thought was *I hope not*, because he was very drawn to Susan and would hate to discover he was being unfaithful, if only in his thoughts. But the more he considered the question, the more certain he became that he wasn't. "No."

Her brow furrowed. "How can you be so sure?"

"Because sleeping beside you today felt… foreign, like I haven't slept beside a woman in a very long time." Though her face didn't reflect it, he could feel her disappointment at his assertion and wondered at the cause.

"Maybe you're gay."

Amusement kick-started a chuckle. "I'm not gay, Susan."

"How can you be so sure?"

"Because even in my weakened state, I'm attracted to you."

Her eyebrows rose. "Oh."

He heard her heartbeat pick up. "I hope that doesn't make you uncomfortable."

"It doesn't. I guess it just surprised me a little."

"I don't know why. You're beautiful. You're kind. And you have an enchanting singing voice."

A flush mounted her cheeks as she pointed her fork at his plate. "You need to eat more. Hunger has made you delusional."

He laughed, then grunted when the pain spiked.

She offered him a look full of sympathy. "Still hurts when you laugh?"

He nodded and dedicated himself to consuming several more forkfuls. "Thank you for letting me sleep beside you," he said softly. "It helped."

Her blush returning, she lowered her eyes to her plate and twirled her fork in her pasta.

"Exhibiting weakness before you makes my stomach clench, but…" He toyed with his dinner. "I needed the closeness, the physical contact. Being alone, buried down there for however long it was…" Irritated by his inability to find the right words to describe the anxiety that rode him, he shook his head. "Having you near comforted me."

Much to his surprise, she slid her free hand across the table, palm up.

His beleaguered heart tried to pound once more as he covered her small hand with his and curled his fingers around hers.

"Anytime you need me," she said, "I'm here. Okay?"

"Okay."

"And I don't think you're weak. No one I know could have survived what you have. So that makes you the strongest person I've ever met."

He squeezed her hand. "Thank you." He winked. "Though now I think hunger is making *you* delusional."

She laughed, and the two tucked into their meal once more.

Several minutes passed in silence. Peaceful, not awkward.

Susan released his hand long enough to carry her empty plate to the sink and refill his. "It's weird," she said as she reclaimed her seat. "I can't read your thoughts anymore."

He nodded, wishing he still held her hand. "Over the years I've learned to guard them so the telepaths won't intrude."

Her eyes widened. "You know other telepaths?"

When he realized what he'd said, his own eyes widened. *Did* he know other telepaths?

He thought for a moment. "I can bring no names or faces to mind, but for some reason am certain it's true. I do. I know other telepaths." Realization struck. "That's it!"

"What is?" she asked, her expression still stunned.

"That must be why they tried to kill me. Whoever did it must have found out. The bastards must be hunting *gifted ones.*"

"What's a *gifted one*?"

"We are," he told her. "You and I. Men and women who were born with advanced DNA that grants us unique gifts ordinary humans lack."

She stared at him. "I don't have advanced DNA."

"Yes, you do." He corrected her with absolute certainty. "That's why you're telepathic." And that was why he was so different.

Wasn't it?

––––––––⊱✦⊰––––––––

Susan didn't know why she was telepathic, but advanced DNA? She found the notion preposterous. "Wait. You said *you and I.* Are you saying you're telepathic, too?"

"No. I'm an empath," he revealed, then consumed another mouthful of pasta. He was clearly starving after his long fast. Yet he had excellent table manners.

"I don't know what that is," she admitted.

"I can feel other people's emotions."

She wasn't sure why that seemed weird when she could read other people's thoughts, but it did. "Like anger, sadness, that sort of thing?"

"Yes."

"Do you have to touch them to do it?"

"No." His look turned uneasy. "But in the interest of full disclosure…"

She groaned. "Nothing good ever follows those words."

His mouth twisted into a slight grimace. "I'm afraid in this instance, you're correct."

"Just tell me whatever it is, because you look like you think I'm going to explode when I hear it."

He set his fork down. "When I concentrate, I don't just feel other people's emotions. I can manipulate them too, should I desire to do so."

A chill skittered through her. He looked guilty as hell. "Are you manipulating mine right now?"

"No. But I did last night."

Dread settled like a heavy stone in the pit of her stomach. "What do you mean? How?"

"When you came down into the basement and found Jax doing his damnedest to dig me up, I dampened your dismay and fueled your curiosity until it overwhelmed you."

Her heart began to pound. He had manipulated her?

Regret filled his haggard features. "I'm sorry, Susan. I would not have done it if there had been any other way I could've gotten out of the ground. But you were my only hope. I needed you to find me, and knew you wouldn't if I didn't quash every doubt that rose and feed your curiosity until nothing else mattered but digging me up."

Rising, she paced away from the table. "No wonder," she mumbled. "No *wonder* I kept digging. I couldn't figure out why the hell I was so desperate to find whatever Jax smelled or heard down there. It made no sense."

Heavy silence fell.

He had manipulated her. The betrayal stung. A lot.

But damn it, she could understand why he'd done it. If he hadn't, he might be dead right now. There was no telling how much longer he could have lasted down there.

She swung around to face him. "Was that it? Was that the only time?"

He shook his head, his lips clamping into a grim line. "You were terrified when you found me. I didn't want you to be, so I banished your fear and replaced it with calm."

Which explained why she had felt no qualms about lugging him up to her bedroom and sleeping beside him—a total stranger she had dug up in her basement.

Her hands began to shake as panic rose. Her breath shortened. "Are you manipulating me right now?"

He shook his head, the amber light in his eyes brightening. "If I were, you wouldn't fear me."

She didn't know why guilt flared inside her at his words, but it did. Or was he *making* her feel guilty? She couldn't tell, because he had manipulated her! "Are you making me feel guilty?"

"No. I don't want you to feel guilty. You've no reason to. And I don't want you to fear me either."

"Show me," she demanded. If she was going to be pissed, she might as well confirm he could actually do what he claimed he could. "Show me you can do it. Change my emotions."

Her fear vanished with her next breath, leaving her calm again. The guilt evaporated as well while her heartbeat slowed. Her hands stopped quivering. "That's amazing," she breathed. "And terrifying."

His lips turned up in a sad smile. "More terrifying than your being able to read my thoughts and use them against me if you wish it?"

Susan bit her lip. She had barged into his mind countless times without a care for his feelings. It seemed kind of crappy to cry foul over him screwing with her emotions.

She stifled a desire to grimace. That made it sound as if they were lovers and he had toyed with her affections in some way. All he had really done was reduce her fear. Susan had to admit she felt better without it crowding her mind.

And he hadn't assaulted her. Or robbed her. Or done anything else heinous. He had been a perfect gentleman. He had even offered to leave. *And* he had removed her feelings of guilt. If he'd had nefarious intentions, wouldn't he have kept the fact that he could manipulate her emotions to himself?

She would've kept her ability to read his mind to herself if she'd been able to. And he really had no idea how often she had violated his privacy and perused his thoughts without permission before he'd begun to block them.

Slowly, she crossed to the table and sat down once more. "Is the advanced DNA you claim we both have the reason your eyes glow?"

He opened his mouth. Closed it. Shook his head. "Since your eyes don't glow, I'm not sure. I fear something else may be responsible."

She couldn't imagine what that something else might be. "Let me read your thoughts."

"Susan..."

"Please," she added. "One last time. I need to know I can trust you."

He sighed. "So be it." And just like that, his mind opened to her.

Once more she marveled over how odd it was to read the mind of someone who couldn't remember his past. Minds usually resembled libraries. The memories were all there, like books sitting on shelves, waiting for her to retrieve and peruse them. Some were shiny and new and on display right in front. Others were dusty and neglected and tucked away in back with pages missing.

But with him, she couldn't see the books — his memories — at all. She knew they were there. She could sense them. Like furniture in a seldom-used vacation home, covered by sheets.

Or maybe it would be more accurate to compare his memories to the recently declassified documents that occasionally made the news. The ones that only let you see a word or phrase here or there and blacked out the rest. His past — his life before he had been buried in her basement — had been obscured by thick dark swipes of a marker. Only those that had formed once he had awakened could be seen.

There were precious few of them. And they whorled around in such disarray with his thoughts that she found it hard to examine them. But she managed to get the gist of it.

He didn't want her to fear him. He actually dreaded that more than he did the idea of being forced back down into that hole in her basement and buried once more. The fact that she *did* fear him now, that she distrusted him as much as she did, that she felt even a moment's discomfort or uneasiness because of him upset him more than his missing memory did.

He was so damned grateful to her for helping him. And he liked her. Admired her strength. Her courage, which she herself found lacking. Loved that she could joke and laugh despite the bizarre and troubling circumstances they found themselves in.

He also needed her and dreaded leaving her. Because after the isolation he had suffered, he craved her company and touch more than he did the food and drink he'd been denied for so long. But if she asked him to, he would leave in a heartbeat.

Her breath left her in a rush.

He just didn't want her to fear him. That was why he had closed his thoughts to her. He had discovered other oddities about himself—oddities like his eyes that she couldn't seem to ferret out amid the tempest of his thoughts—and wished to hide them, because he didn't want to frighten her.

He had no other motivation.

He believed more than ever that calling the police would place her in danger because of the whole *gifted ones* thing. He feared what would happen to her if their differences should come to light. He was convinced that such always prompted dire consequences. And she knew from past experience that he was right.

The reminder of what had happened to her when the wrong people had learned of her telepathy made her shudder before she tamped the memory down.

He wasn't a criminal or a scam artist. He was just... lost.

Lowering his eyes, he curled both hands into fists on the table's edge.

He thought she was going to tell him to leave. She wasn't sure what he worried she was reading in his chaotic, fractured thoughts, but he believed it would turn her away from him.

Did the oddities that concerned him really matter though?

So he was different. She was, too. She had been all her life and had been rebuffed and rejected for it time and time again. She wouldn't turn around and reject him because he was an empath. Particularly since he had accepted *her* differences with grace and without condemnation.

Swallowing hard, Susan slid one hand across the table, palm up. His gaze rose and met hers.

She cleared her throat. "Anytime you need me," she reaffirmed, "I'm here. Okay?"

His Adam's apple bobbed. Reaching out tentatively, he took her hand in his. "I'm sorry I betrayed you."

"I'm not. I mean, I was at first. But if you hadn't, I wouldn't have found you." She squeezed his hand. "And I'm really glad I found you."

He covered their clasped hands, sandwiching hers between both of his. "I don't deserve your kindness."

"Yes, you do." He was a good guy. Instinct and everything she had read in his mind told her as much. She had found some pretty ugly stuff in the minds of the men she had dated in the past. His mind was a refreshing change. "Now finish your dinner. I know you're still hungry." While in his head, she had seen what a struggle it had been for him to eat slowly for her sake.

Nodding, he released her hand with obvious reluctance and filled his fork.

As Susan watched him, she wondered how they might find their way back to the burgeoning friendship they had found before things had gotten so serious. "I really have advanced DNA?"

He swallowed his latest mouthful. "All *gifted ones* do."

"You make it sound as if there are quite a few of us."

"There are." He frowned. "Damn it, why can I remember that but not remember my own name?"

"Actually, in the interest of full disclosure…" She broached the subject with the same hesitance he had demonstrated when speaking the words earlier.

A muscle in his jaw jumped. *She's right. Whatever follows those words will not be good.*

She laughed.

He cast her a questioning look. "What?" Then his lips formed a rueful smile. "Oh. Right. You're reading my thoughts. Would you be offended if I went back to guarding them?"

"Not as long as you stop manipulating my emotions."

"I already have. Your emotions have been your own ever since I lowered my mental barriers. And I'll not alter them again unless you wish it," he vowed.

"Thank you."

An instant later, she could no longer glean his thoughts. He really must know other telepaths, otherwise he wouldn't know how to do that.

He arched his brows. "What did you wish to tell me?"

"I know this is going to sound weird, but I think I might know your name."

He stared at her. "What?"

"I think I know your name."

Unease crept into his features. "How do you know my name?"

"When I sleep, the thoughts of others nearby tend to creep into my mind, and sometimes I can be pulled into their dreams. It's why I was so desperate to find a place out in the middle of nowhere."

He nodded. "That sounds familiar. Other telepaths must have told me the same."

How she wished she could meet those other telepaths. Being different was hard when you thought there was no one else like you. It was one of the reasons she wanted so badly to trust him. He was the first person she'd met—aside from her mother and brother—who was *different*. "Well, I had a dream when I fell asleep down in the hole with you. Or fainted. Or whatever it was that left me sleeping beside you while you held my hand."

He eyed her curiously as she trailed off. "A dream about me?"

"Sort of. I'm pretty sure it was actually your dream and I was pulled into it, because I was tall like you in the dream. My voice sounded like yours does now that you aren't hoarse. And when I looked into a mirror, I saw…"

"Me?"

"I think so. You're different now. A lot thinner."

"And banged up pretty good?"

She smiled. "Yes. But the resemblance is strong. Anyway, a man in the dream called me by name. Or rather called *you* by name."

"What was the name?"

"Stanislav."

"Stanislav," he repeated experimentally. "Stanislav," he said again, liking the way it sounded. When he let it roll off his tongue a third time, a face briefly surfaced in his mind. A man his height with similar dark hair and eyes, reading beside him in a windowless bedroom.

Susan peered at him. "Does it ring a bell?"

He nodded. "It seems familiar. And I remembered someone."

Her face lit with the same excitement that unfurled in his chest. "Who?"

"A friend, I think. Or perhaps a brother. He had dark hair and eyes like mine and a Slavic look about him. The image was there and gone in a blink. But he was sitting beside me as we both read books."

She smiled. "That's awesome! You see? It'll all come back to you soon."

He hoped so. He also hoped with a desperation that alarmed him that the source of his differences—when it came to light—wouldn't drive her away from him. He hadn't thought he would be able to hide them from her, but she clearly hadn't found them during her search.

His stomach soon began to warn him that too much food too soon might result in him spewing his dinner all over the table, so Stanislav reluctantly lowered his fork.

A half smile still toyed with the corners of Susan's full lips. "Had enough?"

"My mind says no, but my stomach says yes."

She rose, gathering their plates. "I've heard that eating too much after a long fast can result in your losing the meal, so you're probably right to play it safe. If you want more later though, let me know."

"Thank you."

"I need to feed Jax. Would you like to watch a movie or something afterward?"

Not much else he could do right now. "Sounds good."

The only rooms downstairs that Susan had unpacked were the small bathroom, the kitchen, and what she called the breakfast nook. So after dinner, the two of them returned to her bedroom upstairs.

Susan brought a chair in for Stanislav to sit in while she replaced the dirt-encrusted bedding with fresh sheets, pillowcases, and a soft comforter. At one point she glanced over at him and laughed.

"What?" he asked.

She shook her head, her hazel eyes twinkling with merriment. "You just look so disgruntled."

He smiled wryly. "I don't feel comfortable sitting idle while you labor to change bedding I mussed."

"Then we're even. Because I feel awful about not insisting you let me take you to the emergency room."

He shook his head. "I can't risk their discovering my advanced DNA."

"I understand. I just don't like to see you suffer." Done with her task, she patted the bed. "Make yourself comfortable. I'll be right back."

As she left the room, Stanislav rose and—with slow steps— crossed to the bed. He felt a little better, having eaten. But he was still a long way from being whole again. His wounds might not bleed, but they weren't healing. He didn't seem to be gaining strength either, his weakness so great that just climbing the stairs had taxed him. Every movement remained an exercise in torture. Simply lowering himself onto the bed, leaning back against the headboard, and straightening the towel wrapped about his hips hurt like hell.

A very appealing scent carried up the stairs as faint thumping sounds erupted below. A few minutes later, Susan entered, hugging two full glasses of water to her chest with one arm while balancing a huge bowl of popcorn in the other.

He grinned. As soon as she drew near, he took the glasses from her.

"Thank you." Climbing onto the bed, she settled beside him and plunked the bowl down between them.

He handed her a glass and set his own on a coaster on the bedside table.

As soon as she set her glass down, she retrieved the remote from the nightstand on her side of the bed and turned on the large high-def television that graced the wall across from them. "What do you feel like watching?"

He smiled. "Anything that strikes your fancy."

Her own lips curled up as she sent him a look he would've thought flirtatious under other circumstances. "I love the way you talk."

And he loved being with her like this.

"It's funny. Your accent makes me think you're Russian, but your thoughts are more often than not in English."

He puzzled over that one for a moment. "Perhaps I came to the United States when I was a boy and have lived here long enough that thinking in English has become a norm."

"Are you fluent in Russian?" she asked, her face bright with curiosity.

He ran several phrases through his head. "Yes. French, too, it would seem," he added when he was able to call up the other language. "And German. Italian. Spanish."

She stared at him. "Seriously?"

"Yes."

"Maybe you work as a translator for a publishing house."

He tried to picture himself sitting behind a desk all day and couldn't. "Perhaps."

She seemed to sense the frustration rising within him once more and changed the subject. "So you have no movie preferences? No particular genre you'd like to watch?"

He shook his head. "You choose."

They ended up watching a movie about an alien man with a cape who wielded a large magical hammer and another man who turned green and grew huge in size when angered.

Susan winked at him. "I'm glad your eyes glow. I much prefer that to your turning into a crazed green giant."

He laughed. "As do I."

Though he enjoyed her company, Stanislav could barely keep his eyes open by the end of the movie.

Susan brought a hand to her mouth to conceal a big yawn. "I know we haven't been awake for very long, but I'm about to fall asleep."

"I think I may have nodded off a couple of times during the movie," he admitted.

"Let's go ahead and call it a night then." Rising, she groaned. "Oh, man. I am so sore from all that digging. I really need to start exercising again."

His gaze traveled over her slender form. A red T-shirt hugged

AWAKEN THE DARKNESS

alluring breasts and a narrow waist. Her jeans outlined full hips and hugged a tight ass and shapely legs he shouldn't be ogling.

What had she been talking about?

It took him a moment to remember. *Oh. Right.* She was sore. "I'm sorry."

She shook her head. "Don't worry about it."

But he did. He didn't like causing her discomfort. "How are your hands?" He held his out, palm up.

Rounding the bed slowly, she placed hers in them.

Stanislav sat up straighter and examined them closely, then swore. Raw, open blisters marred the skin at the crooks of her thumbs and the base of every finger. She had gripped that shovel for so long that the blisters had all popped and the flap of loose skin on each had torn away. It looked painful. And she had said nothing, not even complaining when she had held one hand over the steaming pot of pasta while stirring it, something that must have made her hand hurt even more.

"Stop beating yourself up about it," she ordered softly.

He raised his head, on a level with hers though he sat and she stood.

"I wasn't intentionally listening to your thoughts," she told him. "You were sort of broadcasting them. And it wasn't your fault."

"I beg to differ. Had I not compelled you to dig me up —"

"You would probably be dead right now," she finished for him. Withdrawing one hand, she drew it over his hair. "It was worth it."

His pulse raced at her touch. His gaze dropped to her lips. He heard her heartbeat pick up.

Swiveling, she turned and retrieved the empty popcorn bowl. "I'll just take this downstairs." In the next instant, she was gone.

Stanislav released his breath on a long sigh. What the hell had he been thinking? He had almost kissed her, and he didn't even know who he was.

When Susan returned, she headed into the bathroom to brush her teeth and change into another set of those tempting pajamas.

Stanislav waited until she finished, then brushed his own teeth. Excitement rose, making his damned eyes flare brighter. Would she let him sleep beside her again tonight?

He cut the light off and strode into the bedroom.

~ 81 ~

She was already tucked between the sheets.

He hesitated.

She patted the mattress beside her.

"You're sure you don't mind?" he asked.

"I'm sure," she replied, no doubt in her voice.

He walked around to the far side of the bed and lay down next to her beneath the sheets, trying to keep the damned towel around his hips.

It felt different tonight, lying beside her. More intimate.

She turned off the lamp on her bedside table, plunging them into darkness his sharp eyes had little difficulty piercing. "Good night."

He stared at her, admiring her pale features. "Good night." Clasping his hands so he wouldn't reach for her, he rested them on his stomach.

Her face turned toward him, but he knew she couldn't find him in the shadows.

Reaching toward him with her right hand, she found his left on his stomach and twined her fingers through his.

He opened his mouth, then closed it.

Did she know how much he needed her touch?

Rolling toward her, he brought her hand to his lips for a kiss, then cradled it against his chest.

She smiled and rolled onto her side to face him.

What did she see when she peered at him through the darkness?

"Your eyes are so beautiful," she whispered.

He could see their amber glow reflected in hers. "It doesn't frighten you, their glowing?"

She squeezed his hand. "You can read my emotions. Do I feel frightened to you?"

"No." Though none of the emotions he felt swirling inside her included fear, he found himself doubting the veracity of the information his gift conveyed. He knew the concern she felt for him was real. But surely she didn't also feel burgeoning affection for him.

Did she?

Closing her eyes, she released a contented sigh. "Good night, Stanislav."

"Good night, Susan," he replied softly.

Slumber claimed her swiftly. Stanislav watched her as long as his drooping eyelids would allow. He should rest.

He might need every bit of strength he could muster tomorrow.

He inched closer to her.

She didn't stir.

Smiling, he pressed his forehead to hers and swiftly sank into a deep healing sleep.

# Chapter Five

SUSAN SANG UNDER HER BREATH *as she carried the mail into the kitchen and set it on the counter, riffling through it.*

*Junk. Junk. Previous owner crap. Junk. Bill. Junk.*

*A large warm body stepped up behind her.*

*Dropping the envelopes, she spun around and tilted her head back.*

*Stanislav.*

*He looked different. His wounds were gone. His shoulders were broad, clad in a black T-shirt that hugged muscled pecs and washboard abs. The biceps left bare by the dark fabric were large and well defined. Black cargo pants covered thighs thick with muscle and fell to the tops of big black boots.*

*She returned her gaze to his face. Fuller now. And so damned handsome.*

*Her heartbeat quickened.*

*"Keep singing," he whispered.*

*Excitement skittering through her, she obeyed.*

*He slid his left arm around her waist and drew her up against his hard form.*

*Her breath caught.*

*Clasping her right hand in his left, he began to dance with her. Slowly. Matching the rhythm of the love song she crooned.*

*"Again," he whispered when she ran out of lyrics, their bodies brushing as they swayed from side to side.*

*Once more, she complied.*

*Her blood heated when he bent his head and nuzzled her neck, teasing the sensitive skin there with his lips. Such a strong wave of arousal washed over her that she forgot to sing.*

"Don't stop," he implored.

"That's just what I was going to say," she murmured and felt him smile.

His body was hard against hers. Every inch of him. His erection pressed against her stomach.

He raised his head, those bright amber eyes catching and holding hers.

His head dipped. His mouth met hers.

And her body went liquid.

His lips were warm and soft and teased hers with a skill that weakened her knees. Rising onto her toes, she wrapped both arms around his neck and leaned into him. A growl of approval rumbled in his chest as he locked his arms around her and deepened the kiss, touching his tongue to hers. Stroking. Enflaming. Until she rubbed against him, practically begging for his touch.

She didn't think she had ever in her life wanted so badly to make love with a man.

When he slipped a hand up to cup her breast, she arched into him. Lightning shot through her as he drew a thumb across the hardened peak, then returned to torment her more.

A sound of protest escaped her when he abandoned her breast.

Then he swept his arm across the counter behind her.

The mail fell to the floor. Susan couldn't care less. Her whole body burned for him. And she was hoping that meant he was going to —

"Yes," she hissed when he lifted her and sat her on the counter.

Stepping between her thighs, he urged them farther apart until the hard length behind his fly rubbed against her center. She offered no protest when he yanked her T-shirt over her head, then tore off her bra. Literally tore it off! Because as soon as he did, he bent and took a hardened nipple into his mouth. Sucking. Laving. Nipping it with his teeth until she writhed against him.

She lay back on the cold countertop and buried her fingers in his soft, thick hair. "More."

Reaching up, he grabbed his shirt at the back of his neck and yanked it over his head.

So much muscle. She couldn't wait to feel it against her bare skin.

He returned his mouth to her breasts, rested his warm hands on her thighs, and slipped his fingers beneath the hem of her skirt. Susan squirmed beneath him as he splayed his fingers, sliding them up, then down, then up again, his thumbs teasing her by coming just a little closer *to the heart of her with each caress.*

*"Stanislav," she begged. "Touch me. Please."*

*He growled something in Russian.*

*His thumbs skimmed over her clit, sending a jolt through her. Then he tucked his fingers in the waistband of her bikini panties and dragged them down. The skirt swiftly followed, leaving her completely bare to his view.*

*She should feel self-conscious before his perfection, but the heat in his bright eyes as he drank in the sight of her just enflamed her more.*

*He straightened, his hands clutching her hips in a grip that was so tight it was almost painful. The look on his face — the need and desire reflected there as he gazed down at her — left her panting.*

*A slow smile tilted his lips as, holding her gaze, he lowered his head and took her with his mouth.*

*Susan moaned as sensation shot through her. Burying her fingers in his hair, she locked her legs around him and urged him on. She could barely breathe as he worked her with his tongue and his fingers. Throwing her head back, she cried out as a climax rocked her.*

Susan came awake with a start. Eyes wide, she gasped as an orgasm rippled through her, stealing her breath, sending her heartbeat into overdrive and filling her with ecstasy.

What the hell?

It took her several moments to catch her breath and get her bearings as her heart did its damnedest to burst from her chest and her body continued to pulse with pleasure.

She lay on her side in bed, Stanislav spooned up behind her. His face was buried in the hair at the back of her neck. His arms were wrapped about her tightly, one hand clutching her breast, the other tucked between her legs over her panties. The towel he had wrapped about his hips had come loose. And she could feel his unencumbered erection pressing against her bottom and her core.

He was so hard. Every muscle in his body was tight with need. His breathing was strained. But he didn't move.

She peeked into his thoughts.

He was asleep, still caught up in the dream of making love to her on the kitchen counter.

Arousal shot through her once more when he opened his fly in the dream and plunged his hard shaft into her. So big. So good.

"Stanis—" she started to say but broke off as another wave of heat hit her. "Stanislav," she said again, louder this time.

He shifted as the dream faded and consciousness beckoned. The hand on her breast squeezed and kneaded. The fingers between her legs moved.

She bit her lip, barely suppressing a moan.

Then he jerked as he came fully awake and realized just where those large hands of his were. A slew of Russian filled his head as he hastily withdrew them and moved away from her.

Susan knew nothing of that language but guessed from the tone of his mental rant that he was ripping himself a new one. She glanced over her shoulder.

He lay on his back, one arm draped across his eyes, every muscle tense, the covers tenting over his arousal.

She rolled over onto her other side to face him. "Care to repeat any of that in English?"

He gave his head a quick shake, a muscle twitching in his jaw. "It would only offend you more."

"Am I right in guessing they're curse words?"

"A great many of them." He made a sound of disgust. "What you must think of me, fondling you whilst you slept. And after all you've done for me."

"I think," she stated plainly, "that you didn't mean to. You were asleep and caught up in an erotic dream."

He lifted his arm just enough to regard her skeptically.

She arched a brow.

"You don't think me a knave who was taking advantage of you?"

"No, I don't," she assured him and tamped down the temptation to blurt *Take advantage of me. Please.* Because that had been one hell of an orgasm. The first she'd had in a very long time. Kind of hard to regret that.

He looked as though he doubted his hearing. "You truly aren't angry?"

"How *can* I be? We were *both* caught up in the dream." Heat crept into her cheeks. "A dream that I'm pretty sure started out as mine, not yours."

Surprise and intrigue erased the self-recrimination in his features as he lowered his arm. "What makes you think that?"

"Because I was *me* in the dream, not you. If the dream had been yours to begin with, I would've started out as you."

"You drew me into your dream?"

She nodded. "I don't think I've ever done that before. I didn't even know I could."

"Nevertheless, I'm sorry."

"I'm not." She sent him a teasing grin. "I woke up in the middle of a fantastic orgasm."

His lips twitched. "So… not a bad way to wake up?"

She laughed. "Exactly. And if anyone should be angry, it's you. *I* drew you into the dream. You gave me the most intense orgasm I've had in a long time. Then I yanked you out of the dream before you could…" Her voice trailed off as she motioned to the covers tenting over his erection.

It was a big tent. She remembered seeing him plunge his long, hard length into her in the dream and felt heat again sweep through her body.

His eyes brightened.

She swore silently. "You weren't supposed to feel that."

"I'd say I'm sorry, but…"

She chuckled.

His expression lightened as he slowly rolled onto his side toward her. He opened his mouth to speak.

Jax began to bark downstairs.

The doorbell rang.

Eyes flashing even brighter, Stanislav swiftly sat up.

Pain rippled across his features. Clenching his teeth, he sucked in a harsh breath.

Susan lunged up and rested a hand on his shoulder. "What are you doing? You shouldn't move so quickly. Are you okay?"

"The repairmen," he gritted. "I must protect you."

She glanced at the clock on the bedside table. "It isn't the repairmen. It's your clothes being delivered."

An engine rumbled to life outside, then grew fainter as the delivery truck drove away.

Stanislav's brows drew down in a deep vee. "I didn't hear the truck approach."

"I didn't either."

"But I should have," he ground out and seemed furious at himself for having failed to do so.

Poor guy. His face was still way too thin and marred by those harsh gashes. She didn't know what wounds the T-shirt and covers hid, but he was riddled with so much agony that just sitting up too quickly had hurt enough to steal his breath and banish his erection. And he appeared to be mentally kicking himself because he thought he had failed to protect her.

"Well," she told him, "blame me then. You probably would've heard the truck arrive if I hadn't been babbling on about orgasms."

A surprised laugh escaped him.

She sent him a cheeky smile. "Thank you, by the way."

He grinned. "You're very welcome." Shaking his head, he cupped her face in one hand and smoothed his thumb over her cheek.

Affection warmed her at his touch.

"Who *are* you?" he asked with a combination of pleasure and bafflement. "Really."

She shrugged. "No one special."

He drew away with a half smile. "You'll never convince me of that." Shifting over to the edge of the bed, he fished beneath the covers for something.

"What are you doing?"

"Looking for the towel. I need to go down, get the clothes, and prepare for the repairmen's arrival."

Prepare how?

Susan tossed back the covers and rose. "I'll get the clothes. You find the towel." Although she sort of hoped he wouldn't find the towel.

She retrieved the large box from her front porch, then returned upstairs and plunked it down on the bed. "You can have this bathroom to yourself. I'll use the one down the hallway." Grabbing her toothbrush, a change of clothes, and a brush, she headed for the other upstairs bathroom. *Sheesh*, it needed a lot of work. This was the first time she'd used it since moving in.

Glancing around as she brushed her teeth, she grimaced at the horrid floral wallpaper. Updating it all was going to be a pain in the ass.

As quickly as she could, she donned panties, a bra, soft blue jeans, and a gray V-neck T-shirt. Her hair was waving in weird ways as it always did when she didn't braid it before going to bed. So she dampened it and dragged it back into a ponytail.

She studied herself in the mirror.

Stanislav thought she was pretty. Beautiful, actually. She had found as much in his thoughts. But as she stared at her reflection, she really didn't see it. The best thing she could say about herself was that she looked younger than she was. She always had. And she'd hated that when she was in high school. The other girls had teased her mercilessly, repeatedly pointing out that they all looked like women while she still looked like a girl. But it had ended up working in her favor. At thirty-two, she could easily pass for twenty-one.

*Why the hell am I thinking about that now?*

*Because you want to look good for Stanislav.*

She wrinkled her nose at her reflection. *So much for that idea.*

Leaving the bathroom, she went in search of him.

He wasn't in the bedroom.

When she heard a noise downstairs, she skipped down the steps and headed into the kitchen… where she stumbled to a wide-eyed halt. *Holy crap.*

He was garbed all in black. Black T-shirt. Black cargo pants. His big black boots.

And he looked good.

The clothes were loose on him. She had assumed he would gain back the weight he'd lost once he started eating regularly, so she had bought the size she estimated he would need and had thrown in a belt to hold the pants up until he did.

But even with him being too thin and the clothes fitting him loosely…

She let her gaze travel over his back from his head to his heels.

Yeah. He looked good. *Really* good. Especially after that damned dream.

Jax crouched down at Stanislav's feet, happily devouring a bowl of dog food.

Stanislav stood before her cutlery drawer.

As she watched, he slid a steak knife into his back right pocket.

He slid another into the left.

Unease rose. "What are you doing?"

<hr>

Stanislav didn't turn around at the inquiry. "Just making sure all bases are covered," he murmured as he continued to distribute sharp knives to each and every pocket his new pants boasted. Susan had a pretty decent array in her drawer, though he would've preferred daggers, throwing stars, and a couple of katanas.

He heard her heartbeat pick up a bit and glanced over his shoulder. "What's wrong?"

She was fresh-faced and beautiful in jeans that rode low on her hips and a T-shirt that clung to a narrow waist and dipped just enough in front to allow a glimpse of cleavage.

She motioned to the knife he tucked into a pocket on his thigh. "Do you really think that's necessary?"

"Yes." He would take no chances with her safety.

She just stared at him.

Uncertain what she was thinking, he went back to arming himself.

"You look like you've done that before," she murmured. "A lot." And the notion unsettled her. He heard it in her voice even as her unease infiltrated him.

"I must have," he said, unwilling to lie. "It feels familiar."

A scene flashed before his mind's eye. A battle. Firing an automatic weapon. Soldiers running around amidst smoke and explosions.

Pain shot through his head.

Grunting, he pressed the heel of one hand against his forehead and waited for it to pass.

Susan stepped up beside him and touched his shoulder. "Stanislav? Are you okay?"

He shook his head. "I saw something."

She nodded. "I saw it, too. Sorry about that. It wasn't intentional." She rubbed his shoulder in soothing circles. "You must have been in the military at some point."

"That's what it looked like." And that seemed to assuage her... fear?

No. Dread, perhaps. When she had seen him with the weapons, she must have worried about the past he couldn't remember. Who he had been and what he had done that had required him to arm up on a regular basis.

"You don't by any chance have a gun or two, do you?" he asked hopefully.

"Actually, yes."

Surprise struck. "You do?"

She nodded. "But I'd rather they remain where they are, if you don't mind."

He considered trying to change her mind but couldn't blame her. They might have embarked upon friendship and fostered a certain amount of trust in each other, but she still knew little about him. "As you will. What time will the first man arrive?"

She glanced at the clock on the oven. "If he's on time, half an hour. Would you like some breakfast while we wait?"

"Only if you let me help you prepare it."

"Deal." Though her smile returned, it seemed a little forced. The weapons thing had thrown her.

An hour later, he heard gravel crunch beneath tires as the locksmith turned onto her driveway. "He's here," Stanislav announced, setting his dish in the sink. "Keep the dog inside with you. I'll be nearby if you need me."

She stared up him, her hazel eyes full of anxiety.

Taking her hand, he gave it a squeeze. "Don't worry. I'm probably just being paranoid."

"And if you aren't?"

"I'll return in an instant, protect you, and hopefully gain some of the answers I need."

Lips tightening, she surprised him by giving him a quick hug.

His heart singing despite his concern, he slipped out the back door, strode through the shaded yard, and disappeared into the trees.

An eternity seemed to pass while the locksmith introduced himself to Susan, then talked her ear off while he replaced the locks on the front and back doors. He gave all appearances of being exactly what he was: a locksmith with no connections to the men who had buried Stanislav in the basement.

Susan escorted the man out front when the job was finished. Then, with a smile and a wave, she retreated indoors.

The locksmith climbed into his van and guided it slowly down the gravel driveway.

Clenching his teeth, Stanislav sped through the brush at inhuman speed, passed the van, and stopped where the long, winding driveway met a narrow blacktop road. He growled as pain struck him like a sledgehammer. Several colorful epithets spewed forth in a whisper as he tucked a hand in one pocket and fished out the dark sunglasses he'd found in the kitchen. No way would he be able to keep his eyes from glowing.

The van approached and slowed to a stop.

Stepping onto the gravel driveway behind it, Stanislav jogged around to the driver's side, grateful for the shade the old oaks that touched each other overhead provided. "Hey!" he called in his best approximation of an American accent. "Hey, hold up a minute!"

A look of surprise lit the locksmith's features as Stanislav stopped just outside the man's window, then bent forward and braced his hands on his knees as if he had run to catch up and was now winded.

The portly man rolled down his window. "Can I help you?"

Nodding, Stanislav straightened.

The locksmith's eyes widened. "Hey, man, are you okay?"

Stanislav bit back a curse. Right. He'd been so focused on his eyes that he'd forgotten his face was all cut up. Offering the locksmith a friendly smile, he waved a hand in dismissal. "Yeah. I was in a car accident a few days ago. Some dumbass ran a red light and T-boned me. But it looks a lot worse than it feels." Not really. "I'm Susan's husband, Stan. I was sleeping when you arrived. Susan's been worried about me since the accident, so she didn't wake me. But I wanted to ask you about another job."

The prospect of putting more money in his pocket brought a smile to the locksmith's face. "Sure. Sure. What kind of job?"

"The inner doors throughout the house could really use some new hardware. A couple of them lock automatically when we close them. Another won't close at all. It's a real pain in the ass. Would you be interested in taking care of that for us, maybe in another month or two?"

The man smiled and nodded. "Sure. I can do that. What'd you say your name was again?"

He offered his hand. "Stan. Nice to meet you."

The locksmith clasped his hand and gave it a hearty shake. "Devlin. Good to meet you."

Before the man could withdraw his hand, Stanislav shoved the sleeve of his blue uniform shirt up, bent his head, and sank his fangs into the man's arm.

The locksmith emitted a yelp of surprise and struggled briefly before his muscles relaxed as his eyelids drooped.

Stanislav closed his eyes as his fangs siphoned blood into his parched veins. Some of the cursed weakness that beset him eased a bit. *This* was what he needed to eradicate his injuries and restore his strength. A deep healing sleep was far less effective when not accompanied by infusions. If he could do this again when the security man came later, Stanislav would be nearly whole again on the morrow. His internal injuries would heal as the day progressed, his broken ribs weaving back together, his not-fully-healed broken limbs growing strong again, bruised organs becoming like new.

If he could manage a second infusion, the next deep healing sleep should repair his exterior wounds as well—every cut, gash and puncture.

He frowned. At least he thought it would. He wasn't sure about his weight though. Or his strength. He had a sinking feeling that might require more than two infusions to correct.

He took as much as he dared from the locksmith, then retracted his fangs, rolled the man's sleeve down, and slipped his arm through the window. The locksmith's head lolled as he sank into unconsciousness.

"Thank you," Stanislav murmured. Reaching through the window, he found the key in the ignition and turned off the engine. When the locksmith woke, he would remember nothing of what had happened.

Stepping back from the van, Stanislav brushed his fingers across his lips to ensure they were clean and wondered once more why he knew things like that but couldn't remember his damned past.

The new blood coursing through his veins began to relieve the pain that racked him as he removed the sunglasses, ducked back into the brush, and headed for the house. His shoulders straightened. His stride lengthened.

Better.

After circling around to the back of the two-story house, he meandered along the path of dappled shade the large oaks and pecan trees in the backyard provided.

Susan stepped out onto the back porch. The furrow in her brow vanished when she saw him. "There you are. I was worried when you didn't come inside after he left."

He smiled. "I thought I would wait a minute or two in case he returned. Did you hear anything suspicious in his thoughts?"

"Not a thing."

He had suspected as much. "When will the security man come?"

"He's supposed to be here between three and six."

"Good. I'll do the same when he arrives."

⚬✦◉◉✦⚬

Susan clipped Jax's leash onto his collar and headed out the front door. She had let him out without the leash only once since moving into their new home. She had been curious to see what he'd do with so many scents floating on his new turf and had ended up spending the next four hours panicking after he took off running and disappeared.

Never again.

The boards on the front porch creaked as she crossed it, then followed Jax down the steps. Bending, she plucked a couple of weeds as she strode down the brick walkway. She wouldn't be able to devote any time to the landscaping out front until her next book released in May, so she uprooted a couple of weeds every day in a weak attempt at short-term improvement.

Jax barked and wagged his tail as he trotted forward, tugging at the leash, sniffing everything in sight.

She grinned. He really loved it here.

He led her down the long winding driveway, veering off course a couple of times to chase a squirrel. The two of them had made a habit of checking the mail together every day, so he knew where she wanted him to take her.

As they rounded a bend, she stopped short.

The locksmith's van was parked at the end of the driveway.

She frowned. He had left two hours ago. What was he still doing in her driveway?

She listened for his thoughts, but heard nothing.

Was he even in the van? If not, where was he? What was he doing?

Had Stanislav been right?

She glanced over her shoulder, wondering if she should call him.

Better to be safe than sorry, she decided uneasily. *Stanislav?* she called mentally.

*Yes?* he immediately responded, unperturbed in the least by her speaking to him in his head. He really *was* comfortable around telepaths, something that continued to astound her.

*Jax and I walked down to check the mail, and the locksmith's van is parked at the end of the driveway. I can't hear his thoughts, so I'm not sure he's still in it.*

What she guessed was a Russian swear word burst through his mind. *Back away into the trees and wait for me. I'm on my way.*

She did as advised, guiding Jax into the brush and letting the overgrown weeds and untrimmed trees swallow them.

A hand touched her shoulder.

Emitting a squeak of surprise, she spun around.

Stanislav stood behind her. "Forgive me," he whispered. "I didn't mean to startle you."

She gaped up at him. "How did you get here so fast?" She'd never measured it, but it was a long driveway. Long enough that you couldn't see the house from the road.

He shrugged. "I ran."

*Faster than a track star and without making a single sound?* she wondered incredulously.

He started to ease around her. "Stay here."

She grabbed his arm. "No way. I'm coming with you."

He looked as though he wanted to protest but thought better of it and nodded. "When we find him, use your gift to let me hear his thoughts."

"I don't know how to do that. I mean, I can listen to them myself. But I don't know how to let you hear them, too."

He patted her hand where it rested on his arm. "Just hold on to me. You're broadcasting pretty loudly right now. So I'll hear whatever you hear when you peek into his mind."

Really? That was so cool.

His lips twitched.

She grinned. "I *am* broadcasting loudly, aren't I?"

"Yes."

Her nerves jangled as she looked toward the van.

Stanislav leaned down and pressed a kiss to her hair. "Don't be afraid. I won't let anyone hurt you."

Susan nodded, her heart stuttering a bit. She liked the feel of his hand on hers. His lips touching her hair. The casual gestures of affection. It made her feel like a teenager in the grips of a first crush.

Glancing down at her, he smiled.

"Damn it," she hissed. "I just broadcast that, didn't I?"

"Yes."

"Well, forget you heard it."

He returned his attention to the van. "Not likely." Palming a knife, he shifted his hand to keep the weapon out of sight and strode forward.

Susan stuck close to him, squeezing the hell out of his arm, but he offered no protest.

He approached the vehicle with caution.

Susan could discern no movement within and still could hear no thoughts.

She and Stanislav continued forward until they reached the driver's side door, then peered through the open window.

The locksmith was slumped in his seat, head back, mouth open, soft snores pouring forth.

Stanislav smiled. "Looks like he's having a little nap."

And not dreaming, apparently, or she would've picked up on it.

Stanislav rapped his knuckles on the car door.

The locksmith jerked awake with a snort. Blinking, he stared blankly through the front windshield, then turned toward them. "What?"

"Everything okay?" Stanislav asked.

"What do you mean? What's uh…?" He blinked owlishly and peered around him. *What the hell?* "What's goin' on?" *Where the hell am I?*

Susan glanced at Stanislav to see if he was catching the locksmith's thoughts.

He dipped his chin in a slight nod. "I was about to ask you the same," he told the man. "You came out to replace the locks on our house and left two hours ago. We were coming down to collect the mail, saw you parked here, and thought we should check to make sure you're okay."

*What? I changed the locks on their house? And what's up with that guy's face? Why is it all cut up like that?*

Stanislav arched a brow. "Everything okay?"

*Ah shit. Shit shit shit shit shit.* "Yeah," the man mumbled, sitting up straighter. "Yeah, sure." *The woman looks familiar.* "I, uh..." *Right. She said she just bought the house and I came out to change the locks. I remember her opening the front door after I stepped up onto her creaky porch. But everything after that is a blank.* "Um..." *Damn it! What the hell was in that weed I smoked last night? I told Jimmy I just wanted to mellow out, but that asshole must have laced it with something stronger. That fucker is into* everything.

Susan barely managed to hold back a laugh.

The corners of Stanislav's eyes crinkled as he smiled. "Long weekend?" he asked, his tone sympathetic.

The locksmith mustered up a wry smile. "Yeah. *Too* long. Hey, thanks for waking me."

"No problem." Stanislav stepped back, taking Susan with him. "Have a good one."

Susan nodded. "Thanks again for changing the locks."

"Anytime." The man started the van and drove away.

Susan laughed as she looked up at Stanislav. "I don't know who Jimmy is, but I have a feeling he's going to get an earful tonight."

"I think you're right." His face bright with amusement, Stanislav crossed to the mailbox and retrieved several envelopes. When he returned, he took her free hand in his and twined their fingers together.

They strolled up the driveway, Stanislav steering her out of the hot midday sun and through patches of heavy shade.

Warmth filled her as she studied his profile.

He stood straighter now and moved less stiffly. The lines of pain in his features had softened a bit.

Glancing down, he caught her staring. "What?" he asked with an appealing smile.

She shrugged. "You look better."

He winked. "Perhaps I've been smoking some of the locksmith's weed."

She laughed.

"Thank you," he said, his voice softening, "for doing as I asked and waiting for me instead of confronting the locksmith yourself."

She paused to let Jax investigate a rustling sound off to their right. "Well, you seem to know what you're doing. And I feel safer with you at my side."

A squirrel raced up the closest tree, Jax nipping at its heels.

Stanislav raised their clasped hands and pressed a kiss to the back of hers. "I meant what I said, you know. I won't let anyone hurt you, Susan," he vowed.

Her skin tingled where his soft lips brushed it, heat zinging up her arm. She met his gaze... and gasped.

"What?" he asked.

"Your eyes. I just realized they aren't glowing anymore." The amber glow had receded, leaving chestnut irises.

His eyebrows rose. "They aren't?"

"No. Now they're a deep, beautiful brown." She winked. "Must have been really good weed."

He laughed.

Jax trotted back onto the driveway, happy to have terrorized another furry friend.

It was a nice moment in time. Peaceful. Her hand so natural in his.

As they headed around a curve, she saw Stanislav glance back in the direction the van had driven.

# Chapter Six

THE SECURITY GUY, WHO INTRODUCED himself as Henry, arrived half an hour early. That in and of itself made Stanislav suspicious as he watched the house from the dense foliage beside it. Repairmen never arrived early.

*Are you listening for my thoughts?* he questioned Susan mentally. Since he wasn't telepathic himself, she wouldn't hear him unless she was keeping an ear out for him.

*Yes.*

*What are you finding in his?*

*Things that are making me nervous as hell. He's totally fixating on the basement.*

*What does he think is down there?*

*I don't know. I'm not even sure* he *knows.*

Henry kept up a rambling stream of jovial conversation while he installed window sensors and door sensors on the first floor. "Do you want them on the second floor, too?"

*Tell him no.*

"No, thank you. The ground floor is fine."

"What about the basement?"

"No windows down there," she responded.

"Is there an exterior entrance to it?"

"No." *He doesn't like that,* she reported. *And even though he mentioned beagles making great guard dogs, his thoughts tell me he doesn't like that I have one.*

Stanislav had already picked up on the irritation Jax engendered in Henry. *Stay sharp,* he advised.

"Do you have any kids?" Henry asked. "I could put a sensor on the door anyway to alert you if they try to go down there. I did that for my sister. She was worried one of the little ones might manage to open the door and tumble down the stairs."

"No kids," she answered brightly. "And I don't even go down there myself. Too many creepy crawlies."

*Smart thinking.* That would lessen the likelihood that she would be linked to him.

An idea struck. *Ask him what will happen if something triggers the alarm. Tell him you're leaving town in a couple of days and want to make sure the place will be secure.*

*Okay.* She did as requested.

Stanislav felt a surge of triumph ripple through the man before he responded casually, "How long will you be gone?"

"A week," Susan improvised. "I'm flying to Miami for my grandmother's birthday. It's going to be a family reunion of sorts."

"No problem. Just set the alarm when you leave. If something triggers it, police will check it out and you'll receive both a call and a text message alerting you that there's been a problem."

*When he leaves,* Stanislav informed her, *I'm going to follow him as far as the end of the driveway. Maybe he'll pause to make a call and I'll hear something useful.*

*Okay. But be careful. And don't overdo it.*

He remained where he was until Henry exited. Though the man kept a moderate pace, excitement rode him and sped his pulse.

Just as Henry passed between Susan's car and his van, he tripped. The clipboard flew out of his hands as he threw his arms out to catch his balance and bit out a curse. Bending, he picked up the clipboard, then searched the ground around him, leaning this way and that. "Ah." He strode around to the other side of Susan's car and knelt, everything but his hat disappearing from view. A second later, he rose with a pen in hand, got in his van and drove away.

Putting on a burst of preternatural speed, Stanislav reached the end of the driveway before the van did. Thankfully, it didn't hurt as much this time.

The security man was looking down as the vehicle slowly rolled to a halt. When he raised his head, he put a cell phone to his ear.

Stanislav flattened himself on the ground and rolled under the van.

"What's up?" a voice asked. Stanislav's hearing was so acute that he had no difficulty hearing both sides of the conversation.

"I just left," Henry told whomever he'd called.

"And?"

"I think the package is still there, down in the basement."

"You *think*?"

"She only wanted me to put sensors on the first floor, so I didn't have an excuse to go down there. I tried the door to it when she wasn't looking, but it was locked."

"You should have made an excuse to check it out," came the caustic reply.

"Like what?" Henry protested, irritation rising. "She said the basement has no windows or doors."

"Did she act suspicious, like maybe she's found the package herself?"

"No. Not at all. She's too afraid of bugs to even go down there."

"Then we'll go in at daybreak and catch her off guard before she's up and about."

"I don't think we have to worry about that. She's going out of town in a couple of days."

"She is? For how long?"

"A week. She wanted to know how the alarm system would work without her there."

"Perfect."

"But she has a dog. What if she leaves it behind?"

"We'll kill it. This is big. I'm not letting any mongrel fuck this up. And that includes you."

Oh yeah. Henry was furious and wrapped up the call as quickly as he could.

Stanislav gripped the undercarriage of the van and pulled himself up off the ground.

A steady stream of curses and smart-ass responses Henry wished he would've made accompanied the rumble of the vehicle as it swung onto the two-lane road and increased its speed until meadows, forests, and pastures flew by in a blur.

Though the effort made pain return full-force, Stanislav held himself in place until Henry had put several miles between himself and Susan's home. After the screwup with the locksmith, he wasn't taking any chances. He hadn't expected Susan to walk down and check her mail so early in the day and had assumed the locksmith would be long gone by the time she did. He wouldn't risk her finding another unconscious man.

Tightening his hold, he suddenly kicked the undercarriage hard enough to make the vehicle bounce, then threw his body to one side. The van veered in that direction.

Swearing, Henry hit the brakes and drew the van to a stop on the shoulder. "Did a fucking deer run into me or something?" he grumbled. "Stupid bastard." Throwing the driver's door open, he stepped out to check the damage. "Gonna run my damned insurance up," he groused as gravel crunched beneath his boots. "I don't see anything." More gravel crunched as he circled the front of the van. "Nothing here either. What the hell?"

As the man stomped around to the back, Stanislav relaxed his hold and lowered himself to the dirt.

"Shit. I don't know what it was," Henry mumbled and started toward the driver's door.

Stanislav rose to his knees on the opposite side and gave the vehicle a hard push.

Henry sucked in his breath. A tinkling sound arose as the man's hand began to shake, vibrating the keys he held. "What the hell?" he whispered.

With hesitant footsteps, Henry returned to the back of the vehicle.

A moment of silence followed. Then keys jangled as Henry unlocked the back doors.

His breath shortening, Henry yanked the back doors open with a roar to confront whatever he thought lay within.

Stanislav raced around and came up behind him so quickly that anyone watching would've only seen a blur.

Henry wasn't watching. He was staring into the van, fists raised, expecting something to leap out at him.

Stanislav gave the man a hard shove, then leapt into the van with him and pulled the doors closed.

Henry yelped as he hit the floor. Flipping over onto his ass, he gawked up at Stanislav. "Oh shit!"

Stanislav struck before the man could go for a weapon or a tool. "You shouldn't have agreed to kill the dog," Stanislav informed the trembling man. "Susan loves that dog."

When his eyes flashed brilliant amber, the man began to scream.

Several minutes later, Stanislav hoisted the unconscious male over one shoulder, carried him around to the driver's side, and dumped him behind the wheel.

The men Henry conspired with weren't the ones who had buried Stanislav. Those two had worked for a mercenary outfit nearby. And though their bodies had never been found, all believed the men had died in a mass shooting or something along those lines that had taken place at the mercenary compound. Henry's friend — the one who had mentioned killing the dog — had received a call from one of Stanislav's attackers about a package he'd buried in the basement of Susan's home shortly before his demise.

Henry had been kept mostly out of the loop because of his tendency to talk too much when he drank. So Henry wasn't sure what exactly the package was but knew his friend intended to sell it to…

Well, Henry didn't know to whom they wished to sell Stanislav and didn't really care. His friend was serious about the money to be made, and Henry wanted his share of the millions he thought *the package* would bring them.

After fastening the man's seat belt, Stanislav started the van and put it in drive. He walked beside it long enough to steer it off the road, then pushed it hard into a tree.

When Henry awoke, he would remember nothing between leaving Susan's home and crashing into the old oak.

⁂

Susan cast Stanislav another surreptitious glance, relieved that he was feeling better. Before, tension had ridden his form, stiffening every movement and appearing to cut deep. But he had seemed to relax as the day, then night had progressed. Seemed to move more easily, too, and had acquired a grace that made it hard not to stare.

The man was handsome even with hollow cheeks and gashes on

his face. And she knew she must be imagining it, but his shoulders seemed to broaden as the hours passed.

His spirits were certainly lighter. She had suggested they test the memory waters with a series of questions to see what would come to him and what wouldn't.

"What's your favorite color?" she asked him.

"Red. What's yours?"

"Green. Favorite season?"

"Winter."

"Mine, too. Favorite song?"

A moment's thought, then a shake of the head. "I don't know."

"Maybe something more general. Favorite type of music?"

Another pause. Another shake of his head. "I don't know."

"Favorite snack?"

"Popcorn," he promptly responded, scooping up another handful from the bowl that rested half on his lap and half on hers as the two of them reclined, shoulders touching, on the bed, watching television.

She suspected popcorn was a *current* favorite. "Favorite thing to do when you get some downtime?"

He winked. "Watch movies with you."

She grinned, loving him like this. Lighthearted. Almost playful.

When the show ended, they split up to get ready for bed.

Susan bypassed her shorty pajamas and donned a silky green chemise nightgown in the bathroom, then questioned her sanity when she looked in the mirror.

Would he take the change in nightwear as an invitation? No more shorts and tanks. Instead, soft silk fell halfway down her thighs, left her shoulders mostly bare, and showed a lot of cleavage.

She bit her lip. *Was* it an invitation?

The fact that no denials immediately flooded her mind probably wasn't a good sign. Stanislav couldn't remember who he was, didn't know if he was married or single. And someone had tried to kill him. How exactly did all of that add up to good lover material?

*Idiot,* she inwardly grumbled.

He was just such a likable guy. She knew he needed to rest and recuperate, so they had pretty much spent the whole day talking.

One didn't have to remember one's past to have a personality, and his was very appealing. She had come to the conclusion that he was quiet natured. Not shy. Just quiet. With an old-world charm that continued to delight her.

He seemed to like touching her. Holding her hand. Brushing her hair back from her face. Resting a hand on her back when they climbed the stairs side by side. She wasn't sure if he was just naturally affectionate or if he simply needed the human contact after his seclusion beneath the soil in her basement. Either way, she didn't mind. She liked how his touch made her feel.

She had been alone for a long time. Too long, perhaps. Was that and the fact that Stanislav was fine with her being different warping her judgment?

"Susan?" he called from the bedroom.

"Yes?"

"I can feel your anxiety. Would you like me to sleep in one of the other rooms?"

Flicking off the light, she opened the bathroom door. "No. I don't want you to sleep on the floor, remember?" He might be moving more easily, but he was still wounded.

"That won't bother me. I'm feeling better now, so a night on the floor won't…" His voice trailed off as she stepped into the light.

Susan dearly wanted to duck back into the bathroom. What the hell had she been thinking? Wanting to look nice for him? Not wanting him to take it as an invitation and—at the same time—hoping he *would* take it as an invitation? Because she hadn't felt such an intense instant attraction coupled with affection for a man in a very long time. And that affection and attraction kept trying to force caution and common sense out the door.

The silence stretched.

Stanislav stood on the opposite side of the bed, his thin form clad in a black T-shirt and boxers that did little to hide the fact that the sight of her in this nightgown aroused him.

His eyes acquired an amber glow. "I should definitely sleep in another room."

Even with the gashes on his face and arms and—her brow furrowed—on his legs, he looked handsome. *Sheesh.* There seemed to be no part of him that had been left unmarred.

"No," she stated firmly. Before she could change her mind, she crossed to the bed, slipped beneath the covers, then looked at him expectantly.

"Where's Jax?" he asked, unmoving.

"Downstairs. He likes to sit on the ottoman at night and watch out the back window for raccoons and opossums. Why?"

"He's the only chaperone available to us."

She grinned. "And you think he'd object to your trying to cop a feel?"

He smiled. "Maybe not. But a dog staring balefully at me from across the room might dampen the temptation somewhat."

Shaking her head with a laugh, Susan relaxed and patted the mattress beside her. "Come here."

He shut off the light, then climbed into bed with her.

She had expected him to lie on his back like her since he seemed disinclined to engage in love play. But he surprised her by turning onto his side to face her.

Susan did the same.

Her heart did a pleasant little dance when he clasped one of her hands in his and carried it to his lips. His big feet found hers under the covers, stroking and tangling with them.

"I think it would be very easy to fall for you," he murmured.

Her pulse raced.

He raised his other hand and brushed her hair back from her face, tucking it behind her ear. "But I need to confirm I'm free to be with you before I let myself give in to this attraction, dredge up whatever rusty charm I can muster, and attempt to woo you."

Even that showed how worthy he was. He might not know his past, but he clearly was an honorable man. "You are so damned appealing," she told him, both a compliment and a complaint.

"Not nearly as appealing as you," he countered, a twinkle of mischief entering his luminescent eyes. "I think my heart stopped beating for several minutes when I saw you in your nightgown."

She wrinkled her nose, self-consciousness blooming. "I should've stuck with the shorts."

"My body responded just as strongly to you in the shorts, or have you forgotten?"

She smiled. "Hell no, I haven't forgotten."

He laughed. Easing forward, he pressed his lips to hers in a kiss so tender she almost forgot the lust he inspired. "What a treasure you are."

She shook her head. "Since I found you in my basement, I think *you're* the one who qualifies as treasure."

Again he laughed. "Roll away from me."

"What?" she asked, not quite catching the request.

"Roll away from me."

She did so, a little disappointed that he —

She sucked in a breath when he spooned up behind her.

He slipped one arm beneath her head and wrapped the other around her waist. His hard, muscled thighs came up against the back of hers, trapping his erection between them. Considering how much taller he was than her, she was surprised by how perfectly they fit together.

"I just want to hold you," he murmured, nuzzling the back of her neck. Clearly he wanted to do more than that, but she understood his reservations. "Is this okay?"

She nodded. Taking his hand, she twined her fingers through his and hugged it against her chest. "More than okay."

Both sighed in contentment.

"It's so odd, not having a past," he said softly.

Susan couldn't imagine it.

"Would you share some of yours with me?" he asked after a moment.

"Sure. What would you like to know?"

"Have you ever been married?"

"No." She thought for a moment. "I think the longest relationship I've ever had only lasted four months."

"Because of the telepathy?"

She nodded. "Some things are meant to remain private. And when I'm tired or sick or distracted or stressed, I can't keep people's thoughts out of my head. Guys tend to not like that. And I tend to not like it when I hear uncomplimentary things about myself in a guy's mind or find him thinking about someone else when he's with me. It just sucks." She smoothed her thumb over his strong hand. "It's nice, not being able to hear your thoughts when you guard them like this. I don't usually get to enjoy quiet when I'm around other people. Now it's so quiet I can hear my own heart pounding at the feel of you against me."

He tightened his hold on her. "Don't tempt me."

"It wasn't intentional. I just meant..." She shook her head. "It's nice. This is nice."

He pressed a kiss to her shoulder. "Did you tell your boyfriends you were telepathic?"

She hesitated. "Some."

"Not all?"

"No." Not that there had been very many.

"Why?"

A long moment passed as she considered how to answer. Or how *much* to tell him if she *did* answer.

"You don't have to tell me if you—"

"It's okay. It's just..." She sighed, reluctant to revisit the past. "I didn't date at all when I was in high school. I didn't really want to since I could hear the hormone-driven thoughts of the male students."

He chuckled. "I'm sure they were all obsessed with your beauty."

She snorted. "Not in the least. They were only interested in my friends who developed earlier than I did. I was a late bloomer, so most of the time when the boys actually deigned to speak to me, they spent the whole time thinking about the other girls' breasts and what it would take to get them to go all the way with them or give them a blow job under the stairs."

"Classy."

She laughed. "In college, the first two guys I dated ended up thinking I was a total flake when I told them I was telepathic. I didn't tell them right away. I was nervous about how they would react."

"People tend to view those who are different from them with suspicion and distrust."

"Exactly. So I waited until we had grown closer and become lovers. But..." She shrugged. "I guess we weren't close enough, or they wouldn't have thought me a nutcase."

"Imbeciles," he muttered. He actually sounded insulted on her behalf.

"My third boyfriend thought it was great when I first told him, then grew more and more frustrated when I couldn't predict the winning lotto numbers."

"What?" he asked, his tone perplexed.

She smiled. "He had never heard of telepaths before and though it meant I was psychic. When I explained that it meant I could read his thoughts, not predict the future, he wanted me to go to Vegas with him and read the minds of the other poker players so he could rack up some winnings. I said I didn't want to. He kept pushing. So I bailed."

"Where did you find these numbskulls?" he muttered.

Amusement sifted through her, taking the ugly edge off the memories. "Clearly I wasn't very good at picking them."

"Was he the last one you told?"

Her amusement died abruptly. "No. There was one more. A graduate student at UCLA I dated a year after I earned my BA there." Unease crept through her, making her stomach flutter. "We had been together exclusively for four months when I started to pick up on thoughts he was having about his ex-girlfriend. Ted had bumped into her at a school function and was thinking about hooking up with her again. I was pissed that he would even consider cheating on me, so I confronted him. And when he wanted to know how I found out, I told him."

Silence fell.

"I take it he didn't react well?" he posed softly.

Her mood darkened as she remembered. "He actually was very intrigued by it all. So intrigued that it drove all thoughts of his ex right out of his head. I was so relieved. He was the first guy who seemed to accept my differences." It had been such a refreshing change that she had fallen head over heels in love with him.

"What happened?"

"A week later, he called me from school and asked me to meet him for dinner. But instead of a romantic table for two, when I met him at the restaurant he led me to a table for four where two men in suits were waiting for us. The first was one of his professors. The second was the professor's colleague. Both were very interested in my telepathy."

He swore softly. "He betrayed your confidence?"

"Without a moment's guilt."

"The bastard. How interested *were* these men?"

"*Too* interested. I was furious that Ted had shared my secret with them."

"Your fury was justified."

"The men were very friendly and casual about it verbally, saying all the right things to put me at ease. But the thoughts I found in their heads — the ones I guess they couldn't hide, or maybe didn't even *try* to hide because they didn't realize just how strong my telepathy was — scared the hell out of me." Just thinking about it gave her chills. "They wanted to study me. In a lab. They wanted to determine the strength of my telepathy, see if they could discover the source of it, then duplicate it."

He tightened his arm around her. "What happened?"

"I lied. I told them it was all bullshit, that I wasn't really telepathic. I had just swiped Ted's cell phone while he was in the shower and found the text messages he had sent his ex. I said I had made up the whole telepathy thing to cover my tracks and manipulate him into thinking I'd know if he ever tried to pull that crap again."

"Did they buy it?"

"Ted did. He was furious." Such an asshole. "But *they* didn't. Not really. They pretended to, but I saw no change in their thoughts. They were still determined to study me in their lab and were racking their brains, trying to think of a way to get me to cooperate."

"What did you do?"

"I told Ted to do several things I still can't believe I said in public, then left." She swallowed. "Before I could reach my car, two other men jumped me."

⋙◦⦿◦⋘

Stanislav swore. He wished he could've been there to protect Susan.

"I keep a canister of pepper spray on my key ring," she continued, "and sprayed them with it. One let me go. The other grazed me with a punch. I think if he hadn't been rubbing his eyes with his other hand, he would've hit me hard enough to knock me out. It hurt like hell. But I managed to stay on my feet and kicked him in the balls."

"Good," he declared, furious that the men had laid their hands on her.

"When he went down, I ran for my car. And a third man came out of I-don't-know-where and tackled me."

He felt fear swell inside her at the memory and wished he hadn't promised not to alter her emotions again.

"The third guy didn't pull his punches. While I was trapped beneath him, he knocked the wind out of me with a punch to my side, then hit me in the face. Twice."

"Son of a bitch," he growled, wanting to hunt the men down and kill them with his bare hands.

"They yanked me up and shoved me into the back of an SUV with tinted windows. I was out of it and still trying to catch my breath, so I didn't struggle. Two of them got in and sat on either side of me. The other stayed behind. To clean up the mess and ditch my car, I guess. I couldn't focus on their thoughts at first."

"Because of the pain."

"Yes. I was hearing everyone's thoughts at once, and there were two men already waiting in the SUV's front seat—the driver and an older man who had orchestrated the kidnapping. That one…" She shuddered. "His thoughts were the loudest. And he was a monster. He was connected to the professor's friend. But he had kept his intentions to take me against my will a secret from Ted's friends, because he knew I would read the impending attack in their minds and get a heads-up."

"Do you know his name?" Stanislav would commit it to memory and hunt the bastard down at the first opportunity.

"No. They just called him sir. And the plans I read in his thoughts shocked and scared me so badly that I didn't look any deeper."

"What were they?"

"He was going to take me to a facility in Texas." Again she swallowed. "I wasn't the first person he had abducted. In his thoughts, I saw another victim. A woman who was different like me. A woman with special gifts." Her voice thickened. "Whoever this man worked for—I couldn't tell if it was the government or what—held the woman prisoner in a lab. The older man was some kind of consultant or something… I'm not sure. I was hurting and I couldn't figure it all out. But the things they did to her, Stan… The things they did to that poor woman were horrible. They tortured her—or as they put it, *studied* her—and planned to do the same to me."

Unable to stand it, Stanislav broke his vow not to manipulate her emotions and took the edge off the fear rising inside her.

Her heartbeat slowed. Her muscles relaxed. "I didn't want to suffer like that. Didn't want to be dissected and tortured. So—as we approached an intersection—I lunged forward, grabbed the driver's head, and gave it a hard twist."

Shock struck. "Did you break the man's neck?" That took a lot of strength.

"Yes. No. Well, maybe. I mean, not at first. But he was so surprised by my attack that he stomped on the gas pedal and ran a red light. A truck hit us and I think knocked us into another truck or car. I'm still not clear on what happened next, if we flipped over or spun around or what. I just know I went weightless and my knees hit the roof. The driver was seat-belted in. I wasn't. So I held on to his head while the SUV flipped or whatever. The guys in back with me weren't belted in and were flying all over the place and bumping into me. When we hit a building and came to a stop, the guy who punched me in the stomach was half in, half out of the back window and covered with blood. The other guy was missing. I think he might have been thrown out a side window. The older man in the passenger seat was unconscious. And the driver was dead… or *looked* like he was dead. I think from a broken neck."

Good. The fucker deserved it. "And you?"

"I was cut up from all the broken glass and could barely breathe because of the pain in my chest. One of my legs was hurting pretty badly. I think I blacked out, because the next thing I knew I was in an ambulance headed for the nearest hospital."

"Did you tell them you had been kidnapped?"

She shook her head. "After what had happened, I was afraid to draw any more attention to myself or to my telepathy. Instead, I pretended I couldn't remember what had happened."

He understood now why she hadn't put up much of a fight

when he had asked her not to call the police.

"A doctor stitched up the worst of my cuts, said my leg was badly bruised but not broken and that I had a couple of cracked ribs. Then he ordered CT scans to confirm the rib thing and to check for head injuries. The other guys in the SUV with me and the drivers of the other vehicles that hit us started pouring in. So I took advantage of the controlled chaos that resulted and slipped away."

"You didn't go home, did you?" Surely they would've followed her if they had been able to.

"Yes," she admitted. "I didn't know what else to do. One of the nurses had given me my purse. I don't know where the hell they found it. I don't even know *who* found it. Maybe the paramedics or whoever pulled me from the SUV. But I called a cab, went home, and packed everything I could as fast as I could, booked an early flight to New York out of LAX, then went to a cheap motel and paid for the room with cash. I was so scared I didn't sleep a wink all night. First thing in the morning, I tucked my hair up under a baseball cap and returned to the apartment complex."

"*What?*" he damned near shouted in dismay.

"I didn't go to my apartment," she hastened to say. "I went to the front office. My lease was up the following month, and I wanted to pay my last month's rent before I disappeared. I was afraid if I mailed it, they would get their hands on it and know where to look for me."

Those monsters had been trying to capture her and turn her into a lab rat, and she'd been concerned about paying her rent?

"I know what you're thinking," she said. "But if those men survived the crash and came looking for me, I figured they'd follow the money trail, which was why I booked the flight out of LAX the night before. I had no intention of flying to New York and hoped it would lure those men away."

He still thought she shouldn't have worried about paying her rent but conceded that the plane ticket had been "Smart thinking."

"Smarter than I realized," she countered. "Sherrie—the woman who worked in the apartment complex's front office—was really nice. She was only a few years older than me. We weren't close friends or anything, but we had chatted several times. Well, as soon as I walked in and tried to give her a check, she took one look at me, turned the **OPEN** sign on the door to **CLOSED** and hustled me into a back room. She motioned to my bruises and asked me if a man had done that. I was so damned tired I started crying and said yes. When she asked if I'd told the police, I told her the police couldn't help me and that I had to leave and asked her to please not tell anyone. The next thing I knew, she called someone to come in and cover her shift, then guided me to her SUV. She told me to keep my head down and drove me to her sister's house. Turns out her sister Erin had been in an abusive relationship with a man who had come very close to killing her before she fled across the country to escape him after a restraining order and the police didn't help her. The two of them hid me at Erin's house until my bruises faded, then helped me get out of town."

"That was damned kind of them."

"It was. They were born and raised in North Carolina and told me about all the tiny towns sprinkled throughout the state." She shrugged. "I thought maybe I could get lost in one of them if I tried hard enough."

"Did the men come looking for you?"

"It's been years and they haven't shown up on my doorstep yet. But Sherrie said two men came by the office and questioned her after I left, wanting to know how well she knew me and who my friends were. She told them all she knew was that I bitched a lot about neighbors making too much noise and was always whining about the dryers not working in the laundry room."

He huffed a laugh. "Did you?"

"No," she said with a smile. "She just didn't want them to think she liked me."

Sherrie and Erin had saved Susan's life.

"I guess those men were like the people you mentioned who always hunt *gifted ones*. Maybe they found out about the advanced-DNA thing."

They most assuredly had, thanks to Ted, whose ass Stanislav intended to kick as soon as he regained his memory and got his life back. He kissed Susan's shoulder and gave her another hug. "I'm glad you got away."

"Me, too. I admit I've never understood why they didn't track me down and follow me here."

"They must not have been connected with the government." Otherwise they could've located her easily enough unless she had changed her social security number and used other illegal means to hide her identity. But it sounded as though she hadn't.

Though she quieted, he knew sleep didn't claim her.

"What is it?" he asked softly. "I can feel your unease." He also felt her hesitation and knew she questioned the wisdom of speaking whatever was on her mind.

She drew in a deep breath. "I know you've discovered what you call *oddities* about yourself that you think will frighten me. Things other than your being an empath and having eyes that glow."

He stiffened. His heartbeat sped up as alarm pumped through him. "You know what they are? You saw them in my thoughts?" He had been sure they would drive her away from him and had tried to hide them even after opening the rest of his mind up to her.

"No. I just know they concern you."

Relief filled him, though it shouldn't. He would have to tell her eventually and already dreaded the day. "I just don't want you to fear me," he whispered.

"I know. And I don't fear you." She squeezed his hand. "Stan…"

When she trailed off, he prompted, "Yes?"

Curiosity replaced her unease. "Is it okay if I call you *Stan*?"

She had called him as much once before, and he had liked it. "Well," he drawled, trying to sound less than enthusiastic, "I guess so. I mean, I'd prefer that you call me Stud Muffin. But Stan will do."

She laughed.

Happy to have lightened her spirits a bit, he squeezed her hand. "Of course you can call me Stan. Now tell me what troubles you."

She toyed with his fingers, putting off whatever she wished to say a little longer. "What if men like the ones who tried to kidnap me in California got their hands on *you*? What if they found out you're an empath, locked you up in their lab and… experimented on you? You said you didn't think you were born with some of your differences. What if someone — I don't know — changed you? Altered you genetically?"

A chilling thought, but it would explain the oddities she had mentioned. "I suppose it's possible." No wonder she felt such sympathy for him. She thought he had suffered what could have happened to her. "Perhaps I acquired the wounds that afflict me while escaping from the lab." He frowned. "I don't know how escaping from a lab would've landed me in your basement though. Is there one nearby?"

"I don't think so. But if it's as secret as the one I saw in that older man's thoughts, I doubt it would be common knowledge if there were."

Either way, believing he had been genetically altered in a lab was far preferable to believing he was a vampire.

Stanislav hoped they would soon learn the truth. *Without* her coming to harm. "Are you from California then?" he asked, changing the subject.

"Actually, I was born in Seattle. But my parents moved us to the Golden State when I was seven."

He smiled. "I can almost see you, a precocious little girl delighting in the sunshine."

She laughed.

"Tell me more," he urged.

She did so, patiently answering all of his questions.

They talked long into the night. And it felt so natural. Lying in bed with her. Bodies coiled together. Toes tangling. Burying his nose in her fragrant hair as they laughed over some anecdote from her past.

In truth, *nice* was too mild a word for it. Stanislav wished it could last forever.

Alas, fatigue strengthened its hold on them until the two reluctantly succumbed to sleep.

# Chapter Seven

SUSAN CAME AWAKE SLOWLY WHEN something squeezed her hand. She didn't know what time it was, but it felt as though she had only slept for three or four hours.

Groaning a complaint, she pried her eyes open. The first hint of dawn lit the room, or what she could see of it. A forehead was pressed to hers, a blurry face blocking most of her vision.

As her gritty eyes brought the man's features into focus, fear struck.

Yelping, she yanked her hand away and scrambled backward out of bed. Her feet tangled in the covers, landing her on her ass. But a brief scuffle with them freed her so she could stagger to her feet.

The man in bed jolted awake at the sound of her cry. Leaping out of bed, he clutched a knife in one hand and held it out before him.

Susan gaped. "Stanislav?"

His big body in a crouch, Stanislav swept the room with his brown-eyed gaze in search of an intruder. When he found none, he straightened and lowered the knife. "What is it? What's wrong?"

She could only stare at him.

He frowned. "Susan?" Tossing the knife onto the bed, he moved toward her.

She threw up a hand and backed away. "Don't."

His face paled a bit. His Adam's apple bobbed. "Susan?" he asked, his voice softer, hesitant. "Why do you fear me now?"

Her mouth hung open for so long it grew dry. Closing it, she swallowed. "I didn't recognize you." Her voice emerged a hoarse rasp. After clearing her throat, she tried again. "When I woke up, I didn't recognize you."

He didn't seem to know what to say to that. Did he really not know?

"Were you dreaming?"

She shook her head. "You look like a new man, Stanislav. I mean, you look like a brand-spanking-new man." The gashes on his face and body were gone. No marks. No scars. No bruises. Just smooth, tanned skin. His cheeks were no longer sunken. His shoulders were broad. *Really* broad, supporting arms with biceps the size of freaking bowling balls. His chest was no longer as sunken as his cheeks. It now bore impressive pecs above abs that rippled with muscle beneath the T-shirt that had hung loosely on him yesterday and now looked too tight.

She let her gaze drift lower.

His hips were slim, but holy crap, his thighs were thick. His calves, too. He had packed on at least eighty pounds of muscle while he slept.

He glanced down at his arms and legs, then met her stare in silence.

She tried to read his thoughts but found only Russian mutterings. "How can you look like a new man?" she demanded. "How can you...?" She motioned to his body. "How can you look like this? Your wounds are gone and... I mean, *look* at you! You're *huge*! You packed on like eighty pounds of muscle overnight! And I have no idea how much someone as tall as you with so much muscle weighs, so it could've been a hundred pounds or even more. What the hell?" She hated the shrill note that entered her voice. She hated, too, the way her whole body trembled and her thoughts slammed into each other like bumper cars.

"Susan," he said, a certain helplessness entering his expression, "let me calm your fear. Please. Then we can talk."

"No." She didn't want him using his gift to alter her emotions, didn't *trust* him to right now.

A pained look flitted across his handsome face, letting her know he had picked up on her distrust.

She tried not to feel bad about that but did. "Tell me how this is possible."

He shook his head. "I don't know."

"Bullshit."

He raked a hand through his hair, biceps bulging, and looked for a moment as if he wanted to throw something. "I don't know," he repeated. "I would tell you if I did, but I don't. I only know it isn't a result of the advanced DNA I was born with. *That* gave me the ability to feel and manipulate other people's emotions. The glowing eyes and the rapid healing come from something else and… Damn it, I can't remember!" He paced away from her, every movement radiating frustration. "There are other things, too. Other differences I recognize but can't explain. I know I'm faster than ordinary men and stronger—a *lot* stronger—but I can't…" He shook his head, emitting a growl. "Damn it, I can't remember why!"

Susan stared at him as he paced back and forth. And as she did, her limbs stopped quaking. Again she found herself wondering if he had been altered in a lab. That woman—the one who had been tortured in the facility Susan's kidnappers had intended to take her to—had healed quickly, too. If those monsters had gotten their hands on Stanislav and altered his DNA with some of that woman's…

Well, that and the terrible condition he had been in after escaping and inexplicably ending up here would explain a lot.

Her pulse ceased racing. "Stanislav—"

He swung back toward her. "I thought that once my wounds healed, it would all come back to me. My past. Why I'm so different. Who the hell put me in the ground in your basement. But it just isn't there. It *should* be. But it isn't. I know I'm not at full strength—"

Her eyes bugged. "Seriously? This is you when you're not at full strength?"

"But I'm getting there and… Something's wrong. I should remember. I know I should. Everything within me is telling me I should have regained my memory. But I haven't and—"

Susan held up a hand to halt him and spoke softly. "It's okay. It's okay, Stan. It's okay."

He shook his head, his expression anguished. "No, it isn't. You fear me now. And without my memory, I have no way of assuaging that fear, of reassuring you."

Susan took a step toward him. "Read my emotions," she requested, keeping her voice gentle in hopes of easing his agitation. "Do I fear you now?"

He quieted. After a long moment, he said, "Yes."

She swore. "Okay, but not nearly as much, right?"

The lines of strain that had formed near his eyes eased. "Right."

It was true. His dismay over her fearing him and his memory not returning had gone a long way toward reducing her fear. He wasn't lying. His thoughts were chaotic, but those she picked up reflected his words.

He shook his head and offered her a sad smile. "I'm still me," he promised softly. "I'm still the man who peppered you with questions about your past and shared a bowl of popcorn with you while we bend-watched *Stranger Things*."

"Binge-watched."

"Binge-watched *Stranger Things*. I'm just..." He shrugged. "Bigger now."

She nodded. He actually kind of reminded her a bit of the girl from *Stranger Things* in that moment. Like El, he was lost, trying to find his way, and had special abilities that ordinarily would defy belief. And the knowledge that she feared him once more was killing him. She didn't have to read it in his thoughts. It was all there in his glowing amber gaze.

Taking a step forward, she held her arms out to him. "Come here."

She didn't have to ask him twice. Closing the distance between them, he wrapped his strong arms around her and squeezed her close, lifting her feet off the floor.

Susan slid her arms around his neck and held on tight.

"Please don't fear me," he uttered hoarsely, burying his face in her neck.

"I'll try," she promised, unwilling to lie and say she wouldn't. She doubted this would be the last thing about him that would freak her out. "Just give me time to adjust, okay? Some of the things you can do may startle me, like the whole healing overnight thing, but—"

"I would never hurt you, Susan. I vow it."

She tightened her hold. "I know." Resting her head on his shoulder, she sighed. "I'm sorry I hurt you."

He shook his head. Several long moments passed while both calmed and just held each other. Every movement conveying his reluctance, Stanislav finally lowered her until her feet touched the floor, then stepped back.

Susan stared up at him, stunned all over again by his new size. "Wow," she declared with a grin, "you are freaking *huge*."

He laughed.

Reaching out, she gave one of his biceps an experimental squeeze, then poked the hard muscles of his chest. "I like it. You wear it well."

Smiling, he shook his head. "You're amazing."

His words made her want to hug him again. "And you're delirious again," she teased. "Probably from hunger. I'm guessing someone with that much muscle needs to put away a lot of food on a regular basis. Let's go see about breakfast."

"Are you sure you don't want to go back to sleep?" he asked. "You only got three or four hours."

They had talked late into the night.

She silently told herself to stop feeling all mushy whenever he showed concern for her. "I'm totally wired now and couldn't sleep if I tried. Besides…" She gave him an apologetic look. "I would feel like I was sleeping with a stranger… again. I know you're still you, but you look so different—"

"That you need time to adjust."

"Yes. I'm sorry."

"Don't be. You're still here instead of running downstairs, screaming at the top of your lungs or calling 911. I'm fine with your taking time to adjust."

She eyed him curiously. "Do *you* need time to adjust?" How weird must it be to go from being dangerously underweight one day to being packed with heavy muscle the next?

He glanced down at his arms and chest. "No. This feels normal to me. Or mostly normal. As I mentioned, I'm not yet at full strength."

She couldn't seem to stop ogling him. "What must full strength look like?"

He laughed.

Susan ducked into the bathroom and changed out of her nightgown into comfy yoga pants and a tank top while Stanislav donned a new set of blacks.

He looked good. Edible good. And judging by the amber glow that entered his eyes as his gaze swept from her head to her bare toes, he thought the same of her.

He was so different from anyone she had ever met. And he was okay with *her* being different, something she had never found outside her own family. It was nice. And attracted her like candy attracted children.

Susan hoped he would regain his memory soon, because she was becoming dangerously attached to him, peculiarities and all. She already felt closer to him than she had to the last man she had dated. So comfortable. Like they were old friends. And kindred spirits.

If she allowed her feelings for him to deepen any more, finding out he was married could very well break her heart.

<hr/>

Stanislav tried not to stare at Susan while the two of them prepared breakfast. He deeply regretted scaring her. He had been so fixated on healing and getting stronger so he could protect her if his enemies—whoever the hell they were—came looking for him that he hadn't considered how the abrupt change in his appearance might frighten her.

How kind and brave she was. Most people would've been out of the house in a trice and zooming down the driveway in their car if they were hit in the face with his oddities. But she had found the courage to stand her ground. And that warm, caring heart of hers continued to reach out to him.

What a remarkable woman.

"Am I keeping you from going to work?" he queried as he helped her make breakfast. He would hate to be responsible for her losing her job.

"No. I work at home. I'm a writer."

Admiration filled him. "How fortuitous. I happen to love

books." He paused a moment, surprised to discover that about himself. Perhaps his memory was coming back to him? "What do you write?"

"Medieval romance."

"May I read one?"

"Really?"

He nodded. "You seem surprised."

She shrugged. "Most people who don't read romance novels assume they're all sex and no substance."

He scoffed at the notion. "I can't see you writing anything that lacked substance."

"Thank you."

"May I read one?" he requested again, curious about the tales she told.

"Sure. I'll get you one after we eat."

"Excellent." Stanislav carried their plates to the table. When Susan followed with tall glasses of water, he drew out her chair for her.

She smiled up at him. "Thank you."

Seating himself, he picked up the gargantuan sandwich on his plate and took a big bite. "Mmmm." He had awakened ravenously hungry. Susan was right. He must need to put away a lot of calories at this weight.

She chuckled. "I hope you don't mind the sandwiches. I've never liked breakfast foods."

"It's delicious," he declared and once more had to struggle not to consume it too quickly.

Susan's sandwich was considerably smaller. While he devoured his, she toyed with hers more than she ate it.

He let her emotions flow into him. "You're worried."

"Yes."

He liked that she didn't deny it or try to change the subject. "Is it me? Do I make you uneasy?"

"No," she swiftly denied. "I mean, the change in your appearance unnerved me at first. But I'm getting used to it now."

That was a relief. "Then what?"

She sighed. "Do you think Henry, the security guy, will come back?"

"Yes," he responded without hesitation. "And he'll bring friends."

"When?"

"Soon. They believe you're going out of town, so it could be as early as tomorrow."

"And you think they're connected with whoever put you in the ground? You think they might be like those men in California?"

"Yes."

"What are we going to do?"

His heart did a funny leap at how naturally she linked the two of them together. "Is there a friend or family member who would be willing to take Jax for a few days?"

"You're afraid they'll hurt him?"

"Yes."

She nodded slowly. "My former next-door neighbor, Anna, will watch him for me. She adores him and volunteered to keep him for a couple of days while I moved."

"Can you take him to her today?"

"Yes."

He studied her a moment, then asked carefully, "Any chance I could talk you into staying with her as well?"

She scowled. "No."

Sensing the anger rising in her, he set what was left of his sandwich on his plate and took her hand. "I want you out of harm's way, Susan."

"I'm not leaving you here all alone." She seemed insulted that he believed she *would*.

"I can take care of myself now."

"You said you aren't at full strength."

"But I'm strong enough." She had no idea just how powerful and fast he was. Even weakened as he had been the day before, he had run faster than the security guy's van and had been able to move it while Henry was driving.

"Strong enough to do what? What will you do if they come for you?"

A heavy silence fell. He didn't want to lie to her. Nor did he want to admit he intended to get information from the men through any means necessary, then kill them if they meant either him or Susan harm.

"Stanislav?" she pressed when he remained quiet and guarded his thoughts. "Answer the question. What will you do if they come for you?"

"Overpower them and elicit the information I need."

"Then what? You've already told me you don't want the police involved. And I can understand why now that I see how different you are. Honestly, I don't want them involved either, because I'm afraid they'll find out about my telepathy."

"I wouldn't tell them you're telepathic," he said with a scowl.

"I know. But if they do a background check on me, they'll find out about California, and… I just don't want to do anything that might draw attention to that or to the people who tried to kidnap me. I don't want to end up on their radar again."

He didn't want her to either. They still didn't know who those men were or why they hadn't come for her after she'd moved.

A thought occurred to him. "Do you write under your true name?"

"No. I use a pseudonym. On the off chance that I hit the best-seller lists, I didn't want my kidnappers to see my name."

His lips twitched. "Or their lovers to flash a cover of one of your books with your name on it in bold type?"

"Exactly." She gave his hand a squeeze. "What will you do once the security guy and his friends talk if you're able to overpower them?"

"I'll cross that bridge when I come to it."

"If you come to it. People who break into houses are usually armed. How exactly do you plan to —?"

"I can handle it."

She stared at him, her gaze piercing. "Because you were in the military. Or at least we think you were."

He shrugged. "I had a brief memory of being in a large battle, of holding my own, so…"

"So you can handle yourself," she finished for him. "Well, I can, too. I'm staying."

Since he could feel her determination, Stanislav didn't bother to fight her on the issue. He would simply have to find a way to keep her safe. If that meant snapping the neck of every man who threatened them without extracting any information first, he would.

He only hoped Susan wouldn't turn away from him if — or when — he killed them.

———◦◦◦———

Susan left shortly thereafter to take Jax to Anna's. She told her former neighbor the same thing she'd told Henry — that she was going out of town, couldn't take Jax with her, and was reluctant to board him in a kennel. Anna was a real sweetheart, instantly offering to keep Jax for her and warning she just might spoil him so much that he wouldn't want to go home again when Susan returned. Susan hated to lie to her friend but couldn't very well tell her she needed to get Jax out of the house because she'd found a man with remarkable abilities buried in her basement and the two of them were preparing to combat those who had put him there.

Just thinking about the upcoming confrontation made her stomach flutter with nerves. She couldn't stop remembering the men Ted had introduced her to. The things she had seen in their minds. The experiments they had wanted to perform on her. The way they had tortured that other woman.

If the men who were after Stanislav were in league with whoever had buried him in her basement, they were likely just as bad. Only a monster would have wounded him so severely, then buried him and left him to die or — if they'd believed he *wouldn't* die — left him to suffer like that. No food. No water. Only the pain of his injuries to keep him company.

Men like that would kill Stanislav if he didn't cooperate.

Men like that would take him by force and kill *her* if she tried to stop them.

Why did people have to be so fucked up when it came to those who were different from them? If that weren't the case, she and Stanislav could go to the police and wouldn't have to deal with this themselves. They wouldn't have to risk *everything* to protect themselves and learn the truth. Because she just didn't foresee this going well and doubted Stanislav did either. He wouldn't have asked her to stay away if he'd thought it would be easy.

Susan made a couple of stops on the way home and loaded up

on groceries. As she pulled into her driveway, she glanced at the bag on the passenger seat and felt dread pool inside her.

The sun began to make its descent, dipping behind the trees and painting the clouds above with shades of pink and peach.

Stanislav stepped out onto the front porch as she cut the engine.

The dread in her stomach vanished. Not as a result of any manipulation on Stanislav's part this time but because she was simply happy to see him. Her heart swelled. Something about finding him waiting for her when she got home—a soft smile lighting his handsome features as he descended the steps and strolled toward her, as sleek and graceful as a panther—made her wish for things she shouldn't even be thinking about, not while he still had no memory.

She opened her door.

Stanislav offered his hand while she grabbed her keys and exited the small vehicle. "I missed you," he said, his smile both affectionate and rueful as though he thought perhaps he shouldn't admit it.

She returned his smile. "I missed you, too." She really had. It was a little scary that she had come to crave his company so quickly.

He pressed a kiss to her knuckles, then released her fingers and opened the back door. "I see you went grocery shopping." He filled his arms with bags, then headed for the front steps. When Susan started to grab a bag, he shook his head. "I'll get those. You just keep me company. You've spoiled me. I really did miss you."

She laughed. "I wasn't sure what foods you prefer."

"Anything you like is fine."

They made two more trips. Susan was both surprised and pleased when Stanislav didn't just carry the bags in but also helped her empty them. By the time they finished, her refrigerator and freezer were so full she had to move things around a bit to get the doors to close. And the large walk-in pantry sported shelf after shelf of snack foods.

"Looks like we missed one," he commented while Susan washed her hands.

Glancing over, she saw him nod toward the bag on the table in the breakfast nook. "That isn't food."

"What is it?" he asked curiously. Had he caught the edge that had entered her voice?

Susan dried her hands, uncertain whether he would approve or disapprove of her purchases. Crossing to the table, she removed the contents of the bag and arranged them on the table.

He studied the two 9mms, the extra magazines, and the boxes of ammo stacked beside them. "You purchased weapons?"

She nodded.

"For me or for you?"

"For you. I already have two of my own."

He opened the first gun's case and palmed the weapon. "Do you know how to use them?" Ejecting the empty magazine, he opened a box of hollow-point bullets and began to load the mag with a deftness that left her with no doubt that he was very comfortable with guns.

"Yes. My brother was in the army and took me to the firing range a lot."

"Was?"

She nodded. "He was killed in Afghanistan."

He paused. "I'm sorry."

A familiar burning hit her eyes as tears blurred her vision. Swearing, she closed her eyes in hopes of keeping the tears from falling. "It was long enough ago that it shouldn't still make me cry. I'm sorry."

A faint thunk reached her ears as he set the magazine down. The heat of his body reached her first. Then his hands cupped her face and tilted it up.

When she opened her eyes, the sympathy and concern she found in his made the damned tears spill over her lashes and race down her cheeks.

"You miss him," he whispered, sweeping the moisture away with his thumbs.

She swallowed past the lump in her throat. "I miss him."

He pressed a kiss to her forehead, then drew her into a hug.

Susan buried her face in his chest and wrapped her arms around him, embarrassed by her tears.

"It's okay," he continued in that gentle voice. "You don't ever have to hide your tears from me. They're not a weakness. They're an expression of the love you bore him." He rubbed his hands up and down her back in soothing strokes. "And I can feel your grief."

"We were always close," she told him, her voice thick. "Since we didn't know anyone else who had gifts like us, we could only ever be ourselves with each other. Mom and Dad were killed in a car accident the year before I lost Nick. So it was sort of a double blow."

His hold tightened. "And now I've brought more violence into your life."

She shook her head. "*You* didn't. The assholes who buried you in my basement did."

His lips brushed her hair a second before he released her and backed away. "You can still go," he said softly. His brown eyes now bore a faint amber glow and shone with concern. "Take your guns just in case and stay with your friend Anna or in a hotel. Leave me these." He motioned to the 9mms on the table. "I'll call you when—"

"No."

"I won't think less of you, if that's why you wish to stay. You've already shown great courage—"

"I'm not leaving," she interrupted. "This is my home, Stanislav. And you're…" Well, she wasn't sure exactly what he was to her. Her friend at the very least.

"Susan."

"I'm staying," she insisted.

After a moment, he nodded. "So be it. But I will confront them alone." When she opened her mouth to spout a denial, he held up a hand. "I will confront them alone," he repeated, his voice quiet yet resolute. "Knowing how to shoot a gun doesn't make you comfortable with men aiming and firing theirs at *you*. Remember your experience in California, how terrifying it was and how difficult it was to think clearly. How much more so would it have been if those men had threatened you with weapons or even shot you? You've never been in armed combat before, Susan. I have."

No sooner did he speak the words than Stanislav sucked in a breath. Pain rippled across his features as he bent forward slightly and pressed the heel of one hand to his forehead above his right eye.

And just like that, his mind opened to her.

Battle scenes flashed through it, similar to what she had seen before. Men firing automatic weapons at him while Stanislav fired his own at them. A Humvee plowing through the chaos, the flamethrower it bore spewing fire as men in camouflage raced toward Stanislav, weapons firing.

Her heart began to race.

The memory ended abruptly.

Stanislav squeezed his eyes closed and held his breath, weaving a bit on his feet.

Susan gripped his biceps to steady him.

His thoughts — still open to her — were as chaotic as the battle she'd seen. It had been such a tiny glimpse of his past. He wanted more and was furious that he couldn't have it.

At last he released a long breath and straightened. He opened his eyes, met hers. The barriers he could erect to keep her from reading his mind reappeared, gently pushing her out.

"Are you okay?" she asked softly.

He nodded. "Aside from a blinding headache that is already beginning to fade, yes."

Relinquishing her hold, she stared up at him. "How the hell did you survive that?" So many men had been doing their damnedest to kill him.

Was that what it had been like for Nick during his last moments?

He shook his head, a bitter laugh escaping. "Maybe I didn't. Maybe this is all a dream I'm having whilst I lie dying on that battlefield."

"It isn't a dream." And she supposed bullets wouldn't kill him, now that she thought about it. He had been riddled with wounds last night and all had healed within hours, so… yeah. Bullets probably wouldn't kill him. That was a relief. But it also brought to mind some of the more disturbing things she had found in the security guy's mind.

"What is it?" he asked, his gaze sharpening. "You're uneasy again."

Irritation rose. "You know, that really isn't fair. I can't read your mind, but you can still feel every tiny little change in my mood."

"You're right," he acknowledged. "It isn't fair. But that doesn't answer my question. What troubles you?"

She sighed. "There's something I haven't told you. Something about Henry, the security guy. And before you ask, I didn't tell you because it seemed utterly ridiculous. But in light of the new you" — she motioned to his large, muscled, very healthy body—"I'm thinking it might mean something."

He eyed her curiously. "What is it?"

"You know how I told you Henry doesn't know what exactly the package is, just that he thinks it might still be in the basement?"

"Yes."

"Well, that isn't precisely true. A couple of times…" She didn't want to say it aloud. She really didn't. "A couple of times the word *vampire* flitted through his mind."

Stanislav stared at her while several long seconds ticked past.

"Henry seems to think the package is a vampire," she attempted to clarify. "That *you* are a vampire."

"And what do you think?" Stanislav asked carefully.

Her eyebrows rose. "That his colleagues must know about your rapid healing ability and passed it along to their not too bright yet very imaginative friend. He clearly coupled your rapid healing with your having survived being buried alive and drew a crazy conclusion."

Another stretch of silence.

"You don't think I'm a vampire?" he asked.

A surprised laugh escaped her. "No. Of course not. *One*: vampires only exist in fiction, folklore, and really bizarre dreams. And *two*: even if they did exist, they have fangs and can't go out in daylight. *You* have a very nice set of teeth that are fang-free. And I've seen you go outside during the day at least three times. I even walked beside you, holding your hand, on one of those occasions."

His smile seemed forced. "So I shouldn't fear you'll drive a wooden stake through my heart tonight?"

"Not unless you hog the popcorn bowl while we're watching movies."

The tightness in his face eased at that teasing threat. "Why are you telling me this now?"

Shrugging, she motioned to the ammo on the table. "I guess I thought you should be prepared in case Henry shows up tomorrow draped in garlic and armed with silver bullets."

His lips stretched in a handsome grin. "I believe silver bullets are for werewolves, not vampires."

"I know. But I don't think Henry's too swift."

He laughed. "I agree." His stomach chose that moment to rumble.

"I told you," she crowed with a grin. "You have to put away a *lot* more food now that you're so big. Fortunately, I stocked up. Let's see what we can come up with for dinner, then talk strategy while we cook it."

# Chapter Eight

HENRY AND HIS COHORTS DIDN'T break and enter the following day. Nor the one after that. Stanislav knew they were most likely just waiting long enough to ensure Susan had really left town. After his encounter with Henry, he didn't doubt they would show sooner or later.

Based on the emotions his gift conveyed, Susan was alternately riddled with anxiety as the moment of confrontation was delayed and hopeful that it meant they weren't going to show.

Stanislav filled in the hole in the basement and patted down the dirt so whoever came wouldn't realize Susan had dug him up. They decided to leave Susan's car parked in the driveway and hoped the men would assume she had either taken a cab to the airport or had a friend give her a ride. They also left the front and back porch lights on night and day, something Susan said people often did when they went out of town. They turned on the same three lights inside at the same time every night—a lamp in her bedroom, the light at the base of the stairs near the front door and the kitchen light—to enable Susan to see and give the illusion that the lights were on a timer. They also kept the blinds lowered, the drapes closed, and made sure they never passed between the light and a window so they would cast no shadows in case the house was being watched.

If it *was*, whoever watched it did so from a distance, because Stanislav heard no automobiles. Nor did he hear any footsteps or heartbeats other than his own and Susan's.

To pass the time and distract Susan, he encouraged her to return to her writing during the day. Then when night fell, they feasted on popcorn or other snacks while they lounged on her bed—hips and arms touching—and watched movies. Once they turned the television off, they tucked themselves beneath the covers and talked softly until sleep claimed Susan.

Stanislav slept little, merely catching a quick nap here or there to ensure he wouldn't miss his enemies' approach. He feared too much for Susan's safety.

While she wrote, he read her novels. Most took place in medieval England and contained quite a bit of action. Lots of sword fights, truly despicable villains, and admirable heroes and heroines. Stanislav enjoyed them and couldn't help but wonder if they were the first romance novels he had ever read or if his home library, wherever that might be, boasted dozens of them.

He liked the humor Susan wove through her stories. Even now, as he lounged on the foot of her bed, reading the latest, he laughed at something the bold, quirky heroine said.

Sitting at the head of the bed with her back against the wall, Susan glanced at him over her laptop and smiled.

"I like this woman," he told her. "She's strong, smart, and funny. She reminds me of you."

She winked. "And the hero reminds me of you—tall, dark, and handsome with a heart of gold."

Chuckling, he returned his attention to the paperback in his hands and vowed not to interrupt her work again.

A few pages later, the hero and heroine gave in to the attraction building between them and made love. His breath quickened as he read. He hadn't expected the love scenes to be so explicit. So arousing.

His body hardened. He couldn't help but imagine himself doing all of those things with Susan. Peeling her clothing away inch by inch and touching her pale, silky skin. Caressing her full breasts. Tweaking her taut pink nipples. Pressing his lips to hers, then sliding his tongue within to stroke and tease. Kissing a path down her neck. Drawing a hardened nipple into his mouth. Tantalizing her. Tasting her. Tasting *all* of her.

Heat poured into him, compounding his need as he heard Susan's pulse quicken.

Glancing up, he again found her staring at him over her laptop. But this time her lips were parted slightly, her cheeks were flushed, and desire glinted in her pretty hazel eyes.

His body hardened even more as his pulse leapt.

"Your barriers are down," she whispered, her gaze dropping to his mouth.

"What?" He nearly groaned when she drew her tongue across her lower lip.

"Your barriers," she said louder, her voice husky. "They're down."

Which meant she had seen his thoughts and caught him fantasizing about taking her as passionately as the hero had taken the heroine in her novel. As passionately as *he* had taken *her* in their shared dream. She had felt so good as their bodies had merged. So hot and tight and—

She closed her eyes. "Stan."

Cursing, he raised his mental barriers. "I'm sorry. It wasn't intentional," he muttered and brought a knee up to hide his erection. "I just didn't expect the love scenes in your novels to be so…"

"Graphic?" she proposed, eyeing him as if she wished he would pounce. As if she wanted to feel his hands on her again, stroking her to orgasm.

And damn, he wanted to do it.

The faint rumble of an engine reached his ears.

Stanislav looked to the west, where bright light from a late-afternoon sun illuminated the blinds. Sitting up, he listened intently.

"What is it?" Susan asked.

"Someone's coming."

She shifted her laptop to the bedside table and looked in the same direction he had. She, too, appeared to be listening, though her hearing was not as acute as his. "It's them," she announced after a moment.

"You can hear their thoughts?"

"Yes."

The fact that she could do so from this distance impressed him. "How many are there?"

"Henry and three others."

His senses told him the same. He rose.

Her brows drew together as she swore.

"What?"

Swinging her legs over the side of the bed, she stood. "Henry isn't the only moron in the bunch." Her eyes met his, full of furious disbelief. "They *definitely* know about your swift healing capabilities. And they all think you're a freaking vampire. Can you believe that?"

Yes, he could. His fear that the men might be right effectively banished his desire. "Are they coming to kill me or to capture me?" He shoved his feet into his discarded boots, then knelt to lace them up.

"Capture." Dropping to her knees, she fished her sneakers out from under the bed and hurriedly donned them.

"For what purpose?"

She shook her head. "I don't know. They're nervous and excited and their adrenaline is pumping, so they're all thinking very loudly. All I can get is that they plan to capture you, chain you up in a coffin of all things, take you I-don't-know-where, and make a ton of money off you."

He rose. "Then here's hoping they plan to open a cheesy backwoods carnival and think themselves the next P. T. Barnum."

Susan huffed a laugh as she rose. "Stanislav…" Her gaze, somber once more, met and clung to his as she rested a hand on his arm and tilted her head back to stare up at him. "That facility in Texas would pay a hell of a lot to get their hands on you."

He covered her hand with his. "I'm sure it would." Which was why he intended to kill Henry and the others if he determined they worked for such an outfit.

If they worked for that group in particular and had come to claim Susan as well, he would make damned certain they gave him the address so he could personally ensure no one there would ever come looking for her again.

When he would've moved away, she tightened her hold. "Look at me."

He did, and loathed the fear he saw in her lovely features.

"You do whatever you have to do to keep them from capturing

you. Okay?"

"I intend to." When he started to move away, she again tightened her hold on him.

"No. I don't think you're hearing me."

He frowned. "Susan, I—"

"You focus on *you*," she interrupted, speaking very distinctly. "You do whatever you have to do to keep them from capturing you. I don't want you to worry about me. I don't want you to divide your attention between disarming and disabling them and listening to keep track of whatever's going on with me. I've been in your thoughts. I know you would let them take you in a heartbeat if you thought it would enable me to get away safely. But that's bullshit."

He opened his mouth to protest.

"That's bullshit," she repeated. "If whatever's about to happen ends up going really, really wrong and they capture me, I have faith that you will hunt them down and find me."

"Hell yes, I would."

"But if they capture you…" She shook her head, despair entering the eyes that clung to his. "How would I ever find you? How would I free you? Where would I even begin to look for you? I couldn't do it alone, but… who could I trust to help me? Who would even know how to find you without getting the authorities involved?" She poked him in the chest. "Your memory may be gone, but those instincts you gained in the military are still there to guide you. I don't have that, and I—"

He pulled her into a hug. "It won't come to that," he promised.

Her fear whipping him like a cold breeze, she wrapped her arms around his middle and squeezed him tight. "You make damned sure it doesn't."

He pressed a kiss to her hair, then released her.

"Do *not* let them take you," she ordered again.

He nodded but made no promises this time. "Arm up. They're almost here."

She did so without another word, her hands shaking. He admired the hell out of her for remaining by his side and making a stand like this. But he feared for her, too.

Rounding the foot of the bed, he palmed the 9mms he'd left

there. The pockets on his cargo pants were already stocked with the extra magazines and a couple of boxes of ammo. He'd kept them and the weapons close ever since Susan had given them to him.

Gravel crunched in the driveway as what sounded like a truck or SUV pulled up and parked.

He looked at Susan across the bed. "Stay up here," he whispered.

Face pale, she nodded. "Unless you need me."

*I need you safe*, he thought and knew by the tightening of her lips that she had heard him. No way in hell would he let those men get their hands on her. *Stay out of sight.*

The only light in the room poured from a lamp near the window. Susan glanced at it, then eased over into the darkest shadows on the other side of the room. He could hear her heart pounding in her chest.

*Let me ease your fear*, he implored mentally.

She shook her head. *You focus on you. Don't worry about me. I'll be fine.*

Boots thudded on the front steps.

The bastards weren't even trying to hide their approach. They must really believe she was out of town.

Stanislav slipped from the bedroom and made his way down the stairs, avoiding every creaky board.

"You sure no alarm is gonna go off?" a gruff voice asked.

"Yeah," Henry said. "I rigged it so the indicator lights would light up when she armed and disarmed it, but the control panel is a dud and doesn't actually activate anything."

*Asshole*, Susan muttered mentally.

Stanislav's lips twitched.

"You two go around back," the leader ordered. "Paul, you're with me."

Footsteps clomped on the wraparound porch, heading for the back door.

Stanislav cursed silently. If all four had instead opted to pour through the front door, taking them out would've been fairly easy. No one could've come up behind him. All bullets would've been fired from the same direction. And bullets *would* be fired. His acute sense of smell picked up the scent of gun oil.

But their divide-and-conquer approach nullified that.

Ideally, he would simply slip outside and face them there to keep them from even entering the house. But the sun hadn't sunk close enough to the horizon for the trees to the west to provide him with adequate shade. Stanislav was stronger, but full strength continued to elude him. And with his memory lacking, he wasn't sure how quickly the sun would damage him and sap his strength.

*Vampire.*

He cursed as the word again floated through his mind. He wasn't a vampire. He couldn't be. As Susan had said, vampires weren't real. They were fiction and folklore and… hell. He just didn't want to be one. Vampires were monsters. If the oddities Susan knew about didn't drive her away from him, surely that would.

A tall shadow appeared behind the frosted glass window in the front door.

At the same time, boots shuffled to a halt at the back door.

Stanislav eyed the entrance to the basement, located about halfway between the two. Henry and the others seemed convinced the *package* was in the basement. Why not let the four of them come to him and lure them farther away from Susan?

On silent feet, he dashed over to the basement doorway and ducked inside. Avoiding creaky boards was harder to do here, so he simply leapt from the top of the steps to the dirt floor, landing as nimbly as a cat.

Several loud thuds sounded above as one of the men applied either a boot or his shoulder to the front door. It flew open with a pop, then slammed into the wall.

Similar sounds erupted from the other door.

Stanislav eased back into the farthest part of the basement, letting darkness enshroud him. He had been down there often enough to know where the light would strike and where it wouldn't once they flipped the switch.

His eyes on the doorway above, he tucked the 9mms into the back waist of his pants. This was Susan's home, and he might end up killing these men. If possible, he wanted to do so without bloodying up the place and splattering the walls and floor with evidence that would implicate her if police came knocking.

"The basement's over here," Henry said above.

"Don't you think we should make sure the place is empty first?" the first man drawled.

"Oh. Right."

"Dumbass," one of the other two muttered. "Go check upstairs."

*Well, hell. There goes plan A.* Scowling, Stanislav strode forward. *Guess I'll have to settle for plan B.*

*What's plan B?* Susan asked.

Damn it. He'd slipped and forgotten to shield his thoughts. *Don't worry about it. Just get out of sight. Henry is on his way up.*

Henry was actually stomping up the stairs like a petulant teenager who had just been grounded by his parents.

Stanislav shook his head. Sweeping a hand across Susan's workbench, he knocked a few of her tools to the floor.

The stomping stopped.

Four heartbeats picked up as everything above went silent.

Then a floorboard creaked.

*They're heading for the basement,* Susan told him mentally.

*All of them?* he thought.

*I think so.*

A moment later, slow thuds confirmed Henry was descending the stairs to rejoin his friends.

Stanislav melted back into the shadows once more.

A figure suddenly filled the doorway above, the silhouette of a man with his arms extended, his hands aiming a gun into the darkness.

"You see anything?" Henry whispered.

"No. Hit the lights."

Henry's hand appeared as he reached in, felt around the wall, then found and flipped the switch.

Dim yellow light spilled down from one bulb at the top of the stairs and a second at the bottom.

Stanislav breathed deeply, concentrating on keeping his fury under control so his eyes wouldn't glow and give away his location.

"Paul," the leader grunted.

Another man elbowed Henry out of the way and joined the

leader on the landing. "I got your back, Ed."

Stanislav studied the leader as the man cautiously descended the stairs, aiming his gun in front of him, then to the side as he examined the basement. Ed appeared to be in his late forties. His head was shaved but showed the shadow of a receding hairline. His skin was leathery from too many hours in the sun. His jaw thrust forward as he squinted and searched for the source of the sound he'd heard. His shoulders were broad and muscled. But he carried extra weight around his middle like a former athlete who had let himself go.

The beefy hands clutching the handgun were poised to pull the trigger as Ed planted his boots on the dirt floor at the base of the stairs. "This as bright as the light gets?" he asked softly.

Paul glanced at the light switch. "Yeah."

"Charlie," Ed muttered, "get your ass down here."

A fourth man entered the basement and crept down the stairs.

"Henry," Ed ordered, his beady eyes still searching for Stanislav, "check the place and make sure we're alone."

Henry hesitated. "What if the woman's here?"

"Do whatever you want to her," Ed said, "as long as you keep her from calling 911 while you're doing it."

Stanislav closed his eyes as a blast of fury whipped through him.

*Keep your head*, Susan advised mentally, *and don't worry about me. I can handle Henry. He won't expect me to be armed.*

Nevertheless, a low growl rumbled forth from Stanislav's throat.

Ed and Charlie both jumped and swung their guns toward him.

A second later, Ed straightened. His shoulders relaxed as he lowered his aim. "Shit. It's just the damned dog."

Charlie squinted, trying to make out the beagle in the shadows. "She left her dog behind? Is it a mean one?"

Stanislav shot forward in a blur. Ed and Charlie sucked in sharp breaths, their eyes widening. Stanislav knocked their weapons from their hands before they could squeeze the triggers, then struck them both with his fist.

The two men sank to the floor, unconscious.

Up on the landing, Paul cried out. Panic seizing his features, he squeezed the trigger over and over again.

Stanislav dodged to the side and sprang up the steps. Pain shot through his shoulder as a bullet pierced it. But he didn't slow. In a blink, Stanislav yanked the gun from Paul's hand and slammed it against the man's temple.

Paul collapsed to the floor as thuds sounded above.

Stanislav stepped over Paul into the doorway.

Henry raced up the stairs to the second floor.

When Stanislav started after him, a hand grabbed his ankle.

Swearing, he turned to deal with Paul.

⊷◈◈⊶

Susan's breath caught when gunshots pierced her ears. Her fingers tightened on the grip of her 9mm. The second one remained tucked in the back waist of her pants. *Stan!*

*I'm okay*, he responded instantly. *But Henry is heading your way again.*

Thuds reached her ears. Two sets. According to her telepathy, Stanislav produced several as he fought off a man he'd thought unconscious. The others heralded Henry's flight up the stairs.

*Shit.* She aimed her 9mm at the doorway, holding it in her right hand and supporting it with her left as her brother had taught her. She kept her index finger near — not on — the trigger, ready to squeeze it at a moment's notice.

*First the chest, then the head*, she could almost hear Nick murmur in her ear.

*No. Don't kill him*, she reminded herself. Stanislav needed answers.

Heavy footsteps hit the landing and accelerated into a dead run.

Backing up against the wall near the door, Susan lowered her aim.

Henry burst through the doorway.

Susan fired two shots.

Henry cried out as blood spurted from one of his thighs. His leg buckled. His weapon clattered to the floor. Stumbling forward, he fell to his hands and knees.

Susan's breath quickened. Her heartbeat drummed in her ears. Keeping her weapon trained on the howling man, she glanced down long enough to locate his gun on the floor and kicked it aside.

Henry gripped his thigh and spun around. "You bitch!" His face mottling with fury, he lurched to his feet.

Susan tensed, preparing to fire again.

A large form shot past her in a blur. A breeze accompanied it, whipping her hair forward.

Henry yelped as he flew up and slammed into the far wall.

Susan gaped.

Stanislav pinned Henry high against the wall with one hand wrapped around his neck. Henry's eyes bugged as he frantically tried to peel Stanislav's fingers away from his throat. His worn boots dangled several feet above the floor.

How had Stanislav moved so quickly? Susan hadn't even seen him and she had been staring right at Henry when Stanislav grabbed him.

She eyed the duo with astonishment.

Stanislav held Henry up with only one arm as if the man weighed no more than a cat. But he must weigh at least two hundred and fifty pounds. Henry was *not* a small man.

"Touch her and you die," Stanislav growled, tightening his hold. A growing stain glistened on the back of his shirt where a hole frayed the fabric above one shoulder blade.

Had he been shot?

Susan took a step forward. "Are you okay?"

He glanced at her over his shoulder, his eyes blazing with amber light. "Did he hurt you?" he demanded in lieu of answering. She didn't need his empathic gift to know he was furious over the possibility. Rage poured off him in waves.

"No."

"Why the hell didn't you kill him?"

"Because you need answers."

He returned his attention to his captive. "Can you find any in his mind?"

Susan focused on Henry.

Henry's panicked gaze clung to Stanislav. *Shit! His eyes are fucking glowing! He really is a fucking vampire! Ed was right! He's a fucking vampire! He's gonna kill me! He's gonna drink my fucking blood!*

Frustration filled Susan as she struggled to navigate the man's muddled mind. "It's just more vampire bullshit. I can't find anything helpful."

Stanislav lifted Henry away from the wall, then slammed him back against it.

Henry whimpered and wet himself as pain and fear distorted his features.

"Who sent you?" Stanislav demanded. "Who do you work for?" He had to loosen his hold a bit to enable the man to speak.

"No one," Henry blurted, drawing in a frantic breath.

"Bullshit. You intended to hand me over to someone in return for payment. Who?"

Henry shook his head. "I don't know. Ed didn't tell me his name."

Stanislav addressed Susan over his shoulder. "Is he lying?"

She shook her head. "Not according to his thoughts. I don't think Ed shared many of the details with him."

Stanislav shifted his hold.

Henry's eyes bugged as he fought for breath and continued to pry at Stanislav's immovable fingers. His face reddened. His movements slowed. His eyelids lowered. Then he ceased moving.

Stanislav opened his hand.

Henry dropped to the floor, landing in a heap.

Susan stared down at the man, her heart in her throat.

Was he dead?

"Unconscious," Stanislav said. Turning toward her, he closed the distance between them and swept her into his arms. "Are you sure you're okay?" he asked, lifting her feet off the floor and burying his face in the crook of her neck.

Nodding, she wrapped her arms around him, the 9mm still clutched in one hand. "They shot you?" she asked as her body began to tremble.

"I'm okay," he murmured. "It passed through without hitting any major arteries or organs."

Tears welled in her eyes. "Let me see it."

Lowering her feet to the floor, he shook his head. "No time. I need you to read the others' minds and see what they know about me. Are they working alone? Will others follow? Anything you can find."

"Okay," she choked out.

Stanislav cupped her face in his big hands and bent his knees a little to put their eyes more on a level. "Are you sure you're okay?" When she was unable to prevent a tear from spilling over her lashes, he swept it away with his thumb.

"I've never shot anyone before," she whispered.

He pressed his lips to her forehead. "I know. And I'm sorry you had to do it. But it was self-defense, sweetheart." He backed away, his amber eyes full of regret. "We need to get moving. Are you okay with that?"

She nodded.

He pressed another kiss to her forehead. "Come downstairs with me." Grabbing Henry, he tossed him over his uninjured shoulder and left the room.

Susan followed on shaky legs. How could Stanislav move so smoothly and carry Henry as if he weighed nothing when he had a bullet hole in his shoulder? As far as she knew, he still wasn't even at what he considered *full strength*.

Stanislav dumped Henry on the floor by the back door. "I'll get the others." He retrieved three unconscious men from the basement and dropped them beside Henry. "Can you find anything in their thoughts?"

Susan stared at the man with the shaved head. She braced herself for the ugliness she knew she would find, then drew in a deep breath and read his mind. Or at least she tried to. She frowned. "There's nothing there."

Stanislav scowled. "What do you mean? He's the leader. He must know something."

Susan shook her head. "Whatever he knew is gone. When I say there's nothing there, I mean there's actually nothing there. No memories or anything else."

Stanislav stared down at the man. "You mean he's like me?"

"No. You may not have memories, but you have thought. This guy doesn't."

Squatting beside him, Stanislav pressed his fingers to the man's neck, then swore.

"What?"

Gripping the man's chin, he tilted his head to one side. Blood trailed down from his ear. "I hit him too hard. He'll die before you're finished reading the others' minds." He rose. "Scratch that. He just drew his last breath."

Susan swallowed. The man was dead? They had killed him?

"No." Stanislav corrected her. "*I* killed him. What about the others?"

She pointed to one. "He's a blank slate like the bald one. You must have hit him too hard, too."

He loosed another expletive. "And the last one?"

"Still alive, but as clueless as Henry." She frowned. "Or he's *almost* as clueless. These guys aren't working alone. They're part of a larger group. All friends who banded together and intended to split the reward reaped from Ed's deal, whatever it was."

"Somehow that doesn't surprise me. Can you see who Ed made the deal with?"

"No. But the rest of the group knows Henry and the others came here today."

"Then they'll come looking for them. We need to leave before they do. Do you have any gloves? Dishwashing gloves perhaps?"

"Yes."

"I have to take care of these men."

*Take care of them how?* she wondered.

"While I'm gone, don the gloves and go upstairs. Use toilet paper to wipe up any blood Henry or I spilled. Don't toss it in the trash. Flush it down the toilet so Henry's friends won't find it when they search the place."

The idea of more assholes searching her home and invading her privacy made her shudder. "Should I use cleaner?"

"No. They'll smell it. When they get here, I want them to find only an empty house with two busted door locks. I want no signs of a struggle. As soon as I'm done with this, I'm going to dig another hole in the basement. With any luck, they'll think you're still out of town and believe their buddies have fled with the merchandise." Beneath Susan's astonished regard, he tossed the two dead men over his uninjured shoulder. "Once you're done, make the bed and tidy everything as you would've if you'd gone out of town. Grab your purse, phone, keys, and laptop and come downstairs. Wipe up any blood you see on the staircase, too." Spinning around, he disappeared through the back door.

Susan stepped into the doorway to see where he was going…only to discover he was already gone. Leaning out, she glanced left and right and saw no sign of him. Nor did she hear any rustling nearby.

How the hell had he done that?

Giving the unconscious men a wide berth, she hurried into the kitchen and grabbed a pair of vinyl gloves from the box beside the cleaners under the sink. Setting her 9mm down, she pulled them on, then reclaimed the weapon and headed for the stairs. She had only scaled five or six steps when a noise sounded below.

Heart stopping, she swiftly aimed her weapon over the banister at the back door.

Stanislav stepped inside, his burden gone. Spotting her, he held up his hands. "It's okay. It's just me. I had to come back for the other two. This is going to take me a minute, so call out to me mentally if you hear or see anything that makes you nervous." He leaned down and tossed the other two men over his shoulders.

"What are you—?"

Too late. He was already through the doorway again.

Double-timing it up the stairs, Susan quickly snagged a roll of toilet paper from the bathroom and wiped up every drop of blood she could find, flushing the evidence down the toilet. It seemed to take her forever to make the bed and tidy the room. Her nerves were so frayed that she jumped at every stray sound.

How much time did they have before Henry's friends would come looking for him?

Grabbing her phone, she shoved it into her purse. She did the same with her toothbrush and hairbrush, both of which she would've taken if she had actually gone out of town.

What was Stanislav doing with those men? Was he killing the two who still lived?

She found the thought disturbing, but what choice did he have really? Those men would've killed her had Stanislav not knocked them out. And if he didn't kill them, they would continue to hunt him. Or hunt *them*, she supposed, since she knew about them too, now.

Her stomach knotted. Four dead men were tucked away somewhere on her property. How the hell would that not come back and bite them in the ass?

Slinging her purse over her shoulder, she collected her laptop and the toilet paper roll and headed for the stairs.

———⟨◈◈◈⟩———

Stanislav panted as he slung Paul and Henry to the ground and sought refuge in the shade. He was pretty damned far from Susan's house, way out near the edge of her property. Thankfully, she had no neighbors. Just dense forest interrupted by the occasional small meadow like this one.

The wound in his shoulder throbbed. His breath came in pained gasps. His skin bore pink burns.

Bending, he clenched a fist in Henry's shirt and jerked him up so he could sink his fangs into the man's neck. Disgust filled him. Henry reeked of stale sweat and urine. But Stanislav needed the blood. His shoulder wound had wept too much of his own. And the sun had kicked his ass on the run there.

Time pressed him hard, as did concern for Susan. He didn't want to leave her alone for more minutes than he had to.

When Henry's heartbeat ceased, Stanislav tossed him into the deep hole he had dug the afternoon Susan had taken Jax to her friend's home and gone grocery shopping. He had said nothing to her about it, unsure how she would react.

Henry landed in a heap on top of Ed and Charlie. Stanislav wanted to partake of Paul's blood next, but needed to get back to Susan, so he snapped the man's neck instead and dropped him beside Henry. Bending, he picked up one of the shovels he had borrowed from Susan's basement and left beside the hole. He stuck it into the pile of dirt beside him, then swore as a thought dawned.

Abandoning the shovel, he jumped down into the hole and searched Ed's pockets until he found the keys to the man's SUV. Leaping out again, he snared the shovel and filled in the hole at preternatural speeds.

The run back to Susan's house was a little easier after the infusion of blood. The pink had even left his skin by the time he reached it.

When he entered the back door, he found her carrying crimson-stained tissues to the bathroom off the breakfast nook.

Gasping, she stopped short.

"It's just me," he said, sorry he had startled her.

Sighing, she gave him a jerky nod. When her gaze fell to the shovel he carried, she paled a little.

"Almost done?" He hated that she was having to deal with this, all because of him.

"I think so." She motioned to the floor at his feet with one elbow. "I cleaned here and the basement, too. Would you see if I missed anything?"

"Of course." While she disappeared into the small bathroom, Stanislav did as she asked. He could still smell traces of the men's blood—as well as his own—but could see no evidence of it even with his acute vision. She had done well.

He closed the back door.

Susan returned.

"Let me have those gloves," he said softly.

She pulled the gloves off, turning them inside out in the process.

Stanislav took them and stuffed them into one of the pockets of his cargo pants. "Wait here." It only took him a minute to zip down to the basement and dig a grave-sized hole. As soon as he finished, he returned to Susan's side.

"Let's go." He motioned for her to precede him to the front door. The frame on the inside was cracked and the lock no longer worked, but the latch still caught enough to hold the door in place when he closed it behind them.

Susan's steps slowed as they approached the driveway. A dusty black SUV was parked behind her car.

"I'll drive the SUV," he told her. "I'm going to back up enough to give you room to pull out first, then I'll follow you to the road. I want the SUV's tracks to be the last ones left in the driveway."

"Okay."

"Once we're on the road, I'll pull ahead. Then all you have to do is follow me."

"Okay."

Stanislav dearly hoped he deserved the trust she was placing in him. He watched her get in the car, then climbed behind the wheel of the SUV and inserted the key. The engine roared to life when he turned it. As promised, he backed up enough to allow Susan to head down the driveway ahead of him. Once she did, he floored the accelerator. Gravel and dirt flew as he tore down the long driveway after her. If more men came looking for them and saw the tracks, he hoped they would think Henry and the others had left in a hurry, hoping to sneak away with the prize.

As soon as he guided the SUV onto the blacktop road, he passed Susan and led her to the northwest edge of her property. A quick glance in the rearview showed no other cars on the road. Slowing the SUV, he guided it off onto the grass and into the trees.

Susan followed, slowing her car to a stop at the SUV's back bumper once they were out of sight of any passersby.

Stanislav opened the driver's door. Leaving the engine idling, he walked back to talk to her. "Wait for me here. I'll be back in a minute."

She nodded, her pretty face pale and tense.

"Again, if you see or hear anything that makes you nervous, call out to me mentally."

"Okay."

He wanted to tell her it was going to be okay but honestly didn't know if it would.

Returning to the SUV, he eased the vehicle forward once more and carefully slipped it between two trees. The day Susan had shopped, he had walked every square foot of her property and done what he could to prepare for the worst. He hadn't had much to work with, so the best he had come up with was the hole in which he'd placed Henry and the others and… this.

Bringing the SUV to a halt, he put it in neutral and rolled down all the windows. In front of the bumper yawned a second pit he had dug. This one was substantially larger than the first. Beside it rose a mountain of loose soil.

Stanislav cut the engine, exited the vehicle, and closed the driver's door. One push sent the SUV rolling down the sharp slope to crash into the wall of dirt on the other side.

Crossing to the mountain of soil, he grabbed the second shovel he had filched from Susan's basement and went to work. It took longer to fill this pit. He took pains to ensure the interior of the vehicle was as packed with dirt as the exterior. He spent several more minutes spreading the excess soil around until the ground was mostly even.

He never wanted these men's deaths to be linked to Susan. Human cadaver dogs wouldn't find the empty SUV. And if they found the bodies, one could argue that Susan hadn't even known the bodies were there. They were way at the edge of her property, far enough from the house that anyone could have buried them there without her either seeing or hearing a thing. Since the men had known one of the house's previous owners, one could argue that the bodies had been buried there before she purchased the place.

Nevertheless, he hoped it would never come to that.

His fist tightened around the shovel's handle. He had to *make sure* it wouldn't come to that.

Putting on a burst of preternatural speed, he returned to Susan's car.

She waited in the driver's seat, her wide eyes vigilantly scanning her surroundings. The deep furrow in her brow lessened only a little when she saw him emerge from the trees. Her gaze fell to the shovel he carried, and her throat moved in a hard swallow.

He clenched his teeth, anger and concern warring within him. How was he going to resolve all of this? He didn't remember who he was. He didn't know who the men hunting him were. He didn't know a safe place in which they could seek shelter. And he couldn't remember whom he could trust to help him sort this shit out.

How the hell was he going to keep Susan safe?

# Chapter Nine

SUSAN PERCHED ON THE FADED paisley cushions of the only chair in the cheap motel room and bit her lip as she watched Stanislav.

While they had cleaned up the results of the violence at her home, he had been calm and collected. His cool demeanor had prevented her from freaking out. His smoothly spoken instructions had given her something to do and helped her hold it together. He had evinced a little frustration over having to ask her for directions after he had hidden the SUV and gently insisted on driving when they'd left in her car. The fact that he didn't recognize any of the small towns they had driven through clearly bothered him. But other than that, he had been a rock.

*Her* rock.

Until he had stopped at this timeworn, out-of-the-way motel.

Susan had gone into the front office to secure a room because Stanislav's skin and clothing both bore bloodstains. The proprietor had thought nothing of her desire to pay up front in cash and hadn't asked to see her ID, so she suspected the place was a sleazy rendezvous point for prostitutes and their johns, and cheating couples.

After they'd both showered, she had tended to Stanislav's wound while he sat quietly and let her work. But now he paced the small room like a caged tiger. Back and forth. Back and forth. Back and forth.

"Talk to me," she implored softly. "Your eyes are glowing." From anger? From pain? From worry? "But your mind is closed to me."

"I need my damned memory to return," he growled.

Susan wasn't sure how to respond to that. She wasn't sure she *should* respond while he was wrapped in such turmoil, so she opted to remain silent.

He cast her a penitent glance. "I'm sorry. I didn't mean to snap. It's just…" He raked his fingers through his dark hair. "Having no past is tying my hands. I need to know where I can take you to keep you safe. I need to remember whom I can trust, who can help us extricate ourselves from this safely. There must be *someone* out there looking for me. Someone other than the assholes who just tried to kill us. Someone I trust or who cares about me."

He stopped short. A look of dread eclipsed his features.

Rising, she took a step toward him. "Stan? What is it?"

His stark, amber gaze met hers. "What if no one is looking for me?"

The notion made her chest tighten. "I'm sure someone is looking for you. Friends and family. They *must* be."

He shook his head. "Then why haven't they found me?"

"It hasn't been that long," she told him. "A week and a half. Maybe two. They just need more time to—"

"I was down in that basement for a hell of a lot longer than that," he interrupted. "They've had plenty of time to find me."

She stared at him. He seemed certain of it, but… "That's not possible. Without food or water—"

"Gaining a hundred pounds of muscle overnight is impossible, but I managed to do that, didn't I?"

Yes, he had. Because of his rapid healing ability.

Had that same ability enabled him to survive being buried alive for more than a week?

She remembered with sudden clarity hearing a voice whisper to her the first time she had gone to see the house. *Please*, it had entreated.

Dizziness struck. That had been three months ago. Had he been buried down there for three months? Because she had seen him do a lot of impossible things since digging him up, so being buried for three months suddenly seemed frighteningly plausible.

Tears welled in her eyes as she thought of him suffering down there in the cold earth for so long. The isolation. The constant agony of his many wounds. The hopelessness he must have felt as day after day passed with no rescue. No respite.

Crossing to him, she rose onto her toes, wrapped her arms around his neck and hugged him tightly.

He slid his arms around her waist. "Susan?" The anger left his voice.

She shook her head, her throat too thick to speak.

He rocked her slightly from side to side. "Tell me," he implored softly. "I can feel your distress."

"Was that you?" she choked out. "The first time I came to see the house with the real estate agent, was that you I heard whispering to me?"

His arms tightened, his only response.

"When I was leaving," she said, "I heard a voice say, *Please*. I thought it was my imagination but…" It all made terrible sense now. "I couldn't understand why I wanted the house so badly whenever I was there, then questioned my sanity as soon as I left. It was you, wasn't it? You were there—manipulating my emotions, making me feel happy and eager to buy the house every time I went to see it—weren't you?"

"Yes," he admitted raggedly.

Sobs erupted from her chest.

He swore. "I'm sorry, sweetheart. I didn't want to deceive you."

She shook her head. Breaking his hold, she stepped back and looked up at him. "You were down there the whole time. You had already been buried in the basement when I went to see the place for the first time."

"Yes," he admitted, his face grim.

She shook her head and swiped impatiently at her wet cheeks. "It took me *five* visits to finally decide to buy that house. It took another month and a half for the paperwork to go through. And I was in the house for almost a month after that before Jax led me to you and you compelled me to dig you up."

He said nothing, just stood there as though waiting for her to strike a blow.

"Three months, Stanislav. You were down there for at least three months. Alone and in pain." New tears spilled over her lashes as she shook her head. "I'm so sorry I didn't find you sooner. I'm so sorry I didn't listen to that voice, that I didn't—"

Shock rippled across his features. Then he lunged forward and swept her up against him, squeezing the hell out of her as he buried his face in her neck. "I thought you were angry at me," he whispered raggedly.

Her breath halted. "What?"

"I felt your distress and regret and thought you were angry at me for manipulating you into buying the house."

Curling her arms around his neck she held him close. "No." How could he possibly think she would hold that against him? "No, of course not."

"I could hear your voice." He spoke softly, his lips brushing the sensitive skin of her neck and sending a shiver through her. "The day you came to see the house for the first time, I awoke and heard you speaking to Jax." His arms tightened almost to the point of pain. "Your voice was so beautiful. It soothed me. Brought me some measure of peace. I didn't want you to leave."

"But I did," she whispered. Imagining him down there suffering while she had been dithering over buying a fixer-upper, then puttering around the house above him, unpacking and working on her next manuscript, tore her up inside.

"Don't."

"Don't what?"

"I can feel the guilt and regret pummeling you." Relaxing his grip, he drew back enough to look down at her.

Susan didn't want to abandon her hold and settled instead for lowering her hands to his hips and tucking her fingers in his belt loops.

He cupped her face in his big hands, smoothed his thumbs over her checks while he gazed down at her with eyes that held an amber glow. "I'm here because of you. You gave me the strength to hold on until you found me. And you've done your damnedest to protect me and take care of me ever since, even after discovering the alarming differences I bear."

"I'm *thankful* for those differences. Without them, you would've died before I even went to look at the house and I would've never known you." She shook her head. "And I'm so glad I know you,

Stanislav."

His eyes flared brighter. Lowering his head, he took her lips in a voracious kiss.

Her heart stopped, then slammed against her ribs as lightning struck. This wasn't like the kisses he had claimed each night before they had fallen asleep. Those kisses had been gentle and affectionate.

This one was hungry. Demanding. And set her blood on fire.

Susan met it eagerly, parting her lips and inviting his tongue within.

He moaned, his hard body crowding hers as he backed her up against the nearest wall.

*Yes.* He felt so good against her. So strong and hot.

She hissed in a breath as he leaned into her, letting her feel what she did to him and firing her need for more.

—⊰⊙⊙⊙⊱—

The arousal Stanislav felt coursing through Susan matched his own and burned him like a brand. Her hands slid around and clutched him to her, her fingernails digging into his back.

She tasted so good. He couldn't get enough of her. Wanted to burrow into her. Wanted to strip the clothing from their bodies and feel every inch of her soft pale flesh against his. Wanted to bury himself deep inside her warmth and feel her squeeze him tight as she had in their shared dream.

Every time she learned something new about him and didn't rebuke him was like a gift. He couldn't believe it. That Susan could accept him and his oddities even though he couldn't explain them continued to floor him. He didn't deserve her. Didn't deserve *this*, the feel of her small hands gripping him, of her parting her thighs and inviting him to lean between them.

He had manipulated her into buying a house she didn't want and all she felt was regret that she hadn't found him sooner. Could he really be so lucky? After all of the suffering, to have found a woman he thoroughly enjoyed spending time with. A woman who was kind and courageous. Who made him laugh. Who made his body burn. A woman he could love.

A woman he *did* love.

He slid one hand up her rib cage, needing to fit his palm to her breast.

*Yes.* He heard her whisper in his mind. *Touch me.* He didn't know if she had inadvertently broadcast her thoughts or sent them on purpose, and he didn't care, too eager to comply.

Inserting a thigh between hers, he rubbed it against the heart of her as he closed a hand over her breast.

She moaned and arched into him.

He was so hard for her. Every time she rocked against him, pleasure shot through him, heightening his need. He kneaded her breast, tweaked the hardened nipple through her shirt.

*More,* she pleaded mentally, sliding her hands down to grip his ass and urge him on.

Stanislav's control began to fray. He needed her so damned badly. He wished they weren't in such a shitty motel room. She deserved better than to be taken here in this seedy dive. But he'd make it up to her. As soon as his memory returned, he'd…

He froze. Harsh reality came crashing down, landing on him like a bucket of ice water. Swearing, he released her breast and planted both hands on the wall to either side of her. But he couldn't bring himself to move away. Not yet.

Tearing his lips from hers, he dropped his head forward and rested it on her shoulder. His breath came in gasps. His whole body trembled.

"Stan?" she questioned breathlessly.

Even something as simple as her speaking his name made him want her. What the hell was he doing? He might be married. Or engaged. He didn't think he was, but he couldn't make love to Susan without knowing for sure whether or not he was committed to someone else.

A growl of frustration rumbled up from his chest as he curled his hands into fists.

"Stanislav?" Susan repeated breathlessly. He could hear her heart thudding wildly in her breast and felt her confusion over his abrupt withdrawal.

The desire that tightened her nipples and drove her to rock against him tempted him to abandon all honor and claim her.

Pushing away from the wall, he instead turned and strode away from her, needing to put some distance between them and regain a little clarity. "Why the hell can't I remember?" he snarled, frustration battering him once more. Cool air embraced his overheated body but did little to quell his lust or keep anger from rising within him.

Susan remained silent, her breaths uneven. But he felt understanding replace her confusion.

Felt, too, her arousal and badly wanted to satisfy it.

"My body is healed now. I've rested. I've eaten." He gripped his forehead, then slid his hands down his face. "This isn't fair to either one of us. I *need* to remember. Why can't I remember?" The last emerged in almost a shout.

Quiet settled upon the room, broken only by their jagged breaths.

---

Susan stared at Stanislav, both grateful that he had found the strength to pull away (a strength she herself had lacked) and regretting it at the same time. Her body still burned with the fire he'd stoked. Her gaze kept straying to the large bulge in his pants. But Stanislav looked positively tormented. And the need to comfort him overrode all else.

When she spoke, she did so gently, uncertain of his response. "Have you thought that maybe it isn't so much that you *can't* remember now but rather that you don't want to?"

Frowning, he turned to face her. "What?"

"I've heard that sometimes people—particularly those who have experienced something traumatic—don't remember parts of their past not because they're physically *unable* to but because some part of them can't accept it and won't *let* them remember."

He shook his head. "Why would I not want to remember?" A second later, he grunted. Pressing the heels of his hands to his temples, he staggered a step to one side.

Hurrying forward, she steadied him. "Stan? Are you okay?"

Eyes closed, he nodded. "It was just a quick pain. It's already fading."

"Did you remember something?"

"Just the same battle. Men firing automatic weapons.

Explosions. Nothing more."

She hugged him, running her hands up and down his back. "It's okay," she soothed.

"No, it isn't," he whispered, embracing her. "I can't move forward until I know what's behind me." He sighed. "And I can't protect you. Not without knowing—"

"You protected me very well," she protested, looking up at him.

He shook his head. "You know this isn't over, Susan. I need to remember who I am, who I can trust, so I can take you someplace truly safe."

She felt a rhythmic movement and glanced down. He was turning his battered cell phone over and over in his hand. She hadn't realized until then that he had kept it with him, his only link—broken though it might be—to his past.

She stepped back. "I have an idea."

He cast her a questioning look.

"I want to try something. But you have to do exactly what I say, okay?"

"Okay."

The ease and speed with which he answered, his willingness to put his trust in her, sent a rush of emotion through her. "I'm going to ask you a question," she said, tamping it down. "I don't want you to think before you answer it. I don't want you to growl in frustration. I don't want you to do anything but respond instantly. Okay?"

Tilting his head to one side, he studied her. "Okay."

Susan crossed to her purse and retrieved her cell phone. Returning to stand in front of him, she held it out to him. "I mean it," she reiterated as he tucked his broken phone back in a pocket and took hers. "Don't think. Just respond."

"All right."

"Those men at the house were just the tip of the iceberg. More are on the way." She saw no way Henry's friends could possibly locate them but continued nonetheless. "They've tracked us here. They're surrounding the motel right now and are armed with automatic weapons. They want to capture you. And if they think like Henry did when he first started clomping up the stairs to look for me, they will rape and kill me without a second thought. We don't have a hope in hell of getting out of here alive on our own. What number do you call to secure my safety?"

His thumb sped over the surface of the cell phone, dialing a number.

Her eyes flew wide.

His did, too.

"Holy crap," she blurted. "It worked!" Grabbing the phone, she raised it to her ear.

"Hello?" a male voice answered.

"Hi," she greeted him, then wondered what the hell she should say. She hadn't really expected it to work. "Um, you don't know me…"

Stanislav winced.

*I know. I know*, she said mentally. "But—"

"Who is this?" The abrupt interruption offered no welcome. "How did you get my number?"

Susan thought it might be better if Stanislav talked to the man to see if his voice would spark a memory, but when she offered him the phone, he shook his head. "Okay," she said in a rush, making it up as she went along. "I know this is going to sound weird. But my name is Susan and I think my dog found your wallet."

Stanislav stared at her. *Really? You couldn't come up with anything better than that?*

She grimaced. *Apparently I suck at subterfuge. Don't you think you should talk to him yourself?*

He shook his head. *Until I remember who I am and know whom I can trust, I want everyone to believe I'm still buried in your basement.*

"I'm not missing my wallet," the man said, either caution or suspicion entering his voice.

"Oh. Okay. Well, my dog chewed it up pretty good. There wasn't much left by the time he brought it home and I pried it out of his mouth. No driver's license or other ID. I don't even know where he found it. All I could salvage was some cash and this number written on a folded piece of paper."

Silence.

"Honestly, I felt weird calling you," she babbled on, trying to keep the guy on the line. He was their only lead. "I mean, who carries their own number around with them in their wallet, right?

But… I don't know. I just thought it was worth a shot. It's kind of a lot of cash, so I thought whoever owned the wallet would probably be anxious to get it back."

More silence. Then: "The wallet has nothing else in it? Just my number and some cash?"

"Yes."

Stanislav arched a brow.

She shrugged. *Who in today's society will turn down an opportunity to get their hands on a wad of free cash?*

*True.*

"I wouldn't feel right about keeping it without at least *trying* to find who it belongs to," she said when the silence stretched.

"Where can I meet you?" the man asked, his voice clipped. "It isn't mine, but I may be able to tell you who it belongs to and help you get in touch with him."

She grinned in triumph. "Great. Let's see. Um…" *He wants to meet me.*

*Not here*, Stanislav instructed. *And not at your home.*

Susan agreed. *Somewhere public, right? Lots of people around?*

*No*, he said, surprising her. *Someplace isolated. I don't want any witnesses and want to be able to see him coming if he brings friends.*

Well, hell. That sounded grim. "Where are you now?" she asked, thinking furiously.

"Carrboro."

"That's quite a drive." Not really. "I'll tell you what. Why don't we meet halfway?" She named a place out in the country that hosted a farmers' market every weekend but was deserted on weekdays. It was located mere minutes from where she and Stanislav were now and at least forty minutes from Carrboro.

"Sounds good," he said.

"Could you maybe come alone?" she added hesitantly. "I'm not in the habit of calling total strangers—men in particular—and arranging to meet them. You know how it is. A girl can't be too careful."

"Sure," he agreed. "I'll come alone. See you in an hour?"

*Is an hour good?* she asked Stanislav.

He glanced at the window, then nodded.

"Sure. See you then." She ended the call. "Well, he's not very friendly, but that's about all I can tell you." She clapped a hand to her forehead. "Oh crap! I didn't get his name."

"It doesn't matter. His number wouldn't have been in my head if I didn't have a connection to him. Let's just hope he's someone I can trust and not in league with whoever stabbed me in the back and stuck me in the ground."

Dismay filled her. "Do you mean figuratively or literally? Did someone stab you in the back?"

He looked as though he regretted mentioning it. "I'm not sure. That's what the wound in my back felt like, but I couldn't see it well in the mirror."

Susan wondered if—one of these days—he would grow tired of her gaping up at him.

"What?" he asked, shifting his weight from one foot to the other as though uncomfortable beneath her regard.

She shook her head. "Nothing. Are you getting any gut feelings about this guy?"

"Only the one that made me dial his number. He must have been someone I trusted at one time."

"But you don't now?"

"I can't. Not until I remember how I ended up so badly wounded where you found me. You've seen how strong I am, Susan. How fast I can move. Do you really think an enemy could have gotten the jump on me without a little assistance?"

She hadn't thought of it like that. It was a valid point. "No. I'm still hoping he's a friend though. You need someone you can trust."

Smiling, he touched her cheek. "I already have someone I trust. You."

She clasped his wrist and turned her head, pressing a kiss to his palm. "Flirt."

He winked. "Just wait until I confirm I'm not married. Then I'll take flirting to a whole new level."

"Hell yes, you will," she declared.

He laughed. "Let's go ahead and hit the road. I want to get there before he does."

⟞⟨◈◈◈⟩⟝

Stanislav stood in the shadows of the evergreen trees that crowded together fifty yards from the designated meeting place. Susan had done an excellent job choosing it.

Just off the intersection of a couple of two-lane roads, a large patch of asphalt stretched where a structure had once stood. A store perhaps. He wasn't sure since not even a skeleton of the building remained. Everything but the cement foundation and the gravel parking lot was long gone. Now the plot served as a gathering place for a farmers' market that Susan said sprang up every weekend.

He glanced around. There was nothing else for miles. No houses. No places of business. Just fields boasting thigh-high weeds and a crooked border of trees. Very little traffic traveled the roads. Only a handful of cars had passed in the forty-five minutes they had been there. None had spared Susan's car a second glance.

*If he doesn't get here soon, I'm going to fall asleep,* Susan grumbled.

He loved hearing her voice in his head even when she was cranky.

The thought made him smile. *I've been keeping you up too late.*

*Not really,* she replied. *I've always been a night owl. I just haven't been sleeping late the way I usually do.*

And had had one scare after another whilst awake.

*Did I mention I'm still sore from digging your handsome ass up?*

He laughed.

*It was totally worth it, of course,* she went on. *But if we find out you're single, I might hit you up for a nice long massage.*

He cursed when his body immediately responded to the image of her naked and laid out before him, waiting for him to run his hands all over her body. *Now who's flirting?*

*Ooh,* she purred. *That's so cool. Even in your thoughts, your voice deepens and gets all growly when you're turned on.* Before he could respond, she made a sound of impatience. *Damn it. Now I'm turned on.*

He laughed, delighted that she inspired him to do so even in such grim circumstances.

Stanislav caught the sound of another vehicle approaching from the east. This one began to slow down long before the driver caught sight of Susan's car. *Heads up. He's here.*

He felt the spike of fear that shot through her and regretted anew thrusting her into the middle of all this. *It's okay*, he told her. *I won't let him hurt you.*

*I know*, she said, exhibiting no doubt. *Would you take away my fear, please? I don't want it to hinder things.*

He did so in an instant.

*Thank you.*

*Thank you for doing this.* She had really gone above and beyond for him.

A sleek black Tesla Model X slowed, then pulled into the gravel parking lot.

Susan stepped out of her economy car.

*Leave the door open*, he instructed her. *If shit goes down, dive in and get the hell out of Dodge.*

*Yeah, like I'd leave you here to deal with him alone.*

Though day had not yet yielded to night, the sun had dipped low enough to hide behind the tall trees to the west. So if Susan needed him, he wouldn't roast while coming to her aid.

She frowned. *What do you mean, roast?*

He swore. He had forgotten to hide that particular thought.

*Stan?* she prodded. *What do you mean, roast? Does the sun harm you in some way?*

*It's just a minor photosensitivity I discovered I have*, he told her as the Model X's engine quieted. *Roasting was an exaggeration. Stay sharp.*

The driver's door opened and a man stepped out.

Stanislav studied him.

He was about six feet tall with an athletic build and closely cropped dark brown hair. His clothing was nearly identical to Stanislav's: black cargo pants, a black T-shirt, and heavy black boots. Only he wore a black leather jacket as well.

He seemed familiar. But when he sparked no memories, Stanislav wondered if perhaps the sense of recognition wasn't simply because they were dressed alike.

The man studied Susan, then examined their surroundings.

Stanislav had a feeling those sharp eyes missed nothing.

Well, nothing except Stanislav, who stood in deep shadows that camouflaged him.

*What's he thinking?* he asked Susan.

*He's wondering if I really came alone. Do you remember him?*

*No.*

"Susan?" the man inquired.

"Yes."

He shook his head. "Either you're incredibly naïve or this is a setup. No woman in her right mind would arrange to meet a strange man in the middle of the sticks where no one will come to her aid if she needs it."

"Will I need it?" she asked, deadly calm since Stanislav was suppressing her fear.

He lifted one shoulder in a faint shrug. "Depends on whether you're from column A or column B."

"How about column C?"

He arched a brow. "What's column C?"

"Someone who simply found something that doesn't belong to her."

*I belong to you*, Stanislav couldn't resist countering.

Her lips twitched as she rounded the driver's door and cautiously walked forward. *Let's just make sure you're single first, cowboy.*

If he weren't so concerned about her, he would've laughed. *Not too far*, he cautioned, wanting her to remain close enough to seek shelter in the vehicle if necessary.

"I don't believe you mentioned your name when we spoke on the phone," she said.

"Alexei Mikhailov."

An emotion Stanislav couldn't identify rippled through him at the sound of the name, kicking up his heartbeat a bit.

Alexei slowly approached Susan, his eyes constantly skirting the fields and trees around them.

Susan extended her hand. "Nice to meet you."

Alexei shook it. "Let's hope so. Where's this wallet you mentioned?"

"Actually…" Susan drew Stanislav's cell phone from her back pocket. "I didn't find a wallet. I found this." She held it out to Alexei.

Stanislav felt a surge of suspicion strike Alexei. Did he think the phone confirmed it a trap? Or did he fear his part in Stanislav's being wounded and buried alive had been unearthed?

"Whose phone is it?"

"I was hoping you could tell me," Susan said.

Alexei scanned their surroundings once more before taking the phone from her. Birds twittered while he examined the shattered screen. "Where did you say you found this?"

"My dog brought it to me. He found it while he was out exploring."

"Where?"

"Near my home. Why? Do you know who it belongs to?"

Alexei turned the phone over. He started to shake his head, then froze as he examined the damaged casing.

"What?" Susan asked.

Bending down, Alexei drew a sharp dagger from inside his boot.

Susan took a step backward, then another.

Stanislav tensed, preparing to launch himself at the man if he so much as sneezed.

But Alexei didn't attempt to drive the steel blade into Susan's chest. Nor did he pay any attention to her movement. He was too busy using the tip of the knife to pop open the protective case that had failed to shield the phone from damage.

*What's he thinking?* Stanislav asked.

*I don't know,* she responded. *I can't read him now. I'm not sure why.*

Once the case was off, Alexei dropped it and examined the back of the phone.

His eyes widened. His heart began to race. And a maelstrom of emotions flooded him, so many that Stanislav couldn't sort through them all and identify them. "Where did you find this?" Alexei asked, his voice thready.

"I told you, my dog found it near my home."

"What's your address?"

Susan frowned. "I'm not giving my address to a total stranger."

Swearing, Alexei dropped the dagger.

While Susan's eyes followed the falling blade, Alexei lunged forward and grabbed her arm. "Tell me where you found this. I need to know. It's important."

Still free of fear, Susan glared up at him. "Let go of me."

"Tell me where you found it!" he shouted, giving her a little shake. "Did you even find it? Or did you steal it from the person it belongs to?"

Fury suffused Stanislav as he took a step forward.

Before he could leap to her aid, Susan drew her free arm back and punched the man in the face. *Ow! Shit, that hurt!* she exclaimed mentally. But it didn't stop her from delivering a wicked uppercut when the man released her arm and stumbled backward.

Stanislav's jaw dropped.

She really *could* handle herself.

# Chapter Ten

SUSAN SHOOK HER THROBBING HANDS and kept a vigilant eye on Alexei. Punching a man hurt a lot more than she had expected it to. But at least she still felt no fear, thanks to Stanislav.

Alexei swore foully as he brought a hand up to his jaw. Blood trailed from his nose and lips. "I'm not going to hurt you, damn it! I just need to know where you found this phone. I told you, it's important!"

"Why?" Susan demanded. "Who are you? Why is it so important to you?" Why couldn't she read his thoughts? And who was Alexei to Stanislav?

"I can't tell you that."

"Then I'm not telling you where I found the phone."

"I thought you said your dog found it," he challenged.

Susan cursed herself for the slipup.

The man shook his head. "You know damned well whose phone this is, don't you?"

"Do *you*?"

"I don't have time for this shit," he muttered and reached into his jacket.

Susan backed up another step, expecting him to extract a gun. Her own was tucked in the back waistband of her jeans. She lowered her hands to her sides and prepared to grab it.

A breeze ruffled her hair as a blur of motion swept past. Stanislav appeared between her and Alexei just as Alexei withdrew a cell phone. Grabbing the man's hand, Stanislav yanked the phone away and crushed it in his fist as if it were aluminum foil.

Susan's eyes widened. Holy crap, he was strong!

Stanislav dropped the fragments of plastic and metal and fisted a hand in Alexei's shirt. Lifting him with one hand, he tossed the man several yards away.

Alexei landed on the hood of his car with a grunt.

Susan stared at him, then looked up at Stanislav. His eyes glowed bright amber. He practically vibrated with rage. And the thoughts she was able to catch showed her with vivid clarity just what he wanted to do to Alexei for threatening her.

She swallowed. It was pretty gruesome stuff.

Susan took a hesitant step forward. "It's okay. He didn't hurt me."

Stanislav swung toward her, his face a mask of wrath. "He put his hand on you." His voice was low, guttural, almost bestial.

Susan might not feel fear, but she worried that Stanislav would kill Alexei outright before they could question him further if she didn't defuse the situation. "Yes," she said, keeping her voice calm as she took another step toward him, "he did, right before I broke his nose."

Metallic thuds erupted as the man rolled off the dented hood with a groan.

Stanislav looked toward him like a wolf scenting prey.

Gaining his feet, Alexei put a hand to his lower back and arched it. A wince rippled across his features. "Damn it," he groused as he looked toward them. "I—"

Whatever complaint he intended to lodge froze in his throat. His eyes widened. His mouth fell open, revealing bloodstained teeth.

*Ah, hell.* She'd gotten so used to Stanislav's eyes glowing that she had forgotten what a shock it would be to others. How were they going to explain it away?

As she awaited Alexei's next move, she began to wonder if she would even have to. The man looked as though he was having a heart attack.

All color fled his face. His breath sucked in… and just stayed there. All strength seemed to leave his legs as he staggered forward a step, then sank to one knee. He braced a hand on the ground, bent his head, and shook it as though he couldn't believe what he had just seen. Then he looked up again. "Stanislav?" He began to breathe again in jagged huffs. It took him two tries to regain his feet. Tears welled in his eyes. "Stan?"

Stanislav cast Susan an uncertain look.

*I don't know,* she told him. *I don't know what this is.*

Sobs erupted from Alexei, drawing her stunned gaze. Harsh and grating, they chopped up his breath as he stumbled forward.

Stanislav drew a 9mm and aimed it at Alexei's forehead.

Alexei didn't slow.

Was he so blinded by tears that he didn't see it?

"Stop!" Stanislav commanded.

Alexei didn't seem to hear him.

Susan rushed forward and thrust her hands out, planting them on Alexei's hard chest to keep him from walking right into the weapon. She didn't think Stanislav would shoot him but thought it best not to take any chances. "Stay back!"

Alexei blinked and met her gaze. "What?" Tears rolled down his cheeks.

"Stay back," she advised.

He stopped pushing against her hold and glanced from her to Stanislav.

As soon as Alexei stopped struggling, Susan dropped her hands and backed away until her shoulder brushed Stanislav's arm. She glanced up. *Do you know him?*

Stanislav didn't take his gaze away from Alexei. *I don't know,* he replied, the thought conveying both uncertainty and anger. *He seems familiar to me, but that's all, damn it.*

Susan took no offense. She knew his anger wasn't directed at her.

Alexei looked at the gun, then met Stanislav's bright eyes. "What are you doing? And where the hell have you been?" He shook his head. "We thought you were dead."

The grief Susan saw in his stricken features was the same she had felt upon learning of her brother's death.

Stanislav didn't lower his weapon. "You know me?" he asked, his cold voice revealing none of the turmoil she knew churned inside him.

Confusion crinkled Alexei's tear-ravaged features. "What?"

"Do. You. Know. Me," Stanislav repeated, enunciating every

word with cold precision.

Alexei looked at Susan, his bafflement clear.

"He can't remember," she explained.

*Don't tell him*, Stanislav bit out in her head. *Don't give him an advantage.*

*The man is crying!*

*That doesn't mean he didn't betray me. We trust no one until we know the truth.*

Alexei drew a hand down his face, scrubbing away the moisture. And as he did, the barriers in his mind weakened. "What do you mean, he can't remember? He can't remember what? Where he's been all this time?"

Susan gasped as jumbled and disjointed images came to her. Snippets so small they resembled photographs. Alexei and Stanislav sparring with swords. The two of them laughing with a couple of other men who looked enough like them to be their brothers. Alexei trying in vain to show Stanislav how to use an iPad. Alexei and Stanislav sitting side by side at a table with at least a dozen other men and women dressed in black. Alexei combing through the smoking remains of some building.

Alexei motioned impatiently to Stanislav. "Why the hell are you pointing that at me?"

Stanislav shot forward. One moment he stood beside Susan. The next he was pressing the barrel of the gun into Alexei's neck, forcing the man's chin up and his head back and to one side. "Because you put your hand on her," he growled with such menace that a chill skittered down Susan's spine.

Alexei went very still. He stared at Stanislav from the corners of wide eyes for a long moment, then slowly raised both hands in a gesture of surrender. "Okay," he said in a calm, take-it-easy voice. "I can see now that was a mistake."

"You're damned right it was," Stanislav snapped.

Alexei looked to Susan. "When you say he can't remember…"

"I mean he can't remember what happened to him. He can't remember you. He can't remember his past. He can't remember anything that happened before I found him a few days ago."

"Susan," Stanislav warned.

*He's on your side. I can see you in his memories now.*

*If he's on my side, then why didn't he come looking for me?*

She couldn't find the answer in Alexei's mind before it closed to her once more. *I don't know. Maybe he really believed you were dead.*

The little bit of color that had begun to creep back into Alexei's features fled once more. He looked up at Stanislav. "Seriously? You can't remember your past? At all?"

Stanislav said nothing.

"Shit." Alexei lowered his voice. "But you remember what you are, right? I mean, you remember you're"—his gaze strayed to Susan momentarily, then returned to Stanislav—"different? You remember your… um… idiosyncrasies, right?"

Something resembling a snort emerged from Stanislav, a laugh he tried to bite back but couldn't. "Idiosyncrasies?"

"Yyyyyeah." Again he shot Susan a glance, then lowered his voice even more. "Does she know what you are?"

The fact that Alexei was trying not to out him in front of her was a good sign, wasn't it?

Stanislav must have thought so, because he lowered the gun and took a step back. "Hell, *I* don't even know what I am," he admitted with disgust.

Alexei shook his head. "How is that possible?"

When Stanislav didn't answer, Susan turned to Alexei. "How do you know Stanislav?"

"I'm his Second."

"His second what?"

He swore. "I'm his second… cousin."

Susan frowned. *Yeah, right. And I'm his Aunt Mable.* "Seriously?"

"Yeah. He's my best friend. He's like a brother to me."

Stanislav scrutinized him carefully, his sharp eyes still glowing amber.

"What?" Alexei questioned defensively.

Tilting his head back, Stanislav drew in a deep breath and held it, nostrils flaring. A low growl rumbled in his throat. "Like a brother?" he parroted. "And not above committing a little fratricide apparently."

Alexei stiffened. "What the hell is that supposed to mean?"

"Two SUVs approach swiftly from the west, carrying at least seven or eight men."

Alexei's scowl deepened. "Are they hunting you?"

His voice rife with sarcasm, Stanislav replied, "Since they reek of gun oil, I'll go out on a limb and say *yes*. But I'm sure you already knew that."

"I didn't lead those men to you!"

"Then who did?"

"Hell if I know. I've only been here five minutes, and you took away my only means of finding out."

"You could've texted them as you arrived."

Now Alexei growled. "I didn't. You would've heard it if I had."

When Stanislav didn't point out that no one could've heard him text someone while he was still in his car with the windows up and the engine running, Susan frowned. Alexei hadn't said it sarcastically. Did he believe Stanislav had some kind of heightened sense of hearing?

Wait. How did Stanislav know two SUVs were approaching? She couldn't hear a thing.

"Look," Alexei said, "I don't know how they found you. But if you give me a phone, I can take care of it." He held out a hand.

Neither Susan nor Stanislav moved to comply.

Alexei looked as though a vessel were about to burst in his head. "Oh, for fuck's sake! I'm on your side, Stan! If you'd just trust me and give me a phone, I can make *one* call and we'll be out of here and safe within seconds."

As the silence stretched, Susan finally heard the SUVs and caught sight of them approaching in the distance. Like Stanislav, she didn't know how the men the vehicles carried could have possibly found them unless Alexei had given them up.

"Let's just go," she urged Stanislav.

A pop sounded.

Pain whipped through her left arm.

Crying out, she clamped a hand over her biceps. Warm blood seeped into her sleeve beneath her hand, the stain spreading and painting her fingers as they all stared at it.

Stanislav's eyes flashed as bright as the sun. Roaring in fury, he raced past her in a blur.

Susan's head snapped around. Holy crap, he was fast! Like as fast as the Flash. She tried to follow his progress but lost sight of him until the lead SUV swung into the parking lot.

The front of it abruptly crumpled as though it had struck a tree and dipped low as Stanislav appeared, crouched down, one fist on the SUV's hood where he had struck it. The back of the vehicle kept going, flying up. And as it did, Stanislav grabbed the bent-all-to-hell front bumper and rose, thrusting upward.

Susan's eyes widened as the SUV flew into the air, flipping over and over as it came toward her. Front bumper. Back bumper. Front bumper. Back bumper. Bodies rolling around inside it as masculine cries split the air.

Alexei swore and tackled her, taking her down to the ground as the SUV flew overhead.

Her palms and elbows burned as gravel abraded them.

A crash sounded when the SUV landed somewhere behind them, sending a vibration through the ground.

Brakes squealed.

The other SUV screeching to a halt?

Gunfire erupted. A *lot* of it.

Alexei grabbed her around the waist, yanked her up, and shoved her behind his car. "Stay down!"

Susan plopped down on her butt, her back pressed against the front tire. Her heart galloped in her chest. Her breath shortened.

The fear Stanislav had been keeping at bay for her returned with a vengeance now that he was too distracted to use his gift to help her. He had stopped that SUV with his fist. He had stopped it and thrown it into the freaking air!

She stared at the crumpled mess the vehicle had become. Blood spattered the front windshield, which now bore a spiderweb of cracks. A body thrown by the crash lay in a heap ten yards away from it, limbs bent at unnatural angles. Two more bodies hung halfway out the driver's window and the window behind it.

All appeared to be dead.

What the hell *was* Stanislav that he could do that? That he could lift a six-thousand-pound vehicle and effortlessly toss it over his head?

Gunshots erupted only a foot away.

Jumping, she looked to her right.

Alexei knelt beside her, keeping his head low and firing a 9mm over the hood of the car.

Concern snapped her out of whatever funk shock had wrapped around her. Scrambling onto her knees, she drew her 9mm from the back waist of her pants and prepared to shoot Alexei if he fired at Stanislav. No way in hell would she let him kill Stanislav while he was distracted by however many enemies had been in that second SUV.

She raised her head enough to peer over the hood.

His face a mask of rage, Stanislav yanked a man up as though he were as light as a beach ball and slammed him down to the ground. Blood spurted from Stanislav's back as a second man fired on him from the cover of the undamaged SUV.

"No!" Susan shifted her aim.

Alexei's gun barked bullets before she could squeeze the trigger.

The second man screamed and dropped to the ground where he writhed in pain.

Susan gaped at Alexei. He was targeting the men from the SUV.

As she glanced back at Stanislav, he jerked. Blood burst from his thigh.

"Damn it! Why isn't he using his swords?" Alexei snapped.

"What swords?" Susan shouted over the din as she tried to locate the shooter. "Why isn't he using the 9mms I gave him?"

Alexei spat more epithets. Setting his gun on the dirt beside him, he reached into his jacket. "Because guns aren't his weapon of choice." Withdrawing a dagger, he bellowed, "Stan!" and tossed it into the air. Then tossed another and another and, to Susan, didn't even seem to be aiming them at anything.

Stanislav raced past. He moved so swiftly Susan had a hard time tracking him. But each dagger Alexei tossed disappeared as the blur that was Stanislav came abreast of it.

Bullets slammed into the Tesla. Susan ducked back down behind it as projectiles burst through the driver's door mere feet away. When they stopped, she risked another peek over the hood.

The man firing at them cried out as a dagger buried itself in his chest. Another man yelped when a dagger found his heart. Then another and another until all of them were down.

The gunfire ceased.

Stanislav appeared in front of Alexei's car. His breath came in gasps. Blood trailed from his mouth and glistened on his clothing. His shirt bore so many holes that Susan didn't know how he remained on his feet.

Silence fell, though her ears continued to ring from the gunshots.

"Susan?" Stanislav sought her out with his fiery gaze.

Alexei rose.

Susan dragged herself to her feet, surprised her quaking knees would support her. Stanislav's wounds appeared fatal. But he and Alexei both acted as if he were fine. Was his healing ability so strong that—?

Something thunked behind her.

Jumping, she spun around.

One of the back doors of the totaled SUV opened. A man lurched out, his face and one arm coated with blood.

Stanislav shot forward.

"Don't kill him!" Alexei shouted just as Stanislav reached the man.

Stanislav halted, one arm already around the wounded man's neck, ready to snap it.

"Use him," Alexei said. "You've lost a lot of blood."

Susan frowned. Use him? What did *that* mean? Use him how?

When she looked back at Stanislav, her stomach sank.

Eyes sparking with amber light, Stanislav peeled his lips back from his teeth in a snarl, revealing long, sharp fangs.

What the hell? Shock froze her breath as he lowered his head and sank his fangs into the man's bloody neck.

"Are you injured?"

Only dimly did she hear Alexei's voice, the booming beat of the pulse in her ears drowning out almost everything else. Her weapon fell from nerveless fingers, hitting the ground with a clatter.

"Are you hurt?" he repeated. "Are you shot? I mean aside from your arm?"

She shook her head. She wasn't shot anywhere else. But she was scared shitless and shaken to her core.

The man Stanislav held slumped as his knees buckled. A moment later, Stanislav let him fall to the ground in a heap.

Susan's eyes began to burn with the need to blink.

Stanislav wiped the blood from his lips and looked her way. Stepping over the dead man, he started toward her.

Susan backed up until her butt hit the car, then began to slide along it to keep him from closing the distance between them.

He halted. "Susan?"

She shook her head, her thoughts rioting. *I did* not *just see that. I did* not *just see Stanislav grow long, sharp fangs and bury them in a man's neck. I did* not *just see him drink that man's blood!*

From the corner of her eye, she saw Alexei's head swivel as he looked back and forth from her to Stanislav.

"Susan," Stanislav said again, his voice soft and entreating.

"They were right?" she blurted incredulously. "Henry and those men who attacked us at my house were right? You're a freaking vampire?"

"No!" both men vehemently denied.

Something between a laugh and a sob escaped her. "Yeah, right. I suppose the next thing you're going to tell me is that the fangs are just for decoration? Like a diamond grill?"

"Susan, please," Stanislav implored, his fangs retracting and disappearing.

"That's how you survived down there, isn't it?" she demanded.

"Down where?" Alexei asked.

Susan ignored him. "Isn't it? And that's why they're hunting you? Why you're so fast and strong and heal so quickly? Not because you're a *gifted one* but because you're a vampire?"

"I'm *not* a vampire," Stanislav said.

"He isn't," Alexei seconded. "He's an immortal."

Stanislav nodded. "I'm an immortal." Then he stopped and looked at Alexei in surprise. "I'm an immortal?"

Now it was Alexei's turn to look flabbergasted. "Well, yeah. You really didn't know that?"

"An immortal what?" Stanislav pressed.

Alexei blinked. "I have no idea how to answer that."

Something small hit the ground at Stanislav's feet.

Susan glanced down at it. "What is that?"

Stanislav eyed her uneasily. "A bullet."

Another hit the ground. Then another.

She focused on the holes in his shirt. "Those came out of you?"

He nodded. "When I..." He glanced at the man whose blood he had drunk, then met her gaze. "It restored some of my strength and will help me heal faster."

Another bullet hit the ground. And though she was still freaking out over him being a vampire or immortal or whatever, sorrow rose. He had been through so much agony already. Now this? "How many times did they shoot you?"

He shook his head. "I don't know."

"Don't lie to me." Tears welled in her eyes and spilled over her lashes as reaction began to set in.

"I'm not. I was too busy fighting them and worrying about you to count."

She swiped at her cheeks. "Does it hurt?" A stupid question. But she was having trouble thinking straight and felt like she would shatter as easily as an egg if she didn't tread carefully.

*I'm still me.* She heard the thought clearly as his gaze bore into hers. *I'm still the same Stanislav. The one you enraptured with your singing long before you saved me. The one who made you laugh while we ate popcorn and watched movies together. The one who has slept beside you every night and come to care for you far more than I should without knowing my past.*

"You're really not a vampire?" she choked out.

He held her stare. "I'm really not a vampire."

Alexei nodded, his gaze ping-ponging between them. "He isn't. He's an immortal."

Another bullet fell to the ground, inspiring more tears she impatiently blinked back. "Are you okay?"

Nodding, Stanislav approached her slowly. "Are you?"

Hell no, she wasn't. She trembled uncontrollably. Her arm hurt like hell. And she was more shaken than she had been when she had awakened to find that he had gained eighty pounds of muscle overnight. "I'm fine." Not by a long shot.

"Will you let me look at your arm?"

She glanced down at her bloody sleeve. "It's fine."

*Will you at least let me hold you then?* he thought to her. *Please. Just for a moment. I was terrified those men would kill you. I need to reassure myself that you're all right. I need to feel your arms around me.*

Biting her lip, she nodded. Because he *was* still Stanislav. *Her*

Stanislav. Fangs and all.

Releasing a ragged sigh, he closed the distance between them and drew her into his arms. "Were you hit anywhere else?"

She shook her head against his chest, swallowing back sobs.

His hold tightened.

"Look," Alexei said hesitantly, "I know… uh, Susan has had a shock. It *is* Susan, right?"

"Yes," they chorused.

"You guys could probably use a minute or two to… I don't know. But we need to clean this mess up and get the hell out of here. And it would be best if we did it quickly, before any cars come along. The last thing we need is for civilians to gawk at the carnage as they drive by, then call 911. Or, even worse, snap a picture and upload it to social media."

Stanislav didn't move. "What do you propose we do?"

Susan turned her head to look at Alexei.

Alexei motioned to the wrecked SUV. "Shove those guys back inside the SUV and disappear it into the woods. Do the same thing with the other group." He strode away from them and bent over a body. After yanking a dagger out of the dead man's chest, Alexei wiped the blade on his pants and tucked it into his jacket. He crossed to another man and did the same. "Susan, can I borrow your phone? I really need to make a call."

Stanislav vetoed that one in a hurry. "No calls."

Alexei swung around to face him. "You still don't trust me?"

No response.

Dropping her arms, Susan stepped away and looked up at him. *He helped you defeat those men. I saw him shoot some of them and toss you his daggers as if he's done it a hundred times before. And he threw himself on top of me to protect me when the SUV rocketed past overhead. I think we should trust him.*

"No calls," Stanislav repeated stubbornly.

Alexei shook his head. "That shit cuts like a knife, but if you can't remember me, I understand. I'm just going to call the Network. Chris Reordon needs to send a cleanup crew to take care of this and see if they can identify the bodies so we can find out who the hell is hunting you. Then I'll call Seth." He hesitated. "Actually, maybe I should call Seth first."

"Who is Seth?"

Alexei regarded him with disbelief. "You really *can't* remember anything, can you?"

Stanislav said nothing.

"Seth is the oldest and most powerful immortal on the planet."

Stanislav's frown deepened. "He's more powerful than I am?"

"A *lot* more powerful."

Susan couldn't imagine such after all she'd seen Stanislav do.

"He can defeat me in combat?" Stanislav asked.

"Easily."

"Then I don't want you to call him."

Alexei shook his head. "He's on your side, Stan."

"I have only your word on that." And his tone indicated that Alexei's word meant nothing to him. At least for now.

"Fine, then I'll just call the Network. We can't risk anyone finding these bodies."

"I don't want this Network to know I'm alive."

"I—" Alexei clamped his lips together, looking as if he wanted to scream. "Okay," he said, making a visible effort to remain patient. "Okay. I get that. I won't mention you or Susan. I'll say they lured me out here and attacked me. As soon as I end the call, we'll hide my car in the woods and leave in Susan's."

"Why not go in your car?" Stanislav asked, suspicion narrowing his eyes.

"Because the Network LoJacks all employee cars. And even though I'm your Second, the Network pays my salary. If we use my car, they'll be able to track us."

Stanislav consented with a brief nod. "Make your call then. But I'll be listening."

Susan took her phone from her back pocket and handed it to Alexei.

Thanking her, he started to make the call, then hesitated.

"What?" Susan asked.

Alexei shook his head. "I've been spending too much time around Roland Warbrook."

"Who is Roland Warbrook?" Stanislav asked before Susan could.

Alexei sighed. "One of your fellow immortals. The antisocial one. He's always pissing Reordon off by accusing Network employees of foul play. In the past, his accusations never panned out, but... Network employees cleaned everything up after the battle you were wounded in. If someone found you before I could and decided to tuck you away somewhere with the intention of using you to make a tidy profit... Hell, I hate to say it, but maybe it was one of them."

Susan looked from Alexei to Stanislav and back again. "So where does that leave us?"

Stanislav grunted. "He's sure as hell not calling the Network."

"I'll call a friend instead," Alexei told them. "Someone I trust. Someone we *both* trust, Stan. Or you would if you could remember him."

Stanislav lowered his gaze to Susan's. *Are you getting anything from his thoughts?*

She tried again to read them, straining to see through the mental barriers Alexei had erected. *Not much. Only a few scattered images of the two of you together that seem to back up his claim that you're like brothers.*

He nodded to Alexei. "Go ahead."

While Susan watched Alexei dial, Stanislav gave her arm a squeeze, then went to work. She found the fact that handling dead bodies didn't appear to faze him at all a little disturbing. And he was moving with that amazing speed again, darting around like the Flash.

"He's a good guy," Alexei murmured, holding the phone to his ear. "If those men were hunting him for the same reason others have in the past, they deserved their fate. Had they caught him, they would've turned him into a lab rat and cut him up to try to identify the causes of his differences so they could duplicate them. And if they'd captured you as well, they would've tortured you in front of him to force his compliance. Don't mourn for them or hold their deaths against him."

She wouldn't but didn't say as much. She did not doubt that those men would've killed her, Alexei, and eventually Stanislav had they met no resistance.

Stanislav pushed the upside-down SUV into the bushes as easily as a child would a Hot Wheels car. That superhero strength of his was going to take some getting used to.

As would the fangs.

Stanislav felt the weight of Susan's gaze as he retrieved the bodies of the men that littered the pavement and stuffed them back into the second SUV.

What must she think of him?

"Hello?" a man answered Alexei's call. As it had earlier when Susan had spoken to Alexei on the phone, Stanislav's acute hearing enabled him to hear both sides of the conversation.

"Dmitry," Alexei said, relief in his voice.

"Alexei?" the male responded.

"Yes. Are you alone?"

"Yeah. Whose phone are you using?"

"It doesn't matter," Alexei told him. "Are any immortals close enough to hear us?"

"No. Why? What's up?"

"I need a favor."

"Name it."

"I need a cleanup ASAP, but can't call Reordon myself. I need you to call him for me."

"Do you need backup?"

"No. I'm good. There's just something I have to do, and I won't be able to do it with Reordon breathing down my neck, wanting to know all the particulars. Tell him I called you from a prepaid cell, have him trace my car, then lose this number, okay?"

"Okay. Are you sure you're all right?" Dmitry pressed.

"Yeah. Just dealing with an unexpected complication."

"Okay. Call me if you need me."

"I will," Alexei vowed. Ending the call, he handed the phone to Susan.

Stanislav pushed the second SUV into the forest.

"I know forewarning you is probably a dumb-ass thing to do," Susan said in a low voice she probably thought Stanislav wouldn't overhear. He glanced over and caught her pinning Alexei with a hard look as she bent to retrieve her 9mm. "But if you betray Stanislav or harm him in any way, I will kill you."

Hope left him light-headed. She wouldn't still feel protective of him if she feared him or wanted nothing more to do with him, would she?

Instead of blustering or bullshitting or getting pissed off, Alexei shook his head. "I'd sooner die than betray him. If we didn't need to haul ass out of here, I'd be sobbing like a baby right now I'm so damned happy to see him."

Stanislav joined them, displeased by the weakness in his limbs. Though his wounds were on the mend, they hurt like hell. He would need a deep, healing sleep in order to regain his strength. More blood would help, too, but didn't appear to be in his immediate future.

He motioned to Alexei. "Now your car."

Nodding, Alexei drew out his keys and headed for the bullet-hole-riddled vehicle. Stanislav was a little surprised it started.

As the man slowly guided the Tesla off the cement slab, Stanislav turned to Susan. *I want him to drive when we leave. If you drove, I wouldn't trust him to sit beside you, nor would I trust him to sit behind us if I took the passenger seat. If he drives, you'll be safely buckled up in back, out of his reach, and both my hands will be free to stop him should he do anything stupid.*

*Okay.*

Awkwardness slithered through him, the first he could recall feeling since he'd met her. Her emotions were all over the place and impossible to read. And her one-word answer lent him no clue to her thoughts.

*Susan…* He got no further. There was so much for which he wanted to apologize that he didn't even know where to begin.

She forced a smile. *It's okay.* When he offered no reply, she reached out and touched his arm. *Really. It's okay. We're okay. I just need time to process everything.*

He covered her hand with his and gave it a squeeze, then cringed when he realized his hand was bloody. "Forgive me."

She wiped her hand on her pants. "Don't worry about it." Would she be so kind when she got a look at the wealth of blood that hugging him had deposited on her face and hair?

Alexei returned, carrying two large duffel bags.

"What's in those?" Stanislav asked.

"Emergency supplies." Alexei headed for Susan's car. "I didn't want to believe you were dead. So I figured as long as Seth continued to look for you, I would continue to lug my gear around, hoping one day you'd miraculously reappear and call me."

Stanislav stared at him. "Seth looked for me?"

"Yeah. He never stopped. I don't think he could bring himself to believe you were gone. It tore him up too much." Opening the back door, he tossed the first duffel in. "I can relate."

Grief wormed its way into Stanislav through his gift. Alexei's grief. Genuine and unfeigned.

"As the leader of the Immortal Guardians, Seth is so powerful that usually all he has to do to locate an immortal is close his eyes and think of him. But you've been off his radar." Alexei tossed the second duffel in. "I don't know why he hasn't been able to sense you all this time, but he refused to give up. And I didn't want him to, because that would've made it all too real." Bracing a hand on the car's roof, he lowered his head. "Man, it was hard losing you. I couldn't wrap my mind around it for the longest and, like Seth, didn't want to accept it. I felt…" Shaking his head, he rubbed his eyes. "I felt like it was my fault. I'm supposed to watch your back. And that day you were watching mine, and it all went to shit. You saw some mercenaries coming up behind me, and while you were distracted cutting them down…" He raised his head, his eyes glistening with tears. "You should have just let them kill me."

Susan gasped.

"You knew the rules," Alexei said, anger entering his features and hardening his voice. "*I'm* supposed to guard *you*." He pointed a finger at himself, then jabbed it at Stanislav. "*I'm* supposed to protect *you*. If either of us was supposed to die protecting the other that day, it should have been me." He clamped his lips together to halt what Stanislav suspected was gearing up to be a nice long rant. "And this is *not* the time to go into it, so let's book." He slammed the back door.

Stanislav stared at him, not knowing what to say other than, "You drive."

Grunting, Alexei stalked around the front of the car, then halted. A second later, he spun around, closed the distance between them and dragged Stanislav into a rough hug.

A rush of affection drove Stanislav to hug the man back, though his memory still eluded him.

"Don't ever pull that shit again," Alexei choked out.

Stanislav met Susan's eyes over the man's shoulder and saw her expression soften. "I won't."

Nodding, Alexei released him. Chin down, he avoided their gazes while he stalked back to the driver's side. "Now get in the fucking car."

Lips twitching, Stanislav and Susan obeyed.

# Chapter Eleven

"WHAT IS THIS PLACE?" STANISLAV asked as the road they traveled came to an end at the base of a gravel driveway. Though night had fallen, his preternaturally sharp eyes had no difficulty picking out the quaint one-story home they approached as Alexei followed the brief drive, rocks crunching under the tires. The windows were dark. No light shone on the porch. Only the moon provided faint illumination.

Alexei brought the car to a halt and cut the engine. "It's okay. No one knows about it except for me and Dmitry. It's my private getaway."

Stanislav unfolded his long form and exited the vehicle, then turned to open the back door. Susan smiled wearily and placed her hand in his when he offered it.

Damned if it didn't make him feel better.

Her slender fingers no longer shook. The color had returned to her formerly pallid features. And every minute that passed without her demanding they take her home or to Anna's lent him hope that the evening's shocking revelations had not turned her away from him.

"Thank you," she murmured.

He nodded, then turned to Alexei. "Explain." Releasing Susan's hand, he leaned in and grabbed one of the duffel bags.

Alexei opened the back door on the opposite side and drew out the other. "I've been with you for a long time, Stanislav, and have lived with you ever since I was assigned to be your Second."

Susan spoke up. "What exactly *is* a Second? Because clearly you're not talking about being his second cousin."

Alexei flushed. "Yeah. Sorry about that. I wasn't sure you could be trusted."

She arched a brow, waiting.

Stanislav bit back a smile as the other man squirmed beneath her regard.

"I'm Stan's guard, I guess you could say. There are people who would hunt him if they knew the things he can do, so I watch over him and keep him safe." He motioned for them to accompany him up onto the porch. "Sort of like Blade's Whistler."

"How long is a long time?" Stanislav asked.

Alexei found the right key on his ring and unlocked the front door. "What?"

"You said you've guarded me for a long time. How long?"

"Twenty-seven years."

Susan's eyes widened. "How old were you when you started guarding him?"

He led them inside. "Twenty-six."

Stanislav stared. "You're fifty-three years old?" He looked like he was thirty, tops.

Alexei laughed. "I look younger than I am, right?"

"A lot younger," Susan professed.

Alexei shrugged. "Most immortals probably don't know this, but the Network sends Seth a notice every five years someone has served as a Second. And every five years, Seth pays the Second a visit to heal what damage he can that's due to aging."

"Heal it how?" Susan asked.

"With his hands," Alexei told her. "Seth is a very powerful healer. He can't stop us from aging altogether, but he can extend our lives." He looked at Stanislav. "And I'm hoping he can restore your memory. It seems like you may have suffered some sort of brain damage. And I know that can be difficult to repair even for Seth. But if anyone can help you remember your past, he can."

Maybe so, but Stanislav was nevertheless loathe to invite the other immortal into their presence. They had only met Alexei an hour ago. It seemed foolhardy to fully place his trust in the man so soon.

Although Stanislav had certainly felt no qualms about putting his trust in Susan. "And this place?" he asked as he took in the small structure they entered.

Alexei shrugged. "As I said, it's my little getaway."

The place looked like it maxed out at nine hundred square feet and required no tour. Stanislav could see every room and amenity from where he stood in a tidy living room. Small connecting kitchen. Tiny breakfast nook. Miniscule laundry room just big enough for stacked machines. Two bedrooms, each with a small closet. One bathroom between them.

"If everyone you work with is as trustworthy as you say," he asked, "why would you need a getaway?"

Alexei glanced at Susan and hesitated.

"It's okay," Stanislav told him. "You may speak freely in front of her. I trust her implicitly."

Susan nodded.

Alexei sighed. "As I said, I've been with you for twenty-seven years. And in that time, I've never seen you date."

Susan's eyes widened. *No way.*

Stanislav doubted she intended for him to hear that particular thought, but it came through loud and clear. He shifted his weight from one foot to the other. "Why not?" He slid Susan an uneasy glance. "What's wrong with me?" Surely she must be wondering the same thing. Now that he was no longer emaciated, Stanislav didn't think he was a bad-looking guy. So why were women not interested in him?

"Nothing," Alexei hurried to reassure him. "Nothing's wrong with you. It's just that immortal/human relationships never end well, so very few immortals bother to embark upon them."

He felt the same dread that slithered through Susan. "Why don't they end well?" Did the immortals lose control and inadvertently kill their mortal lovers or something?

"Immortals don't age," Alexei said.

Susan glanced at Stanislav. "At all?"

He nodded, unsurprised, though he had no past to prove it. "How old am I?" he asked curiously.

Again, Alexei slid Susan an uneasy look. "Are you sure you want me to…?"

"How old am I?" he repeated.

Alexei sighed. "You're four hundred and forty-three years old."

Susan gaped.

Stanislav had to admit shock struck him, too. Shock and alarm. With all of his other differences, did he really need a four-hundred-year age gap to convince Susan to run—not walk—in the other direction?

And forgetting over four hundred years of his life was a hell of a lot worse than forgetting thirty.

Alexei looked at them both. "Humans age. Immortals don't. It doesn't take a genius to guess the kind of problems that can create in a relationship. So you don't date, Stan."

"Ever?" Susan asked.

"Never."

Sorrow crept into her dirt- and blood-smudged features. *He's lived without love for over four hundred years?*

Stanislav winced when he caught the thought. Apparently so.

Alexei broke the heavy silence that followed. "I have never regretted taking this job. I love it and plan to continue doing it for as long as I'm physically able. It *can* get lonely though." Looking more and more uncomfortable, he said, "I'm sorry, Susan. I'm trying to put this as delicately as possible. But I do have certain… needs." He met Stanislav's dark gaze. "Since being transferred here to North Carolina, we've been staying with David. I couldn't very well take a woman back there and…" He combed a hand through his short hair. "Hell, even when we had our own place, I never took women to it because I thought it would be cruel. With your heightened senses, you would've been able to hear every sound we made." He shrugged. "It just felt like it would be rubbing salt into a wound. So in every city or town we've lived in, I've gotten a place like this. Small. Out of the way. Completely off the books and under a different ID so even the Network doesn't know about it. I didn't want Chris Reordon to grill every woman I hooked up with to ensure she didn't learn anything about you."

Stanislav found no emotion in Alexei that would indicate subterfuge. "You weren't exaggerating when you said no one knows about it?"

He shook his head. "Dmitry does, because he's used it himself for the same reason. But he's the only one, and he's like a brother to us. He would never betray us. The only downside to the place is that I don't keep weapons in it. I couldn't risk one of the women I brought here stumbling upon them, so all we have to defend ourselves with is what's in the duffels. I don't keep blood here for the same reason, so you're going to have to take my vein before you go to bed."

Susan blanched.

"No." Stanislav had already fed in front of her once. He wouldn't do it again.

"It's okay," Alexei said. "I think the last time you did it was eight or nine years ago. So it won't infect me."

"What won't infect you?" Susan asked.

"The virus that gives him all the qualities you'd associate with a vampire," he told her, then returned his attention to Stanislav. "You have to bite someone multiple times during a short period to infect them. Either that or drain them almost completely, then infuse them with your blood. So I'm good. You haven't bitten me in years."

"No," he said again.

"I'm afraid I'm going to have to insist," Alexei responded, implacable. "You've suffered multiple gunshot wounds, and I need you to be at full strength in case the bad guys manage to follow us here, although I don't see how they could."

"No."

Susan cleared her throat. "You should do it. Your wounds will finish healing if you do, right?"

He shifted. "I don't want you to—"

"Don't worry about me. Just worry about you. I won't lie. The whole drinking-blood thing makes me uneasy."

"I don't drink it," he told her.

At the same time, Alexei said, "He doesn't drink it. His fangs behave like needles and siphon the blood directly into his veins."

"Oh. Okay. That helps a little," she admitted.

Stanislav shook his head. "Nevertheless, I would rather not—"

"Stan," she interrupted softly.

"Yes?"

"Take off your shirt."

Not what he had expected to hear. "What?"

"Take off your shirt."

With great reluctance, he did so.

Her throat moved in a hard swallow as she examined the many bullet holes he unveiled. None bled. But most wouldn't finish closing and disappear until he succumbed to a deep, healing sleep. And even then some might not heal completely without another infusion of blood.

"It isn't as bad as it looks," he mumbled.

"Bullshit," Alexei countered.

Stanislav shot him a glare.

Susan shook her head. "Take his blood."

He didn't want to, not with her watching. His blasted gift had let him feel the shock and revulsion that had filled her when he had fed on his enemy earlier. He really wasn't up to feeling it again.

Alexei cleared his throat, drawing Susan's gaze. "He may be more inclined to do it if you aren't in the room with us. By all appearances, you've been hit with a lot of shocking revelations today. And I can tell he's worried about you. Would you like a minute a process everything? Maybe take a shower and wash the blood and dirt off?"

Frowning, she glanced down at her clothes and only then seemed to notice the bloodstains Stanislav had deposited on them. "I don't have any other clothes."

"You can borrow some of mine. They'll be too big for you but should suffice until I can wash the clothes you're wearing." He headed into the larger of the two bedrooms. When he returned, he handed her a neatly folded black T-shirt and a pair of black boxer briefs, then topped that with a black robe that looked as soft and fluffy as a kitten.

Stanislav arched a brow.

Alexei shrugged. "Women like it."

Thanking him, Susan cast Stanislav one last glance, then strode into the bathroom and closed the door. A faucet squeaked. Water began to pound tile.

Alexei started rolling back one sleeve. "Who is she?"

"My savior," Stanislav answered, his sharp ears catching every shift of clothing as Susan disrobed.

"She rescued you?"

He nodded.

"From where? Were you being held at another mercenary compound? Or in a research facility somewhere?"

He heard Susan hiss as the water hit her. "Someone buried me in her basement," he murmured absently, frowning. She was in pain.

Alexei stilled. "You were buried in her basement?"

"Yes."

"You don't remember who put you there?"

"No."

"Are you sure it wasn't her and that she wasn't involved?"

Stanislav scowled at him. "Of course I'm sure. I was there long before she bought the house and moved into it. And when four men tried to capture me, she helped me defeat them."

Alexei grunted. "How did she find you?"

"Her dog could hear and smell me. When she caught him digging in the dirt above me, I manipulated her emotions until she felt compelled to discover what he had found."

"Do you know how long you were down there?"

"No. How long have I been missing?"

"About two and a half years."

That stunned the hell out of him. Sure, it had *felt* like years, but to learn it actually *had* been… "I was down there for two and a half years?"

"Unless you were being held somewhere else, then were transferred there shortly before she bought the house."

That didn't sound right to Stanislav. He must have been down there the whole time, yet… "How is that possible?"

Alexei sighed. "Immortals don't die when their—or rather *your*—blood supply gets critically low the way vampires do. Instead, immortals slip into a sort of stasis or state of hibernation."

Hibernation? "This is common?"

Alexei's face twisted in a slight grimace. "Not really. I mean, as far as I know none of the immortals I've met have ever done it. And it's rare enough that I was only warned about it once when I was training to be a Second." He started to offer up his wrist, then stopped. "Oh shit. I forgot. You can't take my vein."

Suspicion rose. "Why?"

"The last time you did, I passed out. Not from blood loss, but from the GHB-like chemical the glands above your fangs release under the pressure of a bite. I need to stay conscious and lucid so I can protect you. I need to stay sharp. So that cancels me out as a donor."

Stanislav studied him thoughtfully. Perhaps he should bite him anyway. If the man were unconscious, Stanislav wouldn't have to worry about being betrayed or double-crossed by him and would be able to relax his guard a little.

"Don't even think it," Alexei warned. "If the fight earlier didn't make it abundantly clear that you need me at your back, then you've lost your common sense along with your memory. Just take Susan's blood."

"I already did, a few days ago."

Alexei frowned. "Does she know?"

"No," he admitted.

"Well, it's too soon to do it again. Would you consider letting me call Dmitry again and have him bring you some—"

"No."

"I told you, he's—"

"No."

"Hardheaded pain in the ass," Alexei muttered.

Amusement diminished some of Stanislav's concern. "I'm beginning to think you *do* know me well."

Alexei laughed. "Yeah. I know you well, Stan."

⁂

Susan's abraded palms stung as she stepped from the shower. Her elbows did, too. The gravel had been annoyingly unforgiving when Alexei had tackled her.

Her arm hurt even more where the bullet had nicked her. She gave it a look as she dried off and grimaced. Instead of leaving entry and exit wounds, it had sort of carved a gash that still bled sluggishly. She had actually forgotten about it until the hot water hit it. Holy crap, that had hurt. And the throbbing only worsened when she dabbed it with her towel, then clenched her teeth and applied pressure.

"Susan?" Stanislav called through the door.

"What?"

"Are you okay?"

"Yes."

"Your breathing changed. It sounded like you were in pain."

Silently she cursed. "Just how heightened *are* your senses?" she groused.

Alexei laughed.

Stanislav didn't. "I'm coming in."

"No, you aren't," she countered in no-nonsense tones. "I'll be out in a minute." No way would she let him make a big deal out of her injury after she had seen the dozen or more bullet holes that had riddled his torso. She would feel like a total wuss.

It took longer than a minute to finish drying off, then to pull on Alexei's T-shirt and boxer briefs. Both were big on her. Alexei was six feet tall or thereabouts and built like an NBA player. Susan had to fold the excess elastic waistband horizontally, then roll it vertically a couple of times to keep them from falling down.

She opted to wrap a smaller towel around her arm before donning the plush robe. The bleeding stopped when she applied pressure but started up again when she moved.

It felt weird, wearing the clothes of a man she barely knew. Wearing Stanislav's clothes would've been different. Though they weren't lovers—not outside her dreams anyway—they had spent almost every minute together since she'd found him, and the affection they shared was undeniable, the connection between them weaving them closer together and strengthening by the minute.

She thought she would enjoy wearing one of Stanislav's T-shirts—just the shirt, nothing else—and seeing desire light his eyes up like candles.

Swiping fog from the mirror, she winced at her reflection. On second thought, she doubted her current appearance would spark desire in anyone. The phrase *drowned rat* came to mind. Even wet, her hair was all over the place.

A brief search yielded a comb that made quick work of the tangles.

"Susan?" Stanislav called again.

"I'm coming." When she opened the door, a figure towered over her, his hands gripping the doorframe overhead. Gasping, Susan jumped back.

"Are you okay?" Stanislav asked, his brow furrowed.

"Yes. Don't do that."

"Do what?"

She waved her hand in a circle in front of him. "*Loom*. It startled me."

Alexei laughed, then unsuccessfully tried to turn it into a cough.

Stanislav's nostrils flared. "I smell blood."

"I'm not surprised. You're covered in it."

"Not mine. Yours." He looked past her and swore, probably catching sight of the red stains on the white towel. "Let me see your arm."

"No. It's fine."

"It isn't fine. It's still bleeding."

"Only when I move," she said, ducking under his arm and striding past him.

He swung to face her. "You're moving now."

She sighed. "How many bullets did you take, ensuring our safety?"

"I don't know."

"But it was a lot, right?"

When he said nothing, Alexei spoke up. "Yeah. It was a lot."

"So why are you making such a big deal about my arm?" she asked. "It's just a nick, nothing more."

Stanislav's mental barriers suddenly fell, letting her hear his thoughts. *Because I care for you and can't bear your being in pain, especially when I'm responsible for it.*

Her heart turned over. *This wasn't your fault.*

*Yes, it was. You were harmed today by men who were hunting* me. *They were most likely aiming at* me *when they shot you. And don't think I didn't notice your scraped hands and elbows.*

Alexei cleared his throat. "You guys are looking kind of intense. Susan, why don't I tend your wound while Stan takes a quick shower? Will that end the face-off?"

"It really isn't necessary," she assured him.

"At least let me take a look at it and see if you need stitches," Alexei pressed before Stanislav could speak. "I have an excellent first aid kit and am very good with a needle. The last thing you need is for it to get infected. Sewing it up will not only help prevent that, it will reduce any scarring that may result."

She didn't care about it leaving a scar. She already had several from the incident in California. But she didn't want it to get infected. "Okay."

"I'm staying," Stanislav stated.

Alexei scowled. "And have you breathing down my neck the whole time? Hell no."

When Stanislav looked as though he intended to insist, Susan caught his eye. *Remember how much you disliked showing any weakness in front of me?*

*Yes,* he grumbled.

*Well, what makes you think it's any different for me?* She narrowed her eyes. *And don't even* think *about saying it's different for you because you're a man, or I will totally kick your ass, bullet wounds and all.*

His lips twitched. *I would never dare suggest such.*

*Good answer.* She touched his arm. *Now go shower. I'll be fine.*

When Alexei turned away and started digging through one of his duffel bags, Stanislav dipped his head and kissed her forehead. *I'll be listening. If he says or does anything that makes you uncomfortable, call me. You can do it telepathically if you don't wish him to know.*

*Okay.*

Alexei turned around, a large bright orange bag in his hands.

Stanislav cast him a warning look, then disappeared into the bathroom and closed the door.

Alexei motioned to the small kitchen table and shook his head. "I wasn't exaggerating earlier. His not trusting me really does cut like a knife."

Susan didn't know what to say to that, so she remained silent as she seated herself.

"Did you really find him buried in your basement?" he asked as he washed his hands.

Stanislav must have told him as much while she was in the shower. "Yes."

He joined her at the table as he dried his hands. "Would you lower the robe, please?"

She shrugged the robe off her left shoulder and eased her arm free. The sleeve of the large T-shirt she wore beneath was already damp, the towel she had wrapped around her arm having slipped down to her elbow.

Alexei gently peeled both away and bent to examine the wound. "Yep," he mumbled, "Looks like they got you pretty good. Assholes. This definitely needs stitches."

Nervousness struck, speeding her heartbeat. She had never liked needles. "Can't you just use some of those skin-closure tape thingies?"

"If it were on your forehead, yes. But this area gets a lot of movement, so stitches would be better."

When he stood and started removing bags of sterilized scissors, needles, thread, gloves, and a small bottle with clear liquid in it, her anxiety multiplied.

Calm abruptly suffused her, eradicating the other and mellowing her out.

*Stanislav. I thought you weren't going to manipulate my emotions anymore*, she thought with no real anger or objection.

Silence.

*Stanislav?*

*I don't want you to be afraid.*

She didn't have to see his face to know how much it upset him. *Thank you.*

*I would take your pain away, too, if I could.*

*I know. But I wouldn't want you to. Not if it meant you would feel it yourself. You've suffered enough.*

Alexei removed the cap from a needle, then partially filled a syringe with clear liquid from a small bottle.

"What's that?" she asked, glad Stanislav had taken away her unease.

"Lidocaine with epinephrine. You'll thank me for it once I start stitching."

It stung a little when he began to inject it into the borders of the wound. Her skin blanched around the edges as he worked.

"If Stanislav heals swiftly," she said curiously, "why did you learn how to do stuff like this?"

"Because I *don't* heal swiftly," he murmured, concentrating on his task. "Seconds can rack up some ugly wounds while fighting alongside or backing up our immortals. And healers aren't always available to take care of the damage for us." After a while, he set the syringe aside and picked up a larger bottle. "That should be feeling pretty numb now."

"It is," she confirmed.

He filled a larger syringe, then sprayed what appeared to be water into the ragged cut. "Sterile water. We don't want any dirt left in there."

Though Stanislav wasn't in the same room with them, he might as well have been. Susan could feel him as strongly as if he were leaning over her shoulder while Alexei donned sterile gloves and began to stitch the wound.

She grimaced. *Gross*. It was kind of cool though, to be able to watch it without feeling any anxiety or discomfort. When that doctor in California had stitched her wounds, she had been flat on her back and unable to see it.

Once Alexei was finished, he topped it all off with a large bandage.

The door to the bathroom opened. Steam spilled out, preceding Stanislav.

Susan's breath halted. She rose, the robe dropping into the chair behind her.

Stanislav's strong jaw was smooth and clean-shaven. And he looked utterly gorgeous. His body was bare, save for a white towel wrapped around his hips. His shoulders were as broad as the doorway, his biceps huge. His muscled chest sported dark hair she wanted to curl her fingers into and give a tug. Rippling abs made her breath quicken despite the pink marks that marred his flesh where bullet wounds had sealed themselves and formed scar tissue. His thick thighs and muscled calves also bore a dusting of dark hair. His large feet were bare.

Damn, he looked good. Soft, tanned skin stretched over hard muscle.

She wanted to feel it all against her with an urgency that shocked her.

A ball of wadded-up clothing in one hand, he strolled toward them in a languid stride that made her want him even more. He moved so fluidly. She could imagine him moving fluidly in other ways. Like when his body slid inside hers as it had in their dream.

He stopped short. His eyes flashed bright amber as he looked at her.

"She's good," Alexei said as he cleaned up the mess. "Weathered it like a pro. I—" He broke off, his gaze swinging back and forth between them. A quick peek into his thoughts revealed only curiosity over why the two of them were standing there as still as statues, staring at each other.

"Does your arm hurt?" Stanislav asked, his deep, husky voice sending an erotic shiver through her.

"No," she answered. *I would want you even if it did.*

His eyes brightened as his hand clenched around the clothing. He looked at Alexei. "I'm not married?"

Alexei's eyebrows rose. "No, you're not married."

His gaze locked with Susan's once more. "Engaged?"

"No," Alexei said.

"Seeing someone?"

"No. I told you, you've never dated *anyone* in the twenty-seven years I've known you."

"You're *sure* I'm not seeing anyone."

"Yeah. One hundred percent. Why are you—?" Breaking off, he looked at Susan. "Oh. Ohhhhh."

Stanislav tossed the wad of dirty clothes at Alexei, hitting him in the chest.

Susan's heart began to pound when Stanislav prowled toward her. And that was how it seemed: prowling. He moved slowly, deliberately, chin down, his eyes locked on hers and promising pleasure beyond anything she had ever experienced.

As soon as he was within touching distance, he slid his arms around her, bent his head, and captured her lips in a hungry kiss.

*Hell yes.* This was no tentative trial. No gentle hello. No slow buildup to something deeper. He crushed her to him as if they had just spent the past twenty minutes tormenting each other with ever-bolder touches. His tongue slipped inside to stroke her own. Rising onto her toes, she wrapped her arms around his neck and met him taste for taste as heat flooded her. She leaned into him, pressing her breasts to his chest, rubbing her hips against the arousal his towel concealed.

Growling, he slid his large hands down to grip her boxer-brief-covered ass. *Wrap your legs around me.*

The harsh demand coupled with the erotic images she found in his head — everything he wanted to do to her, to do *with* her — damn near made her orgasm.

Eager to comply, she jumped up and wrapped her legs around his waist, moaning when her core settled against his hard shaft beneath the Egyptian cotton.

*Holy shit!*

She stiffened. That thought had not been Stanislav's. It had sprung from Alexei, whom she had actually forgotten was in the room the moment Stanislav had touched her.

Heat flooded her cheeks. But Stanislav's ardor didn't cool in the least.

Oh. Right. He could only hear thoughts she *sent* him or inadvertently broadcast.

His lips burned a fiery path down her neck as his arms tightened around her. One hand kneaded her ass. The other slid up to tease the side of her breast.

Alexei cleared his throat. "Um... You guys do know I'm still here, right?"

Stanislav muttered something in Russian, then turned toward the nearest bedroom door.

Susan buried her face in his neck and bit back a moan as their bodies rubbed together with every step.

"Wait!" Alexei called as they passed through the doorway. "Wait, wait, wait."

Stanislav spat what she assumed was a Russian swear word, which pretty much echoed her sentiments. "What?" he snapped.

Undeterred, Alexei said, "You *did* hear me say that immortal/human relationships never end well, right? I mean, I know your memory is gone so... I just want to make sure you know it *never* ends well. Ever." *After all he's been through, the last thing Stan needs is to fall for a woman he can't have.*

Any lingering distrust Susan felt toward Alexei vanished when she caught that thought. He was definitely in Stanislav's corner.

Stanislav reached back and grabbed the edge of the door. "She isn't human. She's a *gifted one*."

Just before he slammed the door, Susan peeked over his shoulder.

Alexei's face lit with a broad grin. "Hot damn!"

# Chapter Twelve

ONCE MORE SETTLING HIS HANDS on Susan's tempting ass, Stanislav strode toward the king-sized bed. "Your arm really isn't hurting?"

"Can't feel a thing," she proclaimed breathlessly. "What about you?"

He knelt on the edge of the mattress. "All I feel right now is a burning need to be inside you."

She nodded. "I can go with that."

He took her lips in another hungry kiss, loving the taste of her, the feel of her small hands roaming his back and urging him closer. "Kneel."

She unlocked her ankles and lowered her legs until her knees hit the mattress.

Stanislav gave her lovely ass another stroke, then slid his hands under the hem of the shirt she wore, dragging it upward as he smoothed his hands over her soft-as-silk skin, brushing the sides of her breasts.

She raised her arms, encouraging him to tug the soft cotton over her head.

His breath left him in a rush as the T-shirt hit the ground beside the bed.

She wore no bra, so her beautiful breasts were bare to his gaze.

"Perfect," he declared hoarsely, cupping them in his palms. When he teased her hard pink nipples with his thumbs, she moaned and let her head fall back. Her hips arched into his as she dug her fingers into the towel still anchored around his hips and tugged him closer.

"Lie back," he whispered against her lips, stealing another kiss.

Her eyes holding his, she did so, easing back to lie on the bed with her head on the pillows.

Leaning over her, Stanislav tucked his fingers in the waistband of the boxer briefs and drew them down slender, shapely legs he wanted to wrap around him again. His gaze went to the triangle of dark curls at the juncture of her thighs. He couldn't wait to taste her, to pleasure her the way he had in the erotic dream they'd shared.

She nodded at his towel. "Now you."

He yanked the towel from his hips and let it fall to the floor with a thump.

Propping herself up on her elbows, she looked her fill, her bold gaze smoothing over him like hands. Her heart beat as swiftly as his. Desire poured off her and swept through him, ratcheting up his own. He was *so* damned relieved that it wasn't accompanied by nervousness or uneasiness or any emotion that would indicate she wasn't sure she wanted this.

"Wow." Her pink tongue slid across her lower lip as her eyes devoured him. "You're big everywhere, aren't you?"

He laughed. And wondered if he had ever laughed before when seized by such desire.

Her legs shifted restlessly on the covers, beckoning him to come between them.

Curling his fingers around each ankle, he eased her feet farther apart, loving the leap in her pulse. He moved forward, his own heart pounding as he smoothed his hands up her calves. He paused when his fingers encountered the raised pink ridge of a scar on her knee.

"It's from the car accident in California," she murmured.

He nodded to the longer one on her hip. "That one, too?"

She nodded.

Forcing back the anger that rose within him, he pressed a kiss to her knee, then smoothed his hand up her thighs, barely grazing the hair at her center before he lowered his body to hers.

She hissed in a breath. "You feel so good."

Claiming her lips once more, he kept the bulk of his weight

propped on his forearms. When she slid her hands around him and gripped his ass, he groaned his approval.

"I want you inside me," she whispered.

And he wanted to be there. But he wanted to taste her first.

Stanislav kissed a path down her neck and over her collarbone, loving her scent and the feel of her soft, soft skin. He closed his lips around a tight pink nipple.

Gasping, she buried her fingers in his hair as he stroked her with his tongue and nipped her with his teeth, careful not to pierce her skin when his fangs descended.

He loved being able to feel what she felt. Every sharp increase in her arousal told him exactly what she wanted. How she liked to be touched. Stroked. Teased. What she wanted more of. What made her buck beneath him and clutch him tighter.

He continued a path down her stomach, dipped his tongue in her navel, then eased lower. She was so ready for him, moaning at just the feel of his warm breath on her clit. She jerked at the first brush of his lips. Writhed beneath him. So hot and wet and eager for every stroke of his tongue. Every lick and flick and undulation. And he devoured her. Intoxicated by her taste. Lust burning through his veins as she arched against him, her cries affecting him as much as her small fingers burrowing through his hair. So fucking good. He wanted more. *Needed* more.

He slid a hand up her side to clasp her breast, kneading and pinching the hard pink tip as he moved his tongue so swiftly it seemed to vibrate against her clit.

She cried out, every muscle tightening as an orgasm tore through her. And the rush of her ecstasy damned near made Stanislav come, too.

<hr>

Susan's breath emerged in gasps as the orgasm seized her and little ripples of pleasure continued long after they usually did. She'd never felt anything like it. So intense and all-consuming.

She stared at Stanislav with no little awe as he kissed his way up her body and settled his hips between her thighs. "Damn, you're good."

She moaned as he teased her center with his hard cock.

His eyes blazed with amber light, his features intense and beautiful. "Are you up for more?"

She felt no fear when she caught a glimpse of sharp fangs. "Hell yes," she declared.

His lips claimed hers.

Susan wrapped her arms around him, clutching him tight, and smoothed her hands over his broad, muscled back. She felt a moment's qualm when her fingers found the scars the bullet wounds had left there. Dragging her lips from his, she met his blazing eyes. "Do they hurt?"

He shook his head. "As I said, all I feel now is a burning need to be with you."

Reaching up, she brushed his hair back from his forehead, then cupped his strong jaw. A rush of affection filled her as she stared up at him. "I'm so glad I found you," she whispered.

Stanislav turned his head and kissed her palm. "I am, too."

Her gaze holding his, she slid her hand down to his chest. She had always loved hairy chests and couldn't resist gripping a fistful and giving it a tug. When she did, his cock jumped against her. And jumped again when she pinched his nipple.

"I love your hands on me," he murmured, his voice nearly an octave deeper than usual. And what a thrill it gave her.

Lust reasserting itself, she smoothed her hand down over his washboard abs and curled her fingers around his shaft. Big like the rest of him. Long and hard.

He dropped his head to her shoulder as she stroked and teased him. "You're killing me, sweetheart." One of his hands clasped her breast, kneading and teasing and tweaking her nipple until her breath quickened and she shifted beneath him, needing more.

Abandoning her play, she guided his cock to her entrance.

Both moaned as he slid in deep, stretching her until he ground against her.

Susan bit her lip as he drew back and plunged inside again. "Yes." Then again. And again. The muscles of his back clenching beneath her hands as she wrapped her arms around him and urged him on. Deep, powerful strokes that hit all the right places. So good. She never wanted it to end.

The headboard began to strike the wall with rhythmic thuds.

Her breath shortened. "More," she pleaded, pleasure rising.

And he delivered, propping his weight on his hands, gazing down at her with brilliant eyes. His lips parted to reveal the tips of those sharp fangs.

It only excited her more.

"Come for me," he whispered.

She nodded, arching up against him, meeting him thrust for thrust until ecstasy again engulfed her. Her inner muscles clamped down around him when the orgasm struck, squeezing him tight until he orgasmed, too, his large body stiffening above her as he shouted his release.

Susan's heart slammed against her ribs as the pleasure went on and on.

Then he lowered his body to hers. Pressing a kiss to her temple, he rolled them to their sides. Bodies still joined, he tucked a hand beneath her knee and slid her leg up over his hip.

Peace settled upon her as she nestled into his chest and toyed with the hair there until her breathing calmed. His frantic heartbeat beneath her palm gradually slowed.

His lips brushed her forehead. "Does your arm hurt?"

She smiled. "No." Her fingers encountered a raised scar just above one nipple. "What about you? Are you in pain?" She found another scar on his shoulder. Another on his side. Three more marred his eight-pack abs. When she lightly explored them, she felt his cock move inside her.

Her eyes widened. He was still rock hard.

"No," he responded, his voice carrying the same desire it had earlier.

She tilted her head back to look up at him. "Seriously?"

He nodded, meeting her gaze with amber light. "I'm fine."

"No, I mean… seriously? You're good to go again? Already?"

His lips twitched. Then he withdrew almost to the crown and slid in deep again.

Her breath caught. And she was even more surprised to feel a spark of renewed desire strike *her* even though she was as limp as a noodle.

"Yes," he responded. "And I'd be *going again* already if I didn't feel your fatigue."

She bit her lip. "Damn." She really was exhausted. "Do you know how much I want to roll you onto your back and ride you until you shout my name?"

Again his cock moved inside her. "Yes," he uttered hoarsely. "But you're too tired."

"Which is why I said *damn*."

He chuckled. Wrapping his arms around her, he rolled onto his back, keeping their bodies joined and settling her atop him. "You could always ride me until you can't, then let me take over."

She sat up, loving the feel of him inside her as much as she loved looking down at his beautiful body stretched out beneath her. "That is just too tempting to pass up." She rotated her hips, dragging a groan from him. "You know, I've never had back-to-back orgasms like that before."

"You haven't?" he murmured, his eyes on her breasts.

Another rotation of her hips. Another low groan.

"I don't know if I can have a third."

He smoothed his large hands up her thighs.

She sucked in a breath when his thumbs brushed her clit, a light touch that produced a strong response.

"You'll have a third," he promised.

Smiling, she began to move.

---

Stanislav sighed as consciousness beckoned. The scent of boiling pasta and bubbling, spicy tomato sauce reached his nose.

He smiled. Alexei was as addicted to pasta as the French immortal Lisette was. It didn't surprise him that his friend kept a ready supply on hand at his getaway.

His eyes opened wide as he sucked in a breath. His smile vanished.

He remembered.

Heart beginning to pound, Stanislav sat up and looked around.

The bed beside him was empty, the sheets cold. He heard Susan laugh softly at something Alexei said while he prepared an evening meal for the three of them.

Alexei loved pasta. He *loved* pasta. *Any* Italian food really. And Stanislav remembered it. He remembered *all* of it. The twenty-seven years Alexei had served as his Second, the two of them becoming closer than Stanislav had been to his brothers while they'd lived.

He remembered his long life as an Immortal Guardian, hunting and slaying psychotic vampires nightly to keep them from preying upon or turning humans. He remembered his own transformation in his twenties at the hands of a sadistic vampire. He remembered Seth asking Yuri to train him.

Yuri! He remembered his best friend!

Jubilation filling him, he laughed and leapt up.

Black clothing, cleaned and folded, lay in a neat stack at the foot of the bed. Stanislav dressed and brushed his teeth in a blink, then headed out of the bedroom.

Susan looked up, in the process of setting the table for three. Alexei had cleaned her clothes as promised, so she was once more clad in tight, low-riding blue jeans and a V-necked T-shirt that hugged her slender curves and bore faint bloodstains his Second hadn't quite been able to remove.

She smiled, her expression full of warmth, affection, and remembered passion.

Stanislav's chest swelled as he shared the emotions. She'd come to mean so much to him so quickly. At last he was free to be with her with no worries over an unknown past.

"Hi," she greeted him softly.

"Hi." Closing the distance between them, he slid his arms around her and brushed a kiss against her lips. "How's your arm?"

She shrugged. "It hurts. What about you? You've slept the day away." After they had spent all night making love. "Are your wounds any better?" *I hope all that sexual energy he expended didn't take anything away from his healing.*

Releasing her, he smiled. "You're projecting again."

A flush mounted her cheeks. "Oh."

"And it didn't. I'm not a hundred percent." His wounds wouldn't heal completely without another infusion of blood. "But I'm getting there." He turned to Alexei, whose face was alight with curiosity as he watched the two of them and stirred the sauce. Crossing to him, Stanislav wrapped his friend in a bear hug.

Alexei dropped the spoon and returned the embrace. "What's

this for?"

"For not giving up on me." Releasing his friend, he turned to Susan with a grin. "I remember my past."

Her face lit up with a bright smile. "Stanislav! That's fantastic!" Skipping across the room, she threw herself into his arms and hugged him tight.

Laughing, he spun her around. "I don't know why or how, but when I woke up" — he shook his head as he set her down — "it was all there. And Alexei was right." Clasping her hand, he brought it to his lips and kissed her knuckles. "You're the only woman in my life." *The only woman I* want *in my life.*

Her heartbeat picked up, matching his as she smiled up at him.

Alexei bent to pick up the spoon he'd dropped. "You remember everything?" he asked, caution entering his tone.

Stanislav nodded, wondering what caused it. "I think so." He even remembered his mortal childhood, and he couldn't wait to share it all with Susan. Couldn't wait to introduce her to his friends. To his immortal family. Yuri was going to love her. "Well, most of it. Some things are still a bit hazy." He vaguely recalled being concerned about Yuri in the weeks before they had converged upon the mercenary compound. Something about his behavior being erratic?

He shrugged it off. It would come to him soon, he was sure.

For now, he smiled as Susan returned to the table to finish arranging plates and silverware for their meal. The world seemed a hell of a lot brighter today.

"Do you remember how you ended up in my basement?" she asked. When she looked over his shoulder, her smile faltered.

Stanislav glanced back at Alexei and caught him shaking his head, his eyes asking her not to mention that. He frowned. "What's wrong?"

Alexei forced an easy smile. "Nothing. We don't need to go into all that just yet."

"No," Susan hastened to add. "Of course not. I'm sorry. We haven't even given you a chance to wake up. And you're probably as hungry as I am."

What didn't Alexei want him to remember? Did he know how Stanislav had ended up in Susan's basement?

His scowl deepened. Wait. How *had* he ended up in her basement?

The last bit of his foggy memory surfaced.

Mercenaries. *Vampire* mercenaries. They had found him after the explosion had knocked him on his ass. What the hell had he been thinking, deflecting a grenade into the armory? He had been in such a hurry to get to Yuri that he…

Grief struck, sucking all the air from his lungs.

*Yuri.* Those bastards had killed Yuri. They had taken his head!

"Stan?" Susan asked, her voice soft with concern.

He met Alexei's gaze, saw moisture well in them as his friend swallowed hard.

Shaking his head, eyes burning, Stanislav staggered back a step. "No." Pain engulfed him as images flooded his mind. He hadn't been there to guard Yuri's back. He had been too far away. Hadn't gotten to him in time. And that fucking vampire had decapitated him. "No," he moaned, his gut clenching. "No, no, no, no, no."

"Stan?" Susan whispered, taking a step toward him.

He bent forward, shaking his head as tears flowed down his cheeks. His friend — his brother — was dead.

Susan hurried forward, pulling him into her arms and supporting his weight when his knees weakened.

Sobs erupted from his chest as he wrapped his arms around her and clutched her tight. "They killed my brother," he moaned. "They fucking killed my brother."

"Oh no. I'm so sorry," she murmured, her voice thickening with tears as she held him. "I'm so sorry, honey."

She must have read his thoughts. Must have seen it unfold in his mind.

Four hundred years. Yuri had been like a brother to him for over four hundred years. A century older, Yuri had watched over him long after Stanislav had honed his battle skills enough to take care of himself and hold his own against vampires. He'd been the proverbial big brother. And when Yuri had needed him most, Stanislav had failed him.

He sank to his knees, taking Susan down with him. But she offered no complaint. She just held him and stroked his back while he wept.

Stanislav didn't know how long they remained like that before a sound reached his ears.

The low rumble of a car engine.

He looked at Alexei, who watched them with moisture glistening on his cheeks. "A car is coming."

Alexei stiffened and looked toward the darkened windows. "This is the last house on the road. Anyone coming this way is coming here. And I didn't make any calls while you were sleeping."

Swearing, Stanislav lurched to his feet and helped Susan up. "Would Dmitry come looking for you?"

"No. Not unless he failed to hear from me for forty-eight hours."

"Does this place have a basement?"

"No. The ground slopes down, away from the house in back, so we can duck under the deck if we have to. And there's a crawlspace beneath the back half that we can access from outside, but it would be a tight fit for you and me."

"What kind of weapons do you have?"

While Alexei grabbed one of his duffels and parked it on the sofa, Stanislav drew his hands down his face to erase his tears. They had left none of the men alive yesterday. So the men couldn't have alerted their comrades to his and Susan's current whereabouts. What the hell?

"Wait here," he ordered the others. Crossing to the front door, he opened it enough to determine the sun had just set, then stepped outside. Though the breeze was a little off, not quite coming from the direction of the approaching automobile, he still managed to pick up the scents of five different males along with gun oil, gasoline, and exhaust.

He slipped back inside and closed the door. "There are five of them. All in the same vehicle. Approximately six minutes out."

Susan stood where he had left her, pale and anxious.

Alexei shoved the dishes aside and began laying out weapons on the kitchen table. Two 9mms, both sporting top-of-the-line silencers. Eight spare magazines. An automatic rifle with a silencer and more spare magazines. A dozen daggers. Two shoto swords.

Susan stared at the array, then looked at Alexei. "Really? You carry all that around with you wherever you go?"

"Yeah."

Stanislav strode over to the table and picked up a dagger.

"Here." Alexei grabbed a black strap and held it out.

Stanislav took it and slipped it over his head and one shoulder so it draped across his chest. As he tucked daggers into the loops it bore, he glanced at Susan. "Can you hear their thoughts from here?"

"I'll try." She closed her eyes, her brow furrowing with concentration.

"She's telepathic?" Alexei asked, tucking magazines in his pants pockets.

"Yes."

"That explains the odd silences and staring contests you two keep engaging in."

He grunted.

"There's a tracker on my car," Susan announced. "That's how they found us. Henry put it there the day he installed the security system."

Stanislav swore. The man must have done it as he was leaving, when he had dropped his clipboard and ducked out of sight for a minute.

"They knew their friends were coming after us yesterday," she continued. "The ones at the house *and* the ones who found us at the farmers' market. They don't know what to think about not having heard from them. Two of them believe all their friends are dead. The other three think the second group killed Henry's crew and took off with the package." She opened her eyes and met Stanislav's. "Took off with *you*. I was expendable."

Fury plowed through him.

Alexei shook his head. "Don't let that shit get in your head and make you do something stupid."

Right. He needed to stay calm.

"Susan," Alexei said, "do you know why they want him?"

"No. Right now their thoughts are all about securing the package and killing their friends if they find out the guys double-crossed them."

Stanislav muttered something in Russian.

Alexei sent him a warning look. "Don't kill them. Incapacitate them. A lot of shit has happened since you disappeared. And the last thing we need is for another fucking mercenary group or someone else to rise up against us. We need to know who the hell these guys are. Okay? Don't kill. Incapacitate."

"Agreed." Grabbing one of the 9mms, Stanislav held it out to Susan. "Here."

She moved forward and took it without hesitation. "Thanks. No way in hell am I going to let those bastards get their hands on you."

Both men stilled and looked at her.

Stanislav's blood heated at the protective and proprietary emotions she exuded.

She glanced up from the weapon and caught them staring. "What?"

Alexei met Stanislav's gaze. "I like her."

He smiled. "I like her more."

His friend laughed. "No kidding." He motioned to Susan. "I noticed you had a 9mm yesterday."

She glanced around with a frown. "Yes, but I don't know where it is."

"Over by the lamp. I cleaned it for you while you were sleeping, but this one's better. You have much experience with them?"

"Yes."

"Good." He handed her two magazines. "When the shit starts, I want you to stay close to me and keep your head down. My job is to protect Stan, and you're clearly important to him, so that job now extends to protecting you. Okay?"

"Okay." She swallowed as her eyes met and clung to Stanislav's. "I don't know if I can kill anyone. I mean, I know I shot Henry, but…"

He shook his head. "I don't want you to kill. I just want you to be able to protect yourself. If any of them get near you and you have to shoot, shoot to wound." Picking up a shoto sword, he looked toward the windows. "Let's head out the back."

Susan's pulse tripped all over itself as fear rose.

Almost immediately, calm suffused her, wiping it away.

*Thank you*, she told Stanislav.

Stepping up beside her, he pressed a kiss to her temple, then took her free hand in his and led her to the back door. *I hate that I've brought such violence into your life.*

*You didn't bring it. They did.*

Alexei exited the house first, body in a crouch, rifle ready to spit bullets. "Hit the lights," he muttered.

Stanislav flicked a switch.

The floodlights on the back deck went dark as Susan exited.

Stanislav nudged her aside and stepped out after her, closing the door behind them.

Not even the light from inside reached them now.

The abrupt shift from light to darkness blinded her. She heard a board creak as Alexei descended the wooden steps. *How does he see so well in the dark?*

Stanislav led her forward. *This may just be a little getaway place for him, but Alexei leaves nothing to chance. The first thing he would've done upon buying the house would be to memorize where everything is and learn to negotiate the place in complete darkness. He does it everywhere we live.*

Wow. Talk about being dedicated to his job. *Why doesn't he use night vision goggles?*

*House lights and streetlights can hamper them. Fog, rain, and smoke can, too.*

And she'd seen a lot of fog since moving to the country.

*Careful*, he warned. *There are five steps here.*

She descended the steps without incident. The ground did indeed slope sharply away from the house in back. Her steps weren't nearly as sure as the men's while they followed the line of the back deck for a bit.

*Duck your head*, Stanislav said. He cupped the top of her head with one large hand and protected it while she ducked under the deck.

Her eyes gradually adjusted to the darkness enough to make out shapes with the moon's aid. From here, she would be able to see any men who crept around the back of the house. But those men wouldn't be able to see her in the shadows.

Stanislav whispered an epithet. "A second vehicle is on the way. I can't tell how many men it carries. While I'm under here, I can only hear it, not smell it."

The first car arrived. Susan guessed the driver had bypassed the driveway and driven up onto the front lawn, shining its headlights directly on the house, because the meadows on both sides brightened a bit.

The backyard, however, remained pitch-black.

Stanislav pressed a kiss to her forehead. *Stay safe.* Seconds later, he slipped away. He made no sound when he did. Nevertheless, she knew he no longer stood beside her.

Metal clunked as car doors opened out front. Boots crunched on gravel.

Alexei touched her arm. *Are you reading my mind?*

*Yes.*

*Stan is going to circle around and come up behind them.*

*How do you know? Are you telepathic, too?*

*No. I've just been with him a long time and know how he operates. I'm going to move over to this corner of the house. I want you to keep an eye on the other one and let me know if you catch any movement.*

*Okay.*

"Hey, Jeff!" a man called somewhere out front. "You in there?" He was one of the two who feared their friends were dead but hoped he was wrong.

"Way to let 'em know we're here, dipshit," another muttered. This one thought their friends had betrayed them, wanting a bigger piece of the pie. Which was why he had opted to come at night. He had wanted to take them by surprise, assuming they would be preoccupied with the vampire.

The first man snorted. "If the package is what Brian says it is, then it heard us coming long before we— *Umph!*"

"Oh *shit!*"

Gunfire erupted.

Cries of pain split the night.

Alexei peered around the corner of the house, then took aim. His bullets made almost no sound when he fired.

Susan kept her eyes trained on the opposite corner, hoping like crazy that no one would move into sight. Just in case though, she raised the 9mm in her right hand—supporting it with her left—and aimed it at chest level.

The front door of the house slammed open. Thuds sounded overhead. Crashes followed. Then a body burst through the back door.

Susan looked up. *Oh shit.* One of the men stood directly above her. Before she could redirect her aim, the man jerked and grunted several times to the accompaniment of soft *thwits*. Spinning around, she found Alexei firing up at him through the deck. The man's weapon hit the wooden deck with a clatter, then his body fell hard.

Dust sprinkled down onto Susan's face, grit landing in her eyes.

Stepping back, she rubbed them furiously with one hand and kept her other on the grip of the 9mm. As soon as she could open her eyes without tearing up, she saw Alexei returning to his corner and looked to the side *she* was supposed to be watching.

A man backed into view, his semiautomatic rifle barking bullets aimed at the front of the house.

Susan didn't hesitate. Raising her 9mm, she pulled the trigger.

Blood spurted from the man's thigh.

Crying out, he ceased firing as his leg buckled, landing him on his ass. He gripped his leg, spewing curses. *Fuckers!* Rolling onto his side, he squinted at the back deck. *How many are there? I can't see them! Where are they?* More curses colored the rest of his thoughts until he pinned his gaze on Alexei, unable to find Susan in the shadows. *There.*

She glanced over her shoulder.

Alexei was turned away, firing toward the front of the house.

*Heads up*, she warned him mentally.

Ducking back into the shadows, Alexei swung around and fired all in one motion.

Susan's jaw dropped as blood spurted from the attacker's right shoulder.

*How the hell did he do that?*

*Lots of practice*, Alexei thought to her. *Stay sharp.*

The downed man swore and gripped his injured shoulder.

Susan divided her attention between keeping an eye on the moaning man and watching for others to come around the corner.

As the man clumsily reached for his gun with his left hand, she tensed.

*Crap. I'm going to have to kill him.*

A blurry form shot past.

A deep gash opened on the man's neck from one side to the other, spilling a stunning amount of blood. Eyes wide, he clamped his left hand to the gaping wound and slumped back, his gun forgotten.

The blurred form slowed to a stop. Stanislav turned glowing eyes upon her, the shoto sword he held glinting crimson. "Susan?"

She swallowed. "I'm all right."

Bright light splashed him as a second car arrived and hit him with the high beams.

Blinded, Stanislav threw up his free hand to shade his glowing eyes.

Blood spurted from his chest as multiple shots echoed in the night.

Susan's heart stopped. "No!"

Alexei swore and took off around the far corner, heading toward the front of the house. *Stay under the deck!*

Stanislav stumbled backward beneath the unceasing volley of bullets and dropped his sword.

*Stan!* Ducking out from under the deck, Susan aimed her weapon at the corner of the house and raced toward him. As soon as the headlights touched her, she opened fire.

*Damn it!* Alexei fired at the same time from somewhere out front. *I told you to stay under the fucking deck!*

Still privy to his thoughts, Susan ignored him and just kept firing.

The attackers ducked for cover, their guns going silent.

Stanislav staggered back a last step as the barrage stopped. Blood poured from his lips to coat his chin as he leaned forward and tried to catch his breath.

Squinting against the bright light, Susan shifted her aim to the open driver's door she thought one or more of the men hid behind and finished emptying her magazine.

A man cried out. Then a second.

Ejecting the empty mag, she slid another from her pocket and inserted it just before she reached Stanislav.

He shook his head. *Get back under the —*

Gunshots rang out. Something struck her hard.

Pain erupted in her chest and raced down her right arm. Her fingers went numb. The 9mm tumbled from her grasp. Her knees weakened.

"Susan!" Stanislav leapt forward and caught her before she could fall.

Alexei continued firing.

Another attacker cried out.

Susan fought to draw in breath as Stanislav clutched her to him and muttered something in Russian.

A figure appeared a few feet away in the headlights, a dark silhouette standing between them and the shooters. He just… appeared… out of thin air.

As the pain in her chest multiplied, Susan stared at him. He had to be at least six feet eight inches tall and had obsidian hair pulled into a ponytail that fell down the back of his long, black coat, all the way to his hips.

Stanislav's jagged breath sawed in and out through blood-coated lips as he clutched her to his chest and limped toward the back deck. "Seth!" he called.

Gasping, the man spun around. His eyes widened, then flashed a brilliant gold.

Bullets struck the newcomer in the back as the remaining attackers resumed fire.

Thunder split the night, as loud as a bomb detonating overhead.

Susan jumped, then moaned at the pain the sharp movement spawned.

Lightning streaked across the sky like skeletal fingers, clawing through rapidly gathering clouds as she watched with wide eyes.

His face darkening with fury, the mystery man vanished.

He didn't move away in a blur of speed like Stanislav. He vanished.

Screams erupted.

Alexei's gun quieted. So did the weapons of their attackers.

Garbled cries of fear and pain accompanied thuds.

Susan closed her eyes and clung to Stanislav with her good arm, not knowing how the two of them remained upright. His shirt was saturated with warm blood. Hers was, too. His breath wheezed in and out of lungs that were clearly damaged. She had difficulty drawing in any air at all. Every movement felt like someone had packed her wound with shards of glass. Her head began to spin. Cold suffused her. Her legs weakened, refusing to support her.

But Stanislav didn't let her fall. *Stay with me, sweetheart.* His hands fisted in the back of her shirt. *I know it hurts, but stay with me. It'll be okay.* He buried his face in her hair. *I promise it'll be okay. Just stay with me.*

The tall mystery man abruptly reappeared beside them.

Susan jumped, then moaned again.

Stanislav lifted his head.

The mystery man stared at him as though he were seeing a ghost while ominous clouds continued to gather overhead.

# Chapter Thirteen

STANISLAV MET SETH'S TORTURED GAZE as lightning flashed and raindrops began to fall with a pitter-patter that swiftly coalesced into a downpour, a reflection of the intense emotion buffeting the powerful Immortal Guardians' leader.

"Stanislav," Seth whispered, his handsome face tight with emotion. "I thought you were dead." Moisture glistened in his eyes as he shook his head. "I reached out to you so many times but couldn't feel you. Not until tonight."

Clenching his teeth against the pain, Stanislav nodded. He didn't think he would be able to remain upright much longer. He wanted to tell Seth he'd explain everything later but had difficulty finding his voice. Tightening his hold on Susan, he choked out, "D-Don't let me drop her."

"Of course." Leaping forward, Seth gently took Susan from him and lifted her into his arms.

Susan cast Stanislav a frantic look. He knew she couldn't read Seth's mind to tell if he was friend or foe. Seth was far too powerful.

And Stanislav was too damned weak to suppress her fear.

Limping forward, he brushed a bloody hand over her hair and wheezed, "It's okay… I trust him… with my life."

Alexei jogged around the far corner and approached them, his boots splashing in the water that rapidly pooled on the lawn and rolled downhill. Blinking against the large drops, he faced Stanislav. "All of them are down. Three dead. Six unconscious." He smiled up at Seth. "You showed up just in time."

Seth nodded to Stanislav. "Help him inside."

Alexei looped his rifle strap over his shoulder and moved forward to offer his support.

Stanislav leaned heavily on his friend as he watched Seth carry Susan up the steps, across the deck, and through the back door, which the body of one of their attackers propped open.

Alexei cursed as he took in the wounds that decorated Stanislav's torso. "I can't remember the last time I saw you with so many wounds. You're off your game."

Stanislav laughed, then grunted as pain knifed through his chest. "Yeah. A little bit."

Once inside, they found Seth kneeling beside the sofa.

Susan lay on it, her eyes wide as she looked from Seth to the large hand he rested upon her chest. That hand acquired a golden glow as Seth healed her wound.

Her breathing grew smoother. The lines of pain in her face receded. Some color returned to her pallid features. Her teeth even stopped chattering as the elder immortal flooded her with warmth and banished the cold produced by autumn temperatures and the sudden rain.

As if on cue, a fire roared to life in the fireplace.

Seth withdrew his touch. His hand ceased glowing.

Susan tentatively tucked bloody fingers into the neckline of her shirt and lifted it a few inches. Tilting her chin down, she eyed the flesh that should have borne an ugly bullet wound but now was completely healed.

Her lips parted as she released the shirt and looked at Stanislav. "That's amazing."

He mustered what he hoped was a smile rather than a grimace. "Susan, this is Seth… the eldest and most… powerful amongst us."

Seth rose and crossed to him.

Stanislav transferred the smile to his friend and leader. "I'm afraid I'm too… weary to explain it all. Just… read it in my mind."

Seth gripped Stanislav's shoulder, his fingers squeezing and releasing as though he needed to confirm again and again what his eyes told him. Placing his free hand on Stanislav's bloody chest, Seth met his gaze.

A soothing heat infused him. Stanislav hadn't realized until then that his whole body trembled from the cold.

The many bullet holes that marred his form began to heal, spitting out any projectiles that hadn't passed through him, the ragged flesh weaving itself back together.

"You were weakened before the battle even began," Seth pronounced hoarsely. "You should have called me."

The muscles in Stanislav's shoulders relaxed as breathing grew easy again and the pain dwindled to nothing. "I didn't remember you until minutes before the attack. I didn't remember *any* of my past."

As soon as he finished healing all of Stanislav's wounds, Seth dragged him into a tight hug. His emotions flowed into Stanislav: joy, grief, guilt, and half a dozen others.

Stanislav tightened his hold, regret filling him over the turmoil his absence had caused.

"We lost Yuri," Seth choked out.

Stanislav nodded, unable to speak past the lump in his throat.

"I thought I'd lost you, too," Seth uttered. Shame and self-loathing entered the mass of emotions writhing within the powerful leader. "I failed you both."

"No," Stanislav insisted, "you didn't." Glancing over Seth's shoulder, he saw Susan sit up on the sofa. Compassion softened her blood-spattered features as she watched them.

Drawing in a deep breath, he loosened his hold and stepped back. "Why couldn't I remember you?" He doubted Seth had wasted any time combing through his memories to discover where the hell Stanislav had been for the past two and a half years. "Was it brain damage caused by the explosion?"

"No." When Seth's voice once more emerged hoarse, he cleared his throat and tried again. "No. It was a consequence of the stasis." He drew a hand down his face, erasing the tears that mingled with the rain on his cheeks. "Even *I'm* not clear on how the odd state of hibernation immortals can slip into affects the various portions of the brain. But I have learned over the millennia that the longer an immortal remains in stasis, the more likely he is to forget his past. It all depends on how long he sleeps. Sometimes the memory loss is partial. Sometimes it's total. Or near total, as it was with you."

Stanislav nodded. "I remembered what a *gifted one* was, but not what an immortal was. I remembered how to shield my thoughts from telepaths but couldn't remember any telepaths. And I kept seeing flashes of the battle."

"It has been centuries since an immortal remained in stasis longer than a day or two," Seth said. "Such has rarely happened since I began assigning you all Seconds to watch over you and keep track of you. But thus far, the memory loss has never been permanent, even for those who slept longer than you. With more blood infusions, you would've regained your memory faster."

Alexei spoke up. "Is the stasis the reason you couldn't feel him? Couldn't locate him?"

"Yes. Until the immortal heals and regains his memory, he remains off my radar, so to speak. I don't know why."

Stanislav inched closer to Susan, needing to be near her. He had come damned close to losing her tonight. If any of those bullets had struck her in the head…

Seth was an exceptionally powerful healer, but he couldn't resurrect the dead.

Reaching out, he took her hand. She started to rise but reeled dizzily and sank back down. Her heart beat quickly in her chest. Her skin, though free of wounds now, remained paler than usual. He cast Seth a look of concern. "Is she okay?"

Alexei spoke before Seth could. "She needs a transfusion. You do, too, Stan."

Seth nodded. "Forgive me. We will see to it now. Do you wish to go to David's place or to the Network?"

Both had infirmaries, but Stanislav would much rather go to David's home.

David—the second eldest and most powerful Immortal Guardian—always opened his doors to immortals and those who served them. Stanislav and Yuri had lived there ever since their transfer from New York. But even if his things had been removed, there would no doubt be a room available for them.

"David's." Stanislav bent over the sofa.

Seth touched his shoulder. "Let me."

Stanislav stubbornly shook his head. "I'll do it." He didn't care how weak he was, he would carry Susan himself now that his wounds were healed.

Susan's emotions flowed into him as she reached for him.

He smiled and lifted her into his arms. She needed his touch as much as he needed hers. The events of the night and nearly losing him had shaken her.

Stanislav cradled her against his chest. At least the rain had washed away most of the blood.

Regret battered him. He'd brought so much violence into her world. Hell, this was what, the third time in two days that men had tried to kill her and take Stanislav captive? The kindest thing he could do would be to get her the medical care she needed, then return her to her life and walk away. He just didn't know if he could find the strength to do it.

Susan curled her arms around his neck. "Don't you dare even try," she whispered. "I don't *want* you to do it."

Closing his eyes, he pressed his forehead to hers. Dizziness assailed him. Eyes flying open, he struggled to right himself as he listed to one side.

Alexei and Seth both clamped hands onto his shoulders to steady him.

"Easy there," Alexei cautioned.

"Let's get you home," Seth murmured.

A feeling of weightlessness engulfed him before he could warn Susan that Seth was going to teleport them. The living room around them blurred and went dark. Then Stanislav and the others stood in the bright, modern infirmary David's large home boasted.

"Darnell!" Seth called.

"What just happened?" Susan blurted, gripping Stanislav tighter.

"Seth teleported us to David's home. David is his second-in-command and—"

"Holy shit," a male whispered.

Stanislav glanced over at the man in the doorway.

Darnell, David's Second, stared at him with wide eyes. "Stanislav?" His brown, cleanly shaven head gleamed in the overhead lights. "We thought you were dead."

"Not quite," he responded with a smile.

Seth caught the Second's attention. "Darnell, Stanislav needs blood and Susan needs a transfusion."

"Right. I'll, uh… I'll need her blood type." Shaking off his shock,

Darnell crossed to what appeared to be a large walk-in closet and opened a case that looked like a refrigerator.

Alexei squeezed Stanislav's shoulder, then gently turned him toward one of the beds in the recovery room portion of the infirmary.

Stanislav lowered Susan onto the closest bed. "Do you know your blood type?"

"No. I'm sorry."

Seth drew a phone from his back pocket and dialed a number.

"Reordon," a familiar male voice answered curtly.

"I need to know the blood type of Susan Meyer," Seth stated, his voice reflecting his confidence that the Network head could tell him as much.

"Susan Meyer?" Chris parroted, surprise entering his voice. "From California?"

"Yes."

"Just a sec."

Stanislav frowned. Did Chris Reordon know Susan?

Darnell returned, carrying several bags of blood he held out to Stanislav.

"Thank you." Stanislav took the bags, then lowered himself to the mattress beside Susan.

Smiling, Darnell clapped him gently on the shoulder. "It's good to have you back."

Stanislav dredged up a weary smile. "It's good to *be* back."

"Looks like she's A negative," he heard Chris say.

"Excellent," Seth replied. "Thank you." Pocketing his phone, he turned to Darnell. "She's A negative."

Susan stared at him. "Do I even want to know how you know that?"

Darnell snorted. "Are you kidding?" He jerked a thumb toward Seth. "This guy knows everything."

"Smart-ass," Seth grumbled as Darnell moved away. But he kept his eyes on Stanislav, as though he feared Stanislav would disappear again if he looked away.

A door slammed open somewhere. The front door, by the sounds of it.

"Seth!" a deep voice called.

Stanislav grinned, recognizing it.

A large dark form filled the doorway. Only an inch shorter than Seth, the powerful elder immortal boasted broad, muscled shoulders, skin as dark as midnight, and pencil-thin dreadlocks that fell to his hips. "I felt your turmoil and—" David, Seth's second-in-command, stopped short and gaped. "Stanislav?"

He nodded. "It's good to see you, David."

An amber glow lit the elder immortal's eyes as they filled with moisture. Sweeping forward, he drew Stanislav into a tight hug. "We searched for you," he uttered hoarsely. "We feared you hadn't survived but couldn't give up hoping…"

Stanislav clapped him on the back. "I'm sorry. I would've contacted you if I'd remembered you sooner."

David released him and stepped back with a frown.

"He's been in stasis," Seth informed him.

David stared at Stanislav intently enough for him to guess the immortal was reading his memories. "No wonder Seth couldn't feel you." He turned his gaze upon Susan. "I'm David. It's a pleasure to meet you, Susan. Welcome to my home."

She offered him a shy smile. "Thank you. It's a pleasure to meet you, too."

David looked to Seth. "Do the others know?"

"Not yet."

Stanislav missed whatever Seth said next because Susan distracted him by nudging him with her elbow. "What?" he asked softly.

"Stop procrastinating and do it," she ordered.

He eyed her warily. "Do what?"

She looked pointedly at the bags of blood in his lap.

He hesitated, still not comfortable infusing himself in front of her.

She sighed. "After all the weird things I've witnessed since I met you, do you really think your drinking blood out of a bag is going to scare me away?"

"Maybe."

She rolled her eyes. "You stopped an *SUV* with your *fist*, Stanislav, then threw it over my head like a freaking basketball. *This*"—she pointed to the bags of red liquid—"is nothing."

"If you're sure," he said doubtfully.

She smiled. "I'm sure."

Darnell returned with a bag of A negative and began to set up an IV for Susan while Stanislav infused himself with the bagged blood.

Susan stared at Seth and David while Darnell worked. "How did you know my full name?" she asked Seth. "Did you read it in my thoughts?"

He shook his head. "I knew your name as soon as I saw you. David and I cleaned up the mess in California when you were nearly abducted." He paused. "Well, we cleaned it up with the help of Darnell, Chris Reordon, and two others: Alena Moreno and Scott Henderson."

Stanislav tilted his head to one side. "Who are Alena Moreno and Scott Henderson?" Were they names he should remember?

"You don't know them," Seth said. "They're the heads of the West Coast and Midwest divisions of the Network. The man Susan refers to as the monster in her memories — the one who orchestrated her attempted kidnapping — was a consultant who frequently visited the facility in which Ami was tortured."

Stanislav gaped. "What?"

"When David and I rescued Ami, we razed the facility, then tied up every loose end, which led us to California and to Susan." He offered her a faint smile. "We're the reason they didn't come looking for you after you moved to North Carolina."

"I always wondered about that," she whispered. "I don't think I began to relax until I'd been here for a couple of years with no sign of them. Thank you."

Seth nodded, then cursed suddenly. "Speaking of loose ends," he muttered and whipped out his cell phone again.

"Reordon," Chris answered once more.

"I forgot to tell you we need a cleanup. All humans. All hostiles. Six unconscious. Three dead."

"Where?"

Seth dictated the address.

"Alexei's love nest?" Reordon asked with surprise.

"Yes."

"Okay. Consider it done."

Stanislav glanced at Alexei as Seth pocketed his phone. Seth and David did, too.

Alexei eyed them all blankly. "What?"

Stanislav lowered the empty blood bag he held and picked up another. "Chris knows about your *love nest* as he called it."

Alexei's jaw dropped. "He does?"

The immortals nodded.

"Damn it. That bastard knows everything. He's as bad as you are, Seth."

Seth and David both laughed.

Susan slipped her hand into Stanislav's.

Lowering the second empty bag, he met her gaze, so damned relieved when he found no revulsion in her eyes.

"Feeling better?" she asked softly.

He nodded. "You?"

She nodded.

"She should be fine," Seth murmured. "But I'd like Melanie to look in on her, if that's all right."

"Sounds good," Stanislav agreed. Melanie Lipton was a phenomenal doctor. All of them continued to hope she and her fellow researchers would find a cure for the vampiric virus. Or at least some way to prevent humans infected with it from going insane.

Seth hesitated. "She'll probably want to examine you as well, Stanislav. She's never met an immortal who has slipped into stasis before and will likely have a lot of questions."

Darnell nodded. "A *lot* of questions. She'll probably want to run some tests, too."

"That's fine." Stanislav didn't care. He just wanted to make sure Susan was all right. He looked to Seth. "Do you know why those men were after me? Why they buried me in that basement? Did you have time to read their thoughts?"

"Yes. They knew you were immortal. The vampires who stole you learned the truth—about vampires going insane while immortals didn't—and thought they could find in you the means of preserving their sanity."

"That's all?" he asked, perplexed. If so, why had their friends continued to hunt him long after their deaths?

"They also," Seth added, "thought you the key to producing a fountain of youth. A serum they could sell to millionaires and billionaires who wished to remain forever young."

Silence fell.

Susan broke it. "Wow. Do you know how much people would pay to get their hands on something like that?"

Stanislav frowned. "The men who hunted me did. No wonder they refused to give up."

She shook her head. "But why wait so long to look for you? I mean, from what I understand, that house was vacant for at least two years before I bought it."

Seth sighed. "There was a lot of confusion after we blitzed the mercenary compound."

"Wait," Susan interrupted. "Mercenary compound? Do you mean Shadow River? That was *you*?"

"Yes."

She gaped at them.

Stanislav squeezed her hand. "Shadow River got its hands on the vampiric virus and began to infect its army."

"Crap."

"Exactly."

Seth smiled. "Though Stanislav was severely weakened when they buried him, he used his gift to manipulate the vampires into killing each other. Due to the nature of the virus that infected them, the vampires left no bodies behind to be identified. So the men had no way of confirming that their vampire friends were dead. It took them quite some time to decide they were. It took them even longer to discover where the possessions of the vampire who lived in your house, Susan, had been sent. Took yet more time for them to plan the burglary that enabled them to get their hands on some of it and learn the package was most likely still buried in the basement. By the time they did, the new owner had installed a security system that included cameras and swiftly brought law enforcement out any time they tried to break and enter. So they waited until you purchased the house and the previous owners discontinued the security service."

Susan tightened her grip on Stanislav's hand. "Sheesh. I'm glad they didn't come back until after I got you out of that hole."

He raised her fingers to his lips for a kiss. "I am, too."

"What hole?" Darnell asked.

While Susan told Darnell how she had found him and dug him up, Stanislav caught the sounds of doors opening below them. The sun had set less than half an hour ago, so that must be the immortals who resided in David's home (or who had simply stayed the day) awakening and emerging from their rooms as they prepared for another night's hunt.

He stared at the doorway. Laughter floated up to him, male and female.

His heart swelled with joy at hearing the voices of his friends. It had been so long.

Suddenly a gasp in the basement silenced the others.

"What is it?" a male asked.

Someone raced up the staircase at preternatural speeds and skidded to a halt in the infirmary's doorway.

Stanislav smiled. "Hello, Lisette." She had been Yuri's sports-viewing buddy since their arrival in North Carolina and had often teased Stanislav about his complete disinterest in baseball. "Did I miss the World Series?"

---

Susan stared at the beautiful woman in the doorway. She was a few inches taller than Susan with a slender build and long, shiny black hair pulled back into a braid. Her eyes glowed amber as they rested upon Stanislav.

"Stanislav," she breathed, tears welling in her eyes.

He grinned. "In the flesh."

Racing forward, she threw her arms around his neck and hugged him tight. "We thought you were dead," she choked out, her words flavored with a French accent.

Jealousy wormed its way through Susan as she watched Stanislav close his arms around the woman. Until, that was, she remembered him and Alexei both vowing that he was single and hadn't taken a lover in years.

Exclamations arose somewhere in the distance. A rumble sounded just before a sea of black poured through the doorway.

Her eyes flew wide. *Holy crap!* She had never seen so many tall—

*really* tall—gorgeous men in her life! All wore the dark clothing Stanislav favored and boasted black hair of various lengths along with brown eyes that lit with an amber glow when they saw him.

As soon as Lisette stepped back, a male with longish black hair shot forward and hugged Stanislav, dragging him to his feet. Then another hugged him. And another and another, passing him around the room. All were clearly overjoyed to see him.

And there were women, too, most significantly shorter than the males, whom they shouldered aside so they could get their own hugs in. One in particular drew Susan's gaze. Small. Delicate. Alabaster skin and bright red hair that really stood out amid the black and dark brown hair of the others. Her green eyes sparkled with joy as she hung back with apparent shyness and watched the reunion with a smile.

Susan stared. *It's her*, she thought, shock tearing through her.

As though feeling her gaze, the woman tilted her head to one side and looked around the room until she caught sight of Susan.

*It's really her. I can't believe it.*

The woman looked indecisive for a moment, then slowly approached, skirting the edge of the celebrating crowd of immortals. When she stood only a few feet away, she stopped. A long moment passed. "Do you know me?" she asked softly.

"No, but I saw you in the mind of…" She swallowed. How could she explain it? "In the mind of a monster."

"She's telepathic." Seth spoke softly as he stepped up beside them and rested a hand on the woman's back. His deep voice carried an accent Susan thought might be British tinged with something else. "Ami, this is Susan Meyer. A consultant who worked with the men who tortured you found out she's a *gifted one* and tried to abduct her right around the time we rescued you. Susan saw you in his thoughts and memories."

Ami's face paled as she returned her attention to Susan. "You did?"

She nodded. "I can't believe you're alive. I mean, I can't believe you survived that."

"She nearly didn't," Seth said, his face grim.

Ami reached out and touched Susan's arm. "Did he hurt you? Did they torture you, too?"

"No. I got away." Tears welled in her eyes as she admitted what she had refrained from mentioning to Stanislav. "But I've thought about you so many times. Thought about the suffering you endured." She shook her head. "I'm so ashamed. I did nothing to help you. I should've told someone or tried to find you or…"

Ami took her hand. "No. You couldn't have done anything. Only Seth and David could. And they did. They saved me and made sure those men wouldn't hurt anyone else."

Seth nodded. "We slew the men who tortured Ami, and anyone who was tied to them, including the ones who would've followed you to North Carolina."

Finally she knew.

On impulse, Susan leaned forward and hugged Ami. "I'm so glad you're okay."

Ami hugged her back, careful not to disturb the IV. "And I'm glad you managed to escape them. Thank you for bringing Stanislav back to us."

Seth nodded. "I am in your debt."

"You saved my life," Susan protested. "And saved it again tonight. If anyone owes a debt, it's me."

"No," the Frenchwoman—Lisette—said, shouldering Seth aside. "We are all in your debt." She wrapped her arms around Susan in a careful hug. "You returned our brother to us."

"But I didn't…" Another woman hugged Susan, interrupting her. Then a man. And another man. And another. Until it seemed as though every person crammed into the room—and there had to be a couple dozen of them—embraced her and welcomed her with open arms.

She glanced over the shoulder of the latest immortal to hug her and met Stanislav's gaze. *What's happening here?* she asked him telepathically, unable to grasp it.

He smiled, affection softening his handsome features. *They're welcoming you into the family.*

Her heart began to pound as a set of handsome identical twins took turns bowing over her hand, then embraced her. A dozen voices spoke at once. Laughter spawned by pure joy erupted periodically. They really did seem like a great big family.

And they might actually accept her as one of them and welcome her into the fold?

*Not might.*

Her gaze returned to Stanislav as she caught the thought.

*They've* already *accepted you into the fold.* He made his slow way toward her through the throng, grinning and responding to the comments of his friends. *You're a* gifted one. *And you saved my life. Whatever the future may bring, you will always be one of us now. You will always be welcome here.*

Her throat thickened at just the thought of it. Of having a family again. Of being accepted by so many. Of just being able to relax and be herself without having to hide her gift.

Of feeling normal.

Stanislav reached her side and wrapped an arm around her shoulders. Leaning down, he pressed a kiss to her hair.

A high-pitched giggle reached their ears.

A moment later, yet another tall warrior bent and entered the room with a redheaded toddler riding on his shoulders. Another giggle escaped the little beauty as she wobbled and grabbed his head to keep her balance, mussing his longish black hair.

Stanislav's arm tightened around Susan's shoulders.

She glanced up and found him regarding the child with shock.

The man glanced around, then focused his brown gaze on Ami. Smiling, he waded through the crowd. The little girl atop his shoulders laughed and patted every warrior's head as she passed them.

All the men grinned up at her with apparent adoration.

Too cute.

The man stopped in front of Ami and smiled down at her. "Adira insisted we sing her new baby doll another lullaby before we came up," he said with a British accent. "What'd I miss?"

Ami looked pointedly at Stanislav.

When the man followed her gaze, the smile on his face froze, then transformed into a look of astonishment. "Oh shit," he whispered.

Stanislav stared raptly up at the child the man carried. "That's just what I was going to say," he murmured. "Marcus... is this your daughter?"

"Yes." Marcus glanced at Ami, then back at Stanislav. Releasing one of his daughter's plump legs, he reached out and poked Stanislav in the chest. "Oh shit," he repeated. "You're really here. You're alive."

Susan frowned. Had Marcus thought Stanislav an illusion?

When Stanislav hugged the man, the little girl patted him on the head. Grinning, he turned to Susan. "Marcus can see spirits."

Susan's gaze shot to Marcus. "You can see ghosts?"

He nodded and extended a hand. "Marcus Grayden."

"Susan Meyer." No wonder he had poked Stanislav. He'd thought him an apparition.

He pointed up. "This is Adira."

Stanislav continued to stare raptly at the toddler.

*You seem stunned*, she thought to him.

*I am*, he replied. *Marcus is the first Immortal Guardian to have fathered a child after his transformation.*

The little girl began to bounce and kick her feet. Marcus lifted her over his head and tucked her against his chest.

"She's beautiful," Stanislav breathed. "And she's...?" He sent Marcus a meaningful look.

Marcus smiled. "She's perfect."

Ami smiled, too. "And perfectly healthy with no sign of the virus."

Stanislav's relief was unmistakable... until little Adira suddenly lunged toward him with outstretched arms. Panic widening his eyes, Stanislav grabbed the child and awkwardly cradled her against his chest. "What do I do? Is this right? Am I doing this right?"

Laughter erupted all around them.

Ami grinned at Susan. "Every male present save Seth, David, and Roland panicked the first few times they held her."

"She's so small and fragile!" Stanislav blurted.

Marcus laughed. "You'll get used to it."

"But my clothes," Stanislav protested. His shirt was wet. And the rain hadn't rinsed all the bloodstains from it. But Adira didn't seem to mind it. Nor did her parents.

"Don't worry about it," Marcus said, then turned to Susan. "Ami tells me you saved Stanislav. That you found him buried in your basement, dug him up, and kept him safe while he recovered.

Thank you. We owe you a great debt."

How had Ami told him as much? Susan was standing right next to her and hadn't heard—

"She's telepathic," Stanislav informed her.

"You are?" Susan had never met another telepath before.

Ami's smile was kind. "Almost every man and woman in this room has special gifts. You're no longer the odd man out." Her smile turned wry. "If *anyone* is the odd man out, it's me."

Marcus wrapped an arm around Ami's shoulders. "I don't know. I think most of us would agree that the oddest person here is Sheldon. And he doesn't have *any* gifts."

"Hey!" a male protested somewhere.

More laughter erupted.

Susan didn't know who Sheldon was but found herself laughing alongside the others even as she fought back tears.

She wasn't alone anymore.

"You'll never be alone again," Stanislav whispered.

Every gaze that locked with hers bore both understanding and acceptance.

She looked up at Stanislav. *I'm so glad I found you in my basement.*

He pressed a kiss to her temple. *I am, too.*

# Epilogue

THE WEEKS THAT FOLLOWED WERE unlike anything Susan had ever experienced. She and Stanislav remained at David's very busy and bustling home. Though only one story, it was huge, with a basement bigger than the ground floor that boasted many bedrooms for immortals or Seconds who wished to spend the night or even live there for long stretches at a time.

Most of the other immortals in the area had been staying there of late because it would seem that while Stanislav had slept in that odd stasis in her basement, a formidable enemy had risen against the Immortal Guardians. And against Seth. And... well... pretty much the entire world. Apparently the bastard had already made two nearly successful attempts at launching a third world war and kick-starting Armageddon.

That enemy—Gershom—was willing to use any weapon he could find against Seth. And though Susan still found it hard to believe, Stanislav had told her she could be one of those weapons. Seth was extremely protective of both immortals and *gifted ones*. So Gershom had decided to hurt Seth by harming those he cared about.

How strange and exhilarating it was to be listed among those he cared about. Those they *all* cared about. The Immortal Guardians and their Seconds had gone out of their way to make Susan feel welcome and part of the family.

Even if they hadn't, now that she had been drawn into his world, Stanislav was afraid to return her to her home and leave her unguarded. And he wasn't shy about admitting that he wanted to keep her close for far more personal reasons as well. He cared for her. As deeply as she cared for him. So she had packed some clothes, picked up Jax from Anna's, and agreed to stay at David's place with Stanislav.

He really hadn't had to do a lot of arm-twisting to convince her. She loved it here. Loved feeling normal for a change. Loved the camaraderie and family atmosphere. All the laughing and teasing despite the grim challenges they faced.

She'd been alone for so long. Every moment she spent with Stanislav made her want to spend a thousand more with him.

"We could go away for a while." Stanislav spoke softly as he tugged at the laces on one of his boots.

Seated at the lovely desk he had added to their bedroom, her laptop open before her, Susan glanced over at him.

He had reluctantly returned to hunting vampires at night and helping his brethren seek their enemy. While he did so, Susan trained with Alexei and some of the other Seconds here at David's, wanting to be better able to protect herself—and Stanislav—should the need ever arise again. Then she spent the rest of her free time writing. "What?"

"We could leave here." Tugging the big boot off, he went to work on the laces of the other. "Go someplace safe. Someplace out of the line of fire. Overseas."

"From what I understand, Gershom can make mischief just about anywhere he pleases because he can teleport and nearly matches Seth in strength and power. I don't think there is anyplace safe."

Eyes still on his task, he shook his head. "There are places I can take you. Places even Seth doesn't know about, where I can keep you safe until this is over."

"And knowing your brethren are fighting this battle without you by their sides will kill you," she pointed out gently.

He removed the boot, then stared down at the floor for a long moment. His gaze rose and met hers. "I just don't want anything to happen to you," he admitted. "I would never forgive myself."

Rising, she crossed the room and knelt before him. "If anything happens to me," she said, resting her hands on his thighs, "it won't be your fault."

He covered her hands. "Nor will it be your fault if something happens to me."

She frowned.

Lifting one of her hands, he pressed a kiss to her palm. "I know why you train so hard each night while I hunt. I know you fear I will sacrifice my life to save yours if I must to keep you safe. I know you hope training and growing stronger will prevent such from occurring."

"How did you —?"

"You tend to broadcast your thoughts whenever you're stressed or worried."

She swallowed hard. "I don't want you to die for me, Stanislav."

His lips turned up in a sad smile. "I don't want you to die. I've waited over four centuries to find you." He raised her other palm to his lips, then drew her forward between his splayed thighs and wrapped his arms around her.

Her pulse picked up.

"I love you, Susan."

Joy flowed through her.

"You don't have to say it back," he whispered. "I just wanted you to know." *Because the next battle may not incapacitate me. It may kill me. And Gershom could bring our time together to an end at any moment.*

She was pretty sure he hadn't meant for her to hear that. But she had been thinking along the same lines. "I love you, too."

His eyes brightened with amber light.

"Admitting that so soon should scare the hell out of me," she whispered, "but honestly, I just don't see any reason to wait." *Especially if waiting means I may never have the chance to tell him.*

His eyes grew brighter.

She whispered a curse. "You heard that last part, didn't you?"

"Yes."

She had been broadcasting again, damn it. She seemed to do that more and more often around him, relaxing her guard as she never had before. "Look." She cupped his handsome face in her hands, loving the dark stubble that abraded her skin. "If the worst happens, it will all have been worth it." When he parted his lips to protest, she pressed a finger to them to silence him. "Don't get me wrong. I don't want to die, Stanislav. I really don't. But if I *do*…" She shook her head. "My time with you has been the best in my life. I finally found love with someone who can accept me for who and what I am. Someone I adore who makes me happier than I ever thought I could be. Someone who makes me laugh and makes my breath catch and has given me a huge new family on top of everything else. It's a dream come true. And it's one I wouldn't have missed for anything."

Wrapping his arms around her, he buried his face in her hair and held her tight. "I don't want to lose you," he whispered against her neck. "The others told me everything I missed while I was away, and Gershom keeps upping his game. The threat has never been greater."

"Then transform me."

His arms clamped down around her. "What?"

"Too tight," she wheezed. "Too tight, honey."

He hastily released his hold and drew back. "I'm so sorry, sweetheart. Did I hurt you?"

"No. And stop looking like you want to kick your own ass. I shouldn't have just blurted it out like that. I caught you off guard."

"You wish to become immortal?"

"Yes."

"This isn't a decision to be made lightly, Susan," he cautioned. But she saw the hope that flared to life in his eyes.

"I'm not making it lightly."

"It can't be reversed." He slid his hands up and down her arms. "Once you're infected with the virus, there is no turning back. There is no cure."

"I know. And I won't lie, I'm not sure how I'll handle the whole hunting and killing vampires every night thing. But if it will mean I can spend the rest of eternity with you, it will be worth it."

"You're sure?" He stared at her with the same awe that had brightened his features when he had seen little Adira for the first time, as though he couldn't believe it was true.

"I'm sure."

Stanislav took her lips in an exuberant kiss. "Thank you. I will do everything in my power to make you happy and ensure you won't regret it. I vow it."

She kissed him again, softer this time, teasing him with the brush of her tongue. "Everything?" she drawled, nipping his lower lip.

The amber light in his eyes brightened. "Everything," he repeated, his voice deepening.

Nodding at the big bed a few feet away, she sent him a sly look. "Care to get started on that right now?"

He gripped her hips. "Absolutely."

A doorbell sounded.

Stanislav swore foully.

Susan laughed as he eased her away and rose. Grumbling over the interruption, he took her hand and drew her up beside him.

The bedroom suites in David's basement had been soundproofed so well to afford the immortals who inhabited them privacy that doorbells had been installed to alert those inside that they had a visitor.

Susan watched Stanislav cross the room.

She loved seeing him like this. Rumpled clothes. Windblown hair. No shoes. His stride languid and relaxed. He was so damned handsome.

When he opened the door, Marcus faced him in the hallway. "Hi. Sorry to disturb you."

"No problem," Stanislav responded.

Susan moved to stand at his side.

"So." Marcus shifted his weight from one foot to the other and seemed uncertain how to phrase whatever he wanted to say. "I've been asked to deliver a message."

Stanislav frowned. "Asked by whom?"

Marcus shook his head and looked at Susan. "Do you know how to pull Stanislav into your dreams? I've heard some telepaths can do that."

She nodded. "As long as we're touching when we sleep, our dreams tend to merge."

"Good. Well, make sure you two cuddle up tonight, because you're going to have company in your dreams."

Stanislav's eyebrows shot up. "A dreamwalker?"

Marcus nodded.

Susan looked up at Stanislav. "What's a dreamwalker? Is that like a telepath?"

"In a manner of speaking. Dreamwalkers can only enter someone else's mind when that person is asleep. The dreamwalker can't read all their thoughts like you can. But he or she can infiltrate and manipulate the person's dreams." He turned to Marcus. "I wasn't aware there were any in the area. Is it someone I know?"

Marcus shrugged. "Not for me to say. I'm just supposed to give you a heads-up. You two sleep well."

Susan stared after him as he strolled down the hallway to his and Ami's room. Pursing her lips, she looked up at Stanislav. "Sleep well, my ass. I'm so curious now I probably won't be able to sleep at all."

He winked. "I believe I can ensure you will sleep *very* well." So saying, he closed the door, picked her up, and tossed her onto the bed.

---

*"When love," Susan sang softly as she stared up at Stanislav, "into my dreams was creeping."*

*Smiling, he tightened his arm around her and tucked her hand against his chest as the two danced in her kitchen.*

*"I gave my heart into your keeping."*

*It would forever be his favorite song, because it was the first he'd heard from her lips.*

*She smiled up at him.*

*How he loved her. Who would've thought that being gravely wounded and buried alive would be the best thing that had ever happened to him in his long, long life?*

*When she reached the end of the song, he pressed a kiss to her lips. "Again," he whispered.*

*The tenderness in her hazel eyes warmed his heart as she complied.*

*The worn Formica countertops around them were gone, replaced by granite. New modern appliances gleamed and reflected a mirror image of them as they circled the room. He would help her remodel every room in the house. Their house now. Make it the dream house she had always wanted.*

*If, he thought with some amusement, he could tear her away from David's home. Susan loved the hustle and bustle and family gatherings that took place there. But he was sure that he could find a way to make* their home more appealing. His hand on her back drifted lower, sliding down over her bottom. He could find many ways to —

"I've known you for over four centuries," a deep voice drawled behind him, his accent identical to Stanislav's. "How did I not know you like to dance?"

Startled, Stanislav spun around. His eyes widened. He sucked in a breath. "Yuri?"

The elder immortal grinned at him from across the kitchen. "It is good to see you, my friend."

A woman stood beside Yuri. But Stanislav saw only the brother he'd lost.

Crossing the kitchen in a blink, he yanked Yuri into his arms.

Yuri pounded him on the back and delivered a crushing bear hug. "I've missed you," he said, his voice rough.

Stanislav's throat thickened as he nodded, unable to speak.

Drawing back slightly, Yuri clasped the back of Stanislav's neck and smiled at him. "I thought you died the same day I did. I thought you crossed over without saying goodbye." Moisture glinted in his glowing amber eyes. "I thought I would never see you again."

"Susan saved me," Stanislav choked out. "But you did die." Tears blurred his vision. "And it was my fault."

Yuri's grip on Stanislav's neck tightened to the point of pain as he gave him a little shake. "Never say that. Never even think it. It's not true."

Stanislav wished it weren't, but... "I shouldn't have left my position. I wasn't there to guard your back. I knew you'd been distracted of late and should have — "

"Done exactly what you did," Yuri interrupted.

Stanislav didn't understand the lack of anger in his friend's expression.

"You made no mistakes, my friend. You did nothing wrong. And my death was actually a good thing."

Stanislav stared at him, appalled. "How can you say that?"

Releasing him, Yuri stepped back and wrapped his arm around the woman, drawing Stanislav's attention to her. "Because it enabled me to be with Cat."

As Stanislav stared at her, uncomprehending, Susan moved to stand beside him and tucked her hand in his. He gripped it tightly, needing the contact. "What?"

"Marcus said you remember all of your past now," Yuri said.

"You talked to Marcus?"

*"I talk to him often, when no one else is around. Your memory is once more intact?" Yuri asked again.*

*"Yes."*

*"Then you remember why I was so distracted in the weeks leading up to the big battle." He smiled down at the woman. "I had fallen in love with a woman I couldn't have."*

*Cat smiled and held her hand out to Stanislav. "Hello. I'm Catherine."*

*Stanislav took the hand she offered and brought it to his lips. "Stanislav. It's a pleasure to meet you…" He trailed off as realization dawned. "You're the dreamwalker?"*

*"In a manner of speaking," she replied with a British accent.*

*Yuri spoke, once more drawing his gaze. "She's a spirit like me, Stanislav. She's Bastien's sister."*

*He stared at her. "Sebastien Newcombe's?" The immortal black sheep's sister had been slain two centuries ago in a fit of madness by her husband after he turned vampire. But Stanislav had thought Yuri had fallen for a human woman who couldn't safely be transformed. A woman he couldn't have.*

*Understanding dawned. He met Yuri's gaze.*

*Like Marcus, Yuri had been born with the ability to see spirits.*

*Yuri nodded. "She haunts David's home."*

*Cat grimaced. "I've always hated that term."*

*Yuri grinned. "That's okay, sweetheart. We both haunt it now."*

*Because his death had freed him to be with her, the ghost he had fallen in love with. "And you're happy?" Stanislav asked, trying to wrap his mind around it.*

*"Very happy," Yuri professed. "Even more so now that you have returned." His gaze shifted to Susan. "Thank you for bringing him back."*

*Disturbed by his lapse in manners, Stanislav hastily introduced her. "Susan, this is Yuri." He had told her all about him. "Yuri, Susan."*

*She smiled. "It's nice to meet you."*

*Yuri took her hand and brought it to his lips for a kiss. "I'm glad Stanislav found you, Susan." He winked. "Or vice versa."*

*Her eyes widened. "You feel so real." Color immediately flooded her cheeks. "Oh. I'm sorry. I shouldn't have said that."*

*Laughing, Yuri covered their clasped hands. "No worries. In the dream realm, we feel as real as you do out of it." He released her hand and winked at Stanislav. "And we can visit you as often as you like."*

*"Often," Stanislav blurted, so damned glad his friend could still be*

*part of his life. He couldn't wait to get to know the woman who had stolen his heart. He turned to Susan. "Is that all right?"*

*She leaned into his side. "Of course it is." She smiled at Yuri. "I'm telepathic and have seen you in his thoughts and memories so much that I feel as though I already know you. If I can get to know you even more here in the dream realm, all the better."*

*Yuri winked. "I can tell you all the embarrassing things he left out while recounting the events of his past."*

*Stanislav narrowed his eyes. "And I can do the same for Catherine."*

*Catherine's face brightened. "Oh yes. Please, do."*

*All laughed.*

*"Does Seth know?" Stanislav asked. Seth seemed to possess all of the gifts the other immortals had combined, so Stanislav assumed he could see ghosts, too.*

*Yuri scowled. "No. Seth is the only thorn in my side."*

*Catherine cast him a reproving look, then turned to Stanislav and Susan. "Seth blames himself for Yuri's death. The wound is still raw, so he — "*

*"Won't face me," Yuri interrupted, his irritation plain. "Every time I enter a room, he leaves it."*

*Catherine leaned into his side and patted his chest. "Be patient, darling. He's hurting. He'll come around eventually."*

*Stanislav nodded. "I'll see to it personally if he doesn't."*

*Yuri smiled. "Damned right you will. If anyone can make him see reason, you can. You're as stubborn as a mule."*

*Susan held up an index finger. "I can attest to that."*

*More laughter.*

*Yuri looped an arm around Catherine's shoulders and began walking backward, leading them out of the kitchen. "Cat and I have become rather adept at controlling and manipulating dreams while you've been gone. And there is something I wish to show you, brother."*

*Smiling, Stanislav gave Susan's hand a squeeze and followed them. "All right."*

*Yuri and Catherine led them to the back door and out onto the deck.*

*Stars twinkled above them in a cloudless midnight sky. A cool breeze rustled leaves as frogs and crickets sang.*

*Stanislav followed Yuri and Catherine down the steps, Susan at his side, so happy to be with the two people he loved most in the world.*

*Moonlight bathed them as they walked across the expansive back lawn.*

*Yuri stopped in the center of it and faced them.*

*Stanislav halted. "So?" he asked. "What did you wish to show me?"*

*Yuri's smile stretched into a grin. "This."*

*The moon above suddenly morphed into the sun, bathing the meadow in brilliant light.*

*Alarm striking, Stanislav threw up an arm to shield his face and prepared to bolt toward the shelter of nearby trees.*

*But Yuri grabbed his wrist, holding him in place. "Wait."*

*Stanislav did, squinting at Yuri in the bright afternoon light.*

*"What are you doing?" Susan blurted, anxiety creasing her features as she tugged at Yuri's arm. "You know he can't be in the sun. It'll hurt him!"*

*Yuri held Stanislav's gaze, his large form unmoving. "No, it won't."*

*When his friend's lips curled up in a smile, Stanislav cautiously lowered his arm and waited. His skin warmed beneath the sun's rays. But the telltale tingle that usually warned him he would soon begin to pinken and burn never came.*

*The sun didn't harm him. Its rays didn't cause his skin to burn and blister. It just bathed him in the gentle, wondrous warmth he had forgotten it possessed.*

*His heart began to pound.*

*Susan stared up at him, her teeth worrying her lower lip.*

*"It's okay," he told her, then met Yuri's gaze. "The sun isn't hurting me."*

*Yuri shook his head, his smile stretching into a grin that flashed straight white teeth. "Outside of the occasional nightmare, it never will here in the dream realm. But we've lived in the darkness for so many centuries, that you and I stopped dreaming of daylight many lifetimes ago." He gave Catherine a smile full of affection. "I didn't know I could enjoy the sun again until Cat showed me. Now you can, too."*

*Here in dreams, Stanislav could stand in direct sunlight without having to wear that insufferable rubber suit the Network had fashioned for immortals. Here in dreams, he didn't have to either remain indoors all day or plot a path through dense shade. Here in dreams, he could feel normal again.*

*Awed by the revelation, Stanislav stared down at Susan.*

*"It really doesn't hurt?" she asked, her brow furrowed.*

*He shook his head, happiness dawning once more as he cupped her face in his hands and studied it for the first time in golden sunlight. "You're even more beautiful when kissed by the sun."*

*Smiling, she wrapped her arms around his waist. "I would much rather be kissed by you."*

*He gladly caressed her lips with his, then held her close as he turned back to Yuri and Cat.*

*Yuri smiled. "We've much more to show you, my friend. Now that you're back, Cat and I intend to fill your dreams with many adventures."*

*Stanislav pressed a kiss to Susan's hair. "I can't wait."*

*She smiled. "Neither can I."*

Thank you for reading *Awaken the Darkness*. I hope you enjoyed Stanislav and Susan's story!

If you liked this book, please consider rating or reviewing it at an online retailer of your choice. I appreciate your support so much and am always thrilled when I see that one of my books made a reader happy. Ratings and reviews are also an excellent way to recommend an author's books, create word of mouth, and help other readers find new favorites.

Thank you again!

Dianne Duvall
www.DianneDuvall.com

Dianne Duvall Books Group
www.facebook.com/groups/128617511148830/

# About the Author

Dianne Duvall is the *New York Times* and *USA Today* Bestselling Author of the **Immortal Guardians** and **The Gifted Ones** series. Reviewers have called Dianne's books "fast-paced and humorous" (*Publishers Weekly*), "utterly addictive" (*RT Book Reviews*), "extraordinary" (Long and Short Reviews), and "wonderfully imaginative" (The Romance Reviews). Her books have twice been nominated for RT Reviewers' Choice Awards and are routinely deemed Top Picks by *RT Book Reviews*, The Romance Reviews, and/or Night Owl Reviews.

Dianne loves all things creative. When she isn't writing, Dianne is active in the independent film industry and has even appeared on-screen, crawling out of a moonlit grave and wielding a machete like some of the vampires she loves to create in her books.

For the latest news on upcoming releases, contests, and more, please visit www.DianneDuvall.com. You can also connect with Dianne online:

Website — www.DianneDuvall.com
**Books Group** — www.facebook.com/groups/128617511148830/
**Blog** — www.dianneduvall.blogspot.com
**Facebook** — www.facebook.com/DianneDuvallAuthor
**Twitter** — www.twitter.com/DianneDuvall
**YouTube** —
www.youtube.com/channel/UCVcJ9xnm_i2ZKV7jM8dqAgA?feature=mhee
**Pinterest** — www.pinterest.com/dianneduvall
**Goodreads** — www.goodreads.com/Dianne_Duvall
**Google Plus** — www.plus.google.com/106122556514705041683

Printed in Great Britain
by Amazon

36774431R00156